The
Spitfire Girl

BOOKS BY ELLIE CURZON

A Village At War Series

The Ration Book Baby

ELLIE CURZON

The
Spitfire Girl

bookouture

Published by Bookouture in 2023

An imprint of Storyfire Ltd.
Carmelite House
50 Victoria Embankment
London EC4Y 0DZ

www.bookouture.com

ISBN: 978-1-83790-637-6
eBook ISBN: 978-1-83790-636-9

To the many brave men and women of the Air Transport Auxiliary and Special Operations Executive who gave their lives during WW2.

PROLOGUE

SEPTEMBER 1939

Sally let out a whoop of exhilaration as she brought her plane out of a barrel roll and saw the village of Bramble Heath laid out beneath her.

The sun flashed off the cottage windows and blazed bright against the weathervane on the church spire and, from up here above it all, the world was peaceful. Down in the lanes she and Freddy would have their very favourite sort of audience as their friends in the village watched. A crowd would be growing outside the George and Dragon pub, and Annie, Bramble Heath's district nurse, would be watching with her friend Betty. And as Sally and Freddy circled over the fields, the Goslings would look up from their cows to see them fly past. It was the sort of display that crowds worldwide usually paid to see, but that was just one of the benefits of life in Bramble Heath: Toussaint and Carr just happened to rehearse in the skies above them.

The other half of that celebrated duo, Freddy Carr, banked his Tiger Moth in front of her, its wasp-like yellow-and-black livery shimmering in the morning sun. Then he raised his hand and waved from the open cockpit.

'You're such a show-off!' Freddy laughed over the radio. 'It's a good job I'm not the competitive type.'

And because Freddy was Freddy, he punctuated that with a perfectly executed barrel roll of his own.

'*I'm* the show-off?' Sally chuckled, and zoomed into a loop, flying out of it upside down, just because she could.

'Well, we can *all* do that!' Freddy laughed as he mirrored her manoeuvre. Sally couldn't remember a time when she and Freddy hadn't been as happy and confident in the sky as they were on the ground. Just like their fathers, they were naturals.

'Time to land, I'm afraid,' Sally said reluctantly with a sigh as she noticed the time. Then she added brightly, 'I'll race you!'

She swooped down, aiming for the landing strip below at Heath Place.

Whenever Sally landed, she was always fizzy with glee from her flight, desperate to turn the plane round right away and head up into the sky again. But she couldn't spend her whole life in the air. Not even birds lived in the sky *all* the time.

Sally pulled off her goggles and helmet, her curly bobbed hair springing free. Then she climbed out of the cockpit and jumped down from the wing onto solid ground. Her legs wobbled like a sailor who'd just landed on the shore.

We'll be flying again soon enough, she told herself, as she watched Freddy taxiing into the hangar.

'That was the best so far!' exclaimed Peter as he dashed into the hangar with Wilbur hot on his heels. The little brown terrier was barking a greeting for Sally up until the moment he realised Freddy's plane had just touched down. Then he turned and hurtled out onto the runway to greet his master instead. At least Peter remained, at ten years old the spitting image of his brother at that same age. 'You outflew Freddy!'

Sally pulled off her gloves and her sheepskin jacket, then threw them aside to give Peter a hug. 'We're always trying to outfly each other!'

'You always win!' He laughed.

'The loyalty of little brothers, eh?' Freddy laughed as he strolled into the hangar. Wilbur was settled happily in the crook of his elbow, the expression on his face smug. Sally could hardly blame him though; anyone would look happy if Freddy had his arm round them. 'You're supposed to stick up for me, squirt.'

Peter shrugged and replied with undisguised cheek, 'You need a bit more practice!'

'Now, now,' Sally joked, pretending to scold them. She went over to Freddy and gently kissed his cheek. 'No fighting, please, boys! We better get these ladies put away.'

At the mention of work, Peter gave his brother and friend a wave and ran out of the hangar towards the house. Freddy stooped to put Wilbur on the ground, then gave Sally's waist a squeeze and smiled. 'He's right, you know. You *are* better than me. And I'm better than most people.'

'I won't hear it,' Sally replied, beaming at him. 'We're both as good as each other. And do you know what? I think we're rather brilliant!'

Now that Peter had run off, Sally chanced another kiss, this time dotting one quickly against Freddy's lips.

'You're good at that too,' Freddy said with a smile.

Sally would happily have kissed him again, but there was a reason they'd had to cut their flight short.

'The wireless,' was all she could say at that moment. She gestured towards it, the wireless that had played dance numbers while they'd happily worked on their planes, looming uncomfortably. She swallowed, before saying, 'Chamberlain's message. I'm sure it'll be good news, though.'

Although she wasn't really all that sure.

'I *hope* it will be.' Freddy switched on the set and turned the dial. The sound of church bells chiming filled the hangar. 'If Adolf's got any sense, he'll blink. Probably at one minute to eleven, but he'll blink.'

Sally slid her arm round Freddy's waist, hoping he wouldn't notice that she was trembling. In reply, he wrapped his strong arm round her shoulders and held her close. The sound of bird-song was as cheery as ever, but here in the hangar the air had grown still. Surely there wouldn't be another war? Sally's family had fled France to escape one war and, though she had been just a child and could barely remember her homeland, the stories her father told of fighting in the north had kept her rapt on many a winter night. It was unthinkable that anyone would be foolish enough to plunge the world into conflict again.

Yet as Neville Chamberlain's voice echoed in the hangar, Sally felt her blood growing colder. Freddy rested his cheek against her hair. She felt him grow tense with each word until the prime minister uttered the announcement that Sally had been dreading.

The British ambassador in Berlin handed the German government a final note stating that unless we heard from them by eleven o'clock that they were prepared at once to withdraw their troops from Poland, a state of war would exist between us. Chamberlain sounded calm, but Sally already knew that this was not the news the world had been hoping for. *I have to tell you now that no such undertaking has been received, and that consequently this country is at war with Germany.*

Sally turned her face, pressing it against Freddy's chest.

'No,' she whispered, her voice muffled. She clung tightly to Freddy. She didn't want a war, no one did, and all she could think of was Freddy being taken away from her.

ONE

SPRING 1941

Sally was flying home to RAF Bramble Heath in a shiny new Spitfire, fresh from the factory. She loved flying them – such agile little machines; she had to fight the urge to loop-the-loop.

But she couldn't. No barrel rolls, or spins, or hammerheads were allowed in the Air Transport Auxiliary. She just had to deliver whatever planes were on the list for that day, flying as soberly and as sensibly as she could.

There was a war on, after all. They couldn't have pilots performing aerobatics. And Sally knew she was very fortunate to be able to do her bit from a cockpit. She couldn't risk losing her job just for the sake of a brief moment of fun.

One little loop, would anyone notice?

Sally shook her head. She was being ridiculous. And what would people think? There'd been so much proud excitement in the press about the Attagirls, the women flying in the Air Transport Auxiliary. She'd be letting the side down. The large number of men in the ATA were already peeved about the amount of press attention the Attagirls got compared to them – if Sally was caught putting on an airshow display, she'd really give them something to complain about.

As much as Sally loved her job, it wasn't free of risks – the ATA flew unarmed planes across the country in all weathers. It was nerve-wracking at times; Sally had heard of terrible accidents suffered by ATA pilots, and she still mourned the friend she had lost. Sally had been lucky, she knew that. She'd limped home in terror on barely any fuel, she'd shaken with fear as she'd dodged bolts of lightning, she'd cried out in alarm as she skidded on an icy runway. Somehow, she was still in one piece.

Sally spotted the village of Bramble Heath up ahead, first the outlying farms, their fields dotted with cattle, then the familiar spire of the church poking up among the trees. She got closer still and saw the neat cottages of the hamlet where the Polish pilots and their families lived, and the river rushing past the mill. Then there were the thatched roofs of ancient houses with splashes of colour in their gardens that always brought a sense of homecoming when she saw them from up here. There were people in the street outside the post office and the butcher's shop, and children were playing in the yard beside the school.

Some of them would tip back their heads to watch the plane flying over, but not everyone would. The sight of a Spitfire over Bramble Heath was hardly unusual since the RAF base had been built beside the village. Things had changed for everyone living here. Once it had been Sally and Freddy flying their stunt planes over the village, but now there were only warplanes.

Sally spotted a large, black shiny car, like some sort of beetle, winding its way through the lanes towards Bramble Heath. Something to do with the RAF, she suspected, so it had nothing to do with her.

Sally felt a pang as she saw Heath Place, her childhood home, now requisitioned and the home of the RAF base instead.

But there's been worse sacrifices than that, she reminded herself. And there were her remaining family in France, who were going through who knew what. Sally's father had tried to bring them to England, but they'd run out of time. All communication had been cut. There were no more letters from her cousin Manon, no more postcards. When scraps of news from France appeared in the newspapers or on the radio, it was never good. There was little food and young men were being sent to factories in Germany. Sally's heart had sunk – what about her cousins, Jules, Baptiste, Michel? Had they been taken from their homes to toil in the factories? Sally's aunts and uncles... what had happened to them? And her grandmother, her dear Mémé. Sally was terrified that she would never see her family again. She knew her father had the same fears, but they never spoke about it. It was too painful to think about.

Sally had her job to do and she focused on that now as she brought the new Spitfire in to land on the airstrip. It had been massively expanded from what her grandfather had built; it was unrecognisable from the days of the aerodrome. Several more hangars had been built, along with a canteen, an ops room and a mess. Planes were sitting out on the runway, and groups of pilots waited here and there.

Sally brought the plane down in a smooth landing, aware that all of the pilots would be watching. As she taxied it, she noticed that one group of them were on their feet, applauding.

And at the centre of her admiring audience, she realised, was Freddy, with his dog Wilbur.

Every time she saw him, relief washed through her. Because he had survived – he'd flown an extraordinary number of times in the Battle of Britain, and he had survived. And Sally would gladly have lost Heath Place a thousand times over just so that Freddy was spared.

She pulled back the canopy and lifted her goggles as she climbed out of the cockpit. 'Freddy!' she called, waving. As Freddy returned her wave, the pilots bombarded him with teasing catcalls. He blushed as red as the scarf he was wearing and dismissed them with a shrug, but Sally knew there was no harm in it. The British and Polish aircrew who shared her old home were a family.

'That's a smoother landing than you managed yesterday!' joked Mateusz, nudging Freddy. 'And she's a lot prettier than you too!'

Freddy laughed and reminded him, 'But only one of us made ace in a day!'

'Not that you ever talk about it,' said Freddy's chum Ginge, running his hand through his flame-red hair. 'You're ever so modest, Freds!'

Sally handed the brand-new plane to the two WAAF officers who'd come over, and pulled off her gloves as she headed to see Freddy and his pals. Her boots felt huge and unwieldy as she walked, and the flying suit was nothing like the elegant one she'd worn as half of Toussaint and Carr, but it wasn't a bad job really.

'Hello, boys!' Sally greeted them, and patted Wilbur on the head. 'Been out on any sorties recently, Flight Sergeant Wilbur?'

'He's too busy being the most handsome chap on the base,' Freddy said, laughing, and earned another round of whistles as he pecked a kiss to Sally's cheek. 'How did she fly?'

Sally returned her boyfriend's kiss. Freddy still looked just as boyish and full of life as he always had, despite what he'd been through. But then he'd always been a happy-go-lucky chap.

'Wonderfully,' Sally sighed. Then she admitted, 'How I longed to loop-the-loop over the South Downs. But I managed to resist, I promise!'

She was sure Freddy had felt the same many times up in the air. Rather than loop or spin or roll to avoid enemy fire, surely he'd longed to do it just for the hell of it. Just to remember what life had been like before the war.

'Are you sure you didn't?' her boyfriend asked, nodding

towards the car that was pulling up in front of the ops room. It was the sleek black vehicle Sally had seen from the air, and it may as well have had AIR MINISTRY painted across it. 'Is he here to slap your wrists for pulling a chandelle over Liphook?'

There was no way anyone from the Air Ministry would want or need to speak to her. Sally joked, 'They work fast, don't they? It's curtains for me, Freddy. I'm done for now!'

'Either that or they're making Wilbur air commodore.' Freddy scratched the top of his dog's head as they watched a tall figure emerge from the rear door of the car. The new arrival barely glanced towards the pilots before making his way towards Heath Place, the walking stick he leaned on tapping as he climbed the steps and disappeared inside.

'Gosh, he looks rather important, doesn't he?' Sally remarked, wondering what the man's presence could mean. Whatever it was, she hoped Freddy would be safe. It'd been a stroke of luck that he'd ended up being based at Bramble Heath. She hoped he wouldn't be leaving any time soon.

Freddy shrugged. 'Maybe he's come to see the best looking Attagirl in England?'

Sally tapped Freddy on the nose. 'If you think that means I'll give you another kiss, well... you'd be right!' And she kissed his cheek again.

'Second Officer Toussaint?' a voice called. 'You're to come to Group Captain Chambers' office at once.'

Sally turned quickly and saw Gladys, Group Captain Chambers' secretary, striding towards them. She was far smarter in her WAAF uniform than Sally felt in her flight gear.

'Someone's in trouble,' said Ginge, laughing. 'What've you been up to?'

Sally patted Freddy's sleeve. 'Best go,' she whispered. 'I hope they haven't banned kissing on the runway or we're both for it.'

'Whatever it is, good luck!' Freddy grinned. 'Do you want Wilbur to lead the way for luck?'

'Why not?' Sally knew that Gladys had a soft spot for the little dog. Maybe he would help Sally's cause.

Sally gave Freddy a smile as she set off with Wilbur trotting just ahead of her. Gladys waved to Wilbur, then gestured for Sally to follow her into the house. Sally's old home, which now no longer smelt of wood polish and fresh flowers, but of tobacco smoke and rush and hurry.

Gladys led the way and Sally tried very hard to push back her memories of life in Heath Place. It didn't do to dwell on such things. The war wouldn't be won like that. And yet, she couldn't get over how unfamiliar her old home now seemed, turned over to offices, accommodation and a sickbay. It was hard to imagine her family had ever lived there.

In the corridor where Sally had played skittles on rainy days when she was a child, Gladys stopped and knocked on a door.

'Come in!' called Group Captain Chambers.

Gladys opened the door, and gestured for Sally to enter. It seemed ridiculous that Sally needed permission to go into a room that she had once used whenever she'd pleased. But there was nothing she could do about it.

'Second Officer Toussaint,' Sally said, as she went into the room. 'Sorry about the get-up. I've only just landed.'

She glanced at Group Captain Chambers, sitting behind his desk. There was a man who hadn't survived the Battle of Britain unscathed, but who had got on with life nonetheless. The man who'd got out of the car was also there. He was rather tall, with a walking stick and a black armband on his sleeve. Sally had never seen him before.

'Thank you,' Group Captain Chambers said as Gladys withdrew and closed the door. Both men rose to their feet. Chambers greeted her with a smile and gestured to a seat. 'Do sit down, Second Officer Toussaint.'

Sally sat. *Was* she in trouble? She wasn't in the RAF, so surely they couldn't tell her off.

'Look, if I'm in trouble for something...' Sally said, her voice trailing off as she glanced from Chambers to the mysterious man.

'Second Officer Toussaint, this is Mr Lane-Bannister,' Chambers explained. 'Mr Lane-Bannister is from the Air Ministry.'

The stranger greeted Sally with a polite nod.

She nodded back, but couldn't help wondering – what on earth had she got herself into?

TWO

Sally, still in her flying gear, followed Lane-Bannister out to his car, which was waiting outside.

Everything had happened so quickly. This man didn't hang around. He wanted to see her fly, he'd said. Immediately. But it was confidential, so she wouldn't be flying from the runway right outside the house.

'You're *certain* you can't see me fly from here?' Sally asked him, still trying to get her head around the level of secrecy.

She glanced over at Freddy, who was sitting with his friends beside the runway, and gave him a small wave. *What on earth will Freddy think of me getting into an Air Ministry car? I can't even tell him why.* If the ministry man didn't want her to fly from Bramble Heath, then this was something very secret indeed.

Freddy furrowed his brow as though to ask 'What's happening?', but gave her a wave in return. Lane-Bannister shot him the briefest of glances, then opened the car door for her.

'I'm afraid not,' he replied apologetically. 'But we won't be going too far.'

'Oh... oh, I see,' Sally mumbled as she got into the car. But she didn't see at all, and she had no idea where he was taking her to. There were no other airfields nearby. That she knew of, at least. The whole thing was an utter mystery.

The man from the ministry didn't reply, but instead gazed from the window as the car pulled away. He turned the gold ring that he wore on his wedding finger absent-mindedly, before offering Sally the briefest of smiles.

He looked very official in his pinstripe suit, his blond hair streaked with silver. But he didn't look that old. There was something rather aristocratic about his accent and his bearing. And somewhere there was a Mrs Lane-Bannister, too. She wondered who he was wearing that black armband for. A brother, lost in the Battle of Britain?

Lane-Bannister's driver took them through the village, along the high street. There were two white-haired men sitting on the bench outside the George and Dragon pub watching the world go by. Reverend Ellis came out of the Parkers' bakery with a small loaf of bread just as Rose was putting an OPEN sign in the tea rooms' window. You'd barely know there was a war on, if it hadn't been for the criss-crossed tape in the windows, and the government posters on the village noticeboard.

The driver left Bramble Heath, taking them into the country lanes. Annie rode past them on her motorbike. Whichever of her patients she was off to see, Sally hoped it wasn't anything too serious.

The driver evidently knew where he was going, even though the signposts had all been painted over or taken down. The lanes were getting narrower and, even though Sally had lived in the area for most of her life, she had no idea where she was.

They turned off onto a farm track, and the car bumped across the ruts.

Her teeth rattling, Sally said, 'Well, this is a jolly strange place for an airbase!'

'You grew up at Heath Place?' Lane-Bannister asked, his tone friendly. 'The family pile, was it?'

And something about his chummy upper-class manner suggested he might know a thing or two about ancestral homes. Sally had met a few such men since the war broke out, and all of them seemed to be connected to the Royal Air Force.

'Yes,' Sally said, a note of amusement in her voice. Because she had to find *some* humour in the sorry situation. 'Requisitioned, as you'll have seen. Worse luck. I blame Grandpa, building a runway behind the house. Absolutely perfect for an airbase!'

'But your father is French?' he asked.

Sally nodded. '*Mais oui, Monsieur Lane-Bannister*. And Heath Place was Mummy's childhood home. So I'm English *and* French at the same time.'

'I suppose you must've seen me flying before the war,' she went on casually. A lot of people had. They had packed out airshows, and Sally and Freddy had been in the pages of *Tatler* and *The Sketch*. 'Don't be shy, Mr Lane-Bannister. If you want my autograph, you only need to ask.'

For a moment he looked utterly thrown, then he laughed and admitted, 'I confess I *did* see your Hyde Park flyover for His Majesty's coronation bash. When Pa told me it was a couple of teenagers, I thought he was having me on!'

Sally chuckled. 'So you *have* seen me fly! And Freddy, too. What a shame – he was on the runway back at Brambles. You could've had *his* autograph as well. The full Toussaint and Carr set!'

Memories of that day, their coronation flyover and meeting the king and his family afterwards came back to Sally. What fun days those were. And now she was in a car with someone from the Air Ministry, heading to the middle of nowhere.

'I'm sorry for all the cloak-and-dagger,' Lane-Bannister said. 'Unavoidable sometimes.'

Sally tapped the side of her nose. 'Careless talk and all that, eh? I'm sure we'll get to the end of this track in a mo.'

As she spoke, her voice was drowned out by the roar of an engine and she was suddenly aware of another car overtaking, dangerously close to the side of theirs. It was a low-slung vehicle, dark blue, and, in the few seconds Sally had to take in the unexpected sight, she had the impression of a man at the wheel, his features hidden by the shadow of the hat he wore. A moment later the speeding car cut in front of them and surged away, leaving her companion shaking his head.

'God forbid he should have to wait in line,' he sighed. It was the first car they'd seen in a while. Surely whoever that was would be heading to the same place.

They reached a hedgerow, and Lane-Bannister's driver took the car through a gap into a long field with a tired-looking barn. The dark blue car was parked up beside it and a man in an overcoat and a fedora was climbing out. Smoke spiralled up from his cigarette.

'Just between us, he can be a little brusque,' said Lane-Bannister as the car drew to a halt. The man in the fedora was already striding towards them, his expression giving away nothing. 'Don't let him scare you.'

Sally swallowed. 'Well, we've already had a demonstration of his driving – that doesn't surprise me at all. He won't scare me. Unless I have to share a car with him.' And yet for all her words, Sally was unnerved. The entire place was remote and as nondescript as it could get. It really did look top secret.

The driver got out and opened their doors for them, and Sally and Lane-Bannister got out of the car.

'Mademoiselle Toussaint,' the man barked. And to Sally's surprise, he went on in French. 'I hear you're one of the best pilots in the country. Now I want you to prove it to me.'

And with that he turned on the heel of one immaculate leather shoe and strode away towards the barn, leaving Lane-Bannister and Sally to follow behind.

Sally was astonished. This all got stranger and stranger by the moment.

'Wyngate,' Lane-Bannister told her as they followed Wyngate towards the barn. 'He's from the Ministry.'

Wyngate. That doesn't sound very French.

Another car pulled up behind them, with Group Captain Chambers at the wheel. Sally didn't recognise his passenger, a man with a neatly clipped moustache and sad eyes. She hoped he would be more polite than Wyngate.

Sally waved to them as they climbed out of the car. 'Afternoon!' she said cheerfully. Wyngate turned and shot her a rather stern glance, but Sally had seen plenty of those over the years of her flight career. It took more than a dark look to cow her.

'Commander Seaton, Group Captain Chambers,' Lane-Bannister said, smiling, as they reached the pair and Wyngate. 'Miss Toussaint, reporting for duty.'

The two men exchanged pleasantries and handshakes with Sally, but by now all she wanted to know was why they'd brought her out here to meet commanders and ministry men in what looked like a broken-down farm building.

Wyngate, obviously done with pleasantries, reached into the pocket of his suspiciously well-cut suit and took out a sheaf of papers. Wherever he got his clothing coupons, they seemed to be going a long way. Without any further explanation, he thrust the bundle of papers towards Sally. 'Read and sign.'

Lane-Bannister shook his head and explained, 'This is a matter of national security, Miss Toussaint. We do need you to fully understand the secrecy of the operation and acknowledge that you won't share what you see and hear.'

'Of course,' Sally said, although she felt rather overwhelmed at the quantity of paper she'd just been handed. 'There's a lot here. Do I need to read it all, or if you could give me a potted version would that suffice? Honestly, I've already had to promise to keep everything under my hat – well, flying helmet! – in the ATA.'

'If you speak to anybody about the business we have here, you'll go to prison,' said Wyngate sharply. 'If so much as the word *barn* comes out of your mouth, I'll hear it all the way from London and have you in Holloway.'

'Steady on,' Lane-Bannister admonished him, though Wyngate looked utterly unconcerned. Then he told Sally kindly, 'It's an addendum to the Official Secrets Act. It just assures us that you accept you can't divulge anything that you see, hear or discuss today. You're welcome to read it through before you sign.'

Wyngate heaved a heavy sigh, as though to say *you'd better not.*

'Not just secret but extra secret, then,' Sally said. 'Righty-ho, I'll read it.'

She read the small type, fidgeting from foot to foot as she did. There were a lot of long sentences that she had to reread in order to understand them, and even then she wasn't entirely sure that she had. But the impression she got was that this was a document so secret, she was surprised she hadn't had to sign something else in order to read it. And she was bound to keep everything utterly confidential.

This is rather fun, actually!

She reached the end and asked, 'Anyone got a pen?'

Seaton reached inside his jacket and produced a fountain pen. He unscrewed it and passed it to her. 'Take all the time you need to think it through,' he advised, glancing towards Wyngate. 'Don't feel as though you need to rush. We want you to be sure.'

'I'm sure,' Sally said confidently. She rested the papers

against her thigh, and signed. A rather wobbly version of her signature, it was true, but she had signed nonetheless. Then she returned the pen to Seaton, and passed the papers back to Wyngate, adding cheerfully, 'I'll sign your autograph book next if you like!'

'Miss Toussaint flew for His Majesty,' enthused Lane-Bannister as Wyngate pocketed the signed papers. 'When she was still a teenage girl!'

Wyngate responded with a curt nod, then turned away and walked towards the door of the barn. When he reached it he said, 'I'm afraid His Majesty wasn't able to join us today.' Then he opened the door. 'After you, mademoiselle.'

Keen to see what all the fuss was about, Sally stepped inside the barn.

She froze. She couldn't believe her eyes.

THREE

Sally blinked. But she wasn't imagining it.

'It's a Spitfire,' she gasped, utterly stunned. What could be so secret about a Spitfire? They were fantastic planes, but she had been flying one only an hour ago. Why was this one so special? It was so out of place here, hidden in a barn that'd been turned into an aircraft hangar.

The windows had been painted out and electric lights hung down from the ceiling. There was a long bench bristling with all kinds of tools, and detailed engineer's blueprints were pinned to the wall. Boxes and crates were neatly stacked, and there were oil drums and spare tyres as well. It all looked incredibly neat compared to some of the hangars Sally had seen in her time.

Two RAF ground crew were standing beside the Spitfire, poring over notes on a clipboard, while another sat at the workbench, running a rasp over a shiny disc that she held in a clamp. A couple of them were rolling up a sheet of tarpaulin, while another was on a ladder, polishing the canopy.

None of this made any sense.

Sally slowly turned to look at the men from the ministry. 'I-I don't understand. Why isn't this plane at Brambles? What's all this for?'

'She's our pet project,' Lane-Bannister said with undisguised enthusiasm. 'Isn't she splendid? Go and look her over!'

'Can I?' Sally asked in awe.

'Of course,' Chambers replied. 'I'm sure you'll appreciate her as much as, if not more so, than anyone.'

Sally went up to the plane and touched her fingertips to the propeller. There was something about this Spitfire, something she couldn't quite explain. Maybe it was because it was out here, in this strange, remote, secret place – but it wasn't only that. Something was different about it. She crouched, peering at the underside of the plane, then rose to her feet again, looking at the panels and the bolts that made this Spitfire.

Just as Sally reached the wing, she had it.

She looked back at the men from the ministry. 'She's a different shape. Just subtly, but... I can see it now. Have you put a different engine in her?'

The man up the ladder looked down at her with a very impressed smile. 'You've got a good eye!' he said as he slung the cleaning cloth over his shoulder. 'Engineer Officer Chabra. She and I have known each other all her life.'

'Are you the proud father?' Sally asked him with a giggle. 'She's *beautiful*. A little bit bigger, but I'm going to take a guess it's because she's got a more powerful engine?'

And I'm *going to fly her.*

Chabra nodded and climbed down the stepladder.

'My wife says I'm the midwife really,' he said with a bright chuckle. 'The boffins created her, but I was there from the first rivet.'

'This is such an honour, seeing a beautiful plane like this,' Sally told him. *And a top-secret one at that.* 'You must be very proud. Have you flown her?'

Chabra laughed and admitted, 'I keep my feet on the ground. Unless I'm up the ladder!' Then he told her, 'It's a real treat to meet you, miss. I've seen Toussaint and Carr fly a dozen times – and now you'll be flying *our* plane!'

Sharp footsteps on the floor of the hangar announced that the men from the ministry had joined them, and Wyngate said, 'Today, at any rate.'

'All we'd like you to do today is to take her up and see what she's game for,' Lane-Bannister explained. 'We know she's not quite there yet, but we need to know her limits. What say you, Second Officer?'

Good heavens above.

'You want me to...' Sally was stunned. But she *had* heard him correctly. They wanted her – they trusted her – to fly this special, secret plane. It was as if Christmas had come early. 'You want me to be her test pilot? I'll look after her, I promise!'

Lane-Bannister smiled. 'Is she ready?' he asked Chabra.

'Raring to go,' he replied.

'She's all yours,' Wyngate told Sally. 'Show us what she can do.'

Sally couldn't believe what was happening. She wasn't just taking a plane from one place to the next, flying in a straight, sensible line. She was going to test it. She was going to see what this new Spitfire could do.

As Sally fastened her helmet and put on her gloves, a tiny voice in her head questioned how safe it all was, but she trusted the men from the ministry, and Chabra and his team. They wouldn't have brought her all this way just to send her up in something that she'd be baling from five minutes later.

They trusted that it would land in one piece, and they trusted Sally to do it.

Sally checked the undercarriage first, then she climbed up, taking a peek at the cockpit before getting in. It looked exactly the same as the cockpits of Spitfires she'd flown before. Satisfied that she knew the lie of the land, she slid down into the seat and got as comfortable as she could.

Everyone in the hangar went outside as Sally made her cockpit check, ensuring all was well with the fuses, and the dials for temperatures and pressures. She pulled the handle to prime the engine, then it was the turn of the brass plunger to draw the fuel. She was impressed at how easily they moved. That was *definitely* an improvement. She switched on the starter magneto, then she pulled the stick back.

She was ready. The plane was primed. With mounting excitement, she started the engine. It was a nice big sound, bigger than she was used to from a Spitfire, and it filled the hangar. She waited, watching the dials again, checking the RPM, the pressures and temperatures. But now she had to taxi it, and she hoped the men from the ministry knew how hard it was to manoeuvre a Spitfire on the ground.

And yet, as Sally rolled the Spitfire out of the hangar, it responded to the controls much better than she had expected. Another improvement, and she wasn't even in the air yet.

Outside the hangar there were more ground crew, and Sally could now see the runway, which had been hidden behind the barn when she'd first arrived. A heck of a lot of work had been done for this secret plane.

She gave a thumbs-up to the waiting ministry men and Chabra and his team. Then, her heart hammering against her ribs, she accelerated along the runway and lifted into the air. The take-off was buttery-smooth, the Spitfire handling it as easily as if it was merely out for a stroll.

'Give us an aerial show,' Lane-Bannister instructed over the radio. It had been so long since Sally had been able to fly for fun that the thought of it sent her blood rushing. 'Just like the good old days.'

'Roger that, Mr Lane-Bannister!' she replied. 'I was hoping you'd say so!'

She flicked the switch to raise the undercarriage. It was a welcome innovation; all the other Spitfires needed the pilot to repeatedly pull on a handpump in the crucial first seconds of being airborne. Sally took the Spitfire up over the fields, over the trees, above the hills, the plane moving easily, responding to even the smallest touch.

So let's see what you can do.

She swooped back towards the waiting spectators, eager to show them what she and the plane were capable of. She plunged low over the runway, skimming the tops of the trees before sharply pulling up, up, up, and into a loop, her heart dancing with excitement.

The Spitfire didn't struggle at all, and Sally whooped with the thrill of it, even though she knew they'd hear her over the radio. It'd been so long, and at the moment when the plane turned upside down at the top of the loop she couldn't help a loud 'Hurrah!' escaping her lips.

She left the loop upside down, a favourite trick of hers from those distant days when she could fly for fun, then she did a barrel roll and, just for Freddy, a chandelle. Every move came off with ease. The secret Spitfire was an extraordinary plane. Freddy would love it, and he'd love to hear about her aerobatics—

Oh blast, I won't be able to tell him.

But on to the next move. Sally almost bounced in her seat with excitement as she pulled back on the stick, pointing the Spitfire's nose straight into the sky as she headed up vertically. The Spitfire obediently climbed. Then she turned, plunging back downwards.

Sally whooped again. 'Oh, a hammerhead, I haven't done one in ages!' she exclaimed to everyone on the ground.

And it was perfect. She might not've pulled that move for

almost two years, but she could still do it. And now it was even more exciting because it was a treat, something Sally had thought she'd never be able to do again. And in this wonderful plane, too. She couldn't believe her luck.

She climbed again, steeply, pushing the plane, but it didn't protest at all. Then she zoomed down again in a corkscrew turn, round and round and round and round, then sped out of the move. Sally didn't wait, she *couldn't* wait, and she flew straight into her next move, flying fast circuits around the field, banking at 180 degrees at each corner.

'How does she handle?' That was Wyngate's voice, clipped and stern. 'We're not here to have fun. Any observations?'

'Like a dream!' Sally whooped as she flew the plane side-ways. 'She's so responsive! Best plane I've ever flown. So much power!'

Sally decided another loop was in order. Then she entered the next loop – and another, and another, flying four loops in a row, and laughing with sheer joy through every one of them. The plane seemed perfectly happy and Sally didn't feel nervous for a moment.

'Did you see *that?*' she asked excitedly. 'And she's not strug-gling or growling at all. In fact, I rather think she's enjoying it almost as much as I am! Hurrah!'

How Freddy would love to see this. The only person who took more delight in Sally's flight skills than she did was her boyfriend. Even in her earliest memories Freddy was there, a playmate before he was a best friend and eventually so much more. Their fathers had run a flight school from Heath Place for nearly two decades before the war saw the house requisitioned, and their fathers had trained their children to fly. Sally and Freddy had never flown with anyone else until war broke out, but now Freddy flew with the boys of number 25 Squadron while Sally had her sisters in the Air Transport Auxiliary.

But, flying like this, climbing and swooping, spinning,

rolling, all the things she'd learned and practised and become famous for – all the things Freddy had been famous for too – reminded her of what their lives had been before the war. *We'll fly together again one day*, Sally promised herself as she spun the Spitfire onto its side before righting it.

If only she could tell him about today.

Soon one of the men from the ministry would give her the order to land, and she would be back to soberly delivering planes again.

The thought of that sent Sally looping-the-loop again, before climbing and flying another corkscrew. She was so lucky to have this chance, this one flight, to do everything she used to do, everything she'd loved and that had been taken from her by war. And in such a remarkable plane, too. She executed another barrel roll, another chandelle, marvelling at how well the plane responded, how it kept up despite Sally packing her impromptu routine with every move she had ever learned.

'Splendid work,' Lane-Bannister announced. 'Bring her down, please. I'm sure you'd like to stay up there all afternoon, but they'd have my guts for garters in Downing Street.'

Sally chuckled. 'I'd like to stay up here *for ever!*' But she wasn't going to ignore an order. She added reluctantly, 'Bringing her in to land now.'

She manoeuvred the plane into position, then flicked the switch to lower the landing gear. But nothing happened. There should have been a cranking sound, but all she could hear was the roar of the plane's engine. Her heart skipped a beat.

'There's a problem with the landing gear,' Sally said over the radio, hoping they wouldn't spot the note of panic in her voice. She flicked the switch again, but still nothing. Was she going to have a ditch landing on her first flight? The plane would be damaged, perhaps taken out of commission completely. *Oh heck, this is bad.* 'I've tried to lower it, but nothing's happening. I'm taking her up again and I'll give it another go.'

Sally pulled up the nose and headed back into the sky. She'd turn and try again. The landing gear would lower now, surely? It had to. She couldn't bear the thought of damaging such an important plane.

FOUR

'Take her round again and I'll gather the boffins. No need to panic,' Lane-Bannister replied with what sounded like forced cheer. But Sally did this for a living, so she wasn't about to panic anyway. Still, the man from the Air Ministry wasn't a pilot himself, so perhaps he thought it was precisely the sort of thing a young lady might panic about.

'The pride of the bloody RAF? It's a glorified baked bean tin!' *That* was Wyngate. 'I can see Göring's lads running a mile from a plane that can't get down once it's bloody up!'

Sally banked, turning the plane, so she could attempt the landing again.

'Come on, come on,' she said under her breath as she flicked the switch once more. But there was still no sound from the landing gear mechanism. What on earth had gone wrong?

'Still nothing,' Sally informed them on the ground. 'I'll try again.'

'Second Officer, we're the only pilots here, so let's examine the options,' Group Captain Chambers said with his characteristic lack of alarm. 'How's the fuel looking?'

Sally glanced at the fuel gauge. 'Still got plenty in the tank.'

She wasn't going to run out of fuel just yet. That was something at least.

Over the radio, she could hear someone barking orders. It sounded a lot like Wyngate, and Sally realised he was giving the engineers a telling-off. She was glad she wasn't in their shoes – but then again... she was in a plane with a broken landing gear.

'It looks like you may have to bring her down on her belly. We'd like you in one piece and ideally the plane too,' Chambers said. Sally thought of Chambers' own crash, and the injuries he'd suffered. He knew what she was risking. She knew what pain lay behind his words. 'You've got plenty of options and I know this won't be your first ditch. You've a cool head, Second Officer; I've every faith in you.'

The field next to the secret airstrip looked like it could offer a soft landing, and it was empty. If the landing gear still didn't come down, she had that option at least. It was possible to land a Spitfire with broken landing gear without damaging it, but she needed to keep a cool head. She'd bellyflopped planes before. She'd bruised her ribs and her teeth had rattled. But she'd survived.

'The field next door looks good for a ditch landing, Group Captain,' Sally told Chambers. And at least it was close to the secret hangar, so the plane could be retrieved easily by the engineers without anyone else getting there first. She gritted her teeth, preparing for the risky landing. 'I'll bring her in.'

Keep a cool head, that's all I need to do.

Sally got the plane into position to land again, aiming this time not for the runway but the field on the other side of the trees.

'Bring her down, Second Officer,' Chambers instructed without the slightest hint of urgency. Sally was buoyed by how much confidence he had in her abilities. 'We'll meet you there.'

As she prepared to make the landing, another voice came

over the radio. This time, it was Wyngate's sharp, tight bark, the same bark she'd heard directed at the unfortunate engineers.

'Before you scratch my paintwork, I have one suggestion,' the man from the ministry said. 'Have you tried punching it? In my experience, it cures most things.'

Punching it?

'No, I haven't tried that,' Sally replied. She didn't generally go about punching planes. Or anything else, for that matter. 'But I'll give it a go.'

Punching the control panel was slightly better than a ditch landing.

Sally flicked the switch to lower the landing gear, then curled her hand into a fist and gave the control panel a thump. She held her breath, then – *clank, clank, clank.*

'The landing gear's lowered!' she exclaimed. 'Can you see it? *Is* it down?'

'It's down!' Chambers exclaimed, seemingly as surprised as he was delighted. 'We'll see you and the unscratched paintwork on the strip.'

With utmost relief, Sally neatly brought the plane down onto the runway, and taxied her back towards the hangar.

Her hands were shaking on the controls. Now that she was on firm ground again, she just couldn't believe what had just happened. She'd flown stunts that she hadn't been able to fly for ages, then managed to bring the plane down safely after a malfunction that could've damaged the experimental machine and held the project back. The ground crew and the ministry men were waiting on the airstrip and Sally could see her excitement reflected in almost every face. Wyngate, as Sally was quickly coming to expect, was giving nothing away.

Sally brought the plane to a halt and, as soon as she was ready to climb down, Lane-Bannister was there to help her. Of all the men who had apparently gathered from London just to watch Sally fly, he was the one who seemed determined to make sure she was at ease. Seaton was amiable if silent, while Wyngate gave the distinct impression of a man who had other places to be.

As soon as her feet met the runway, her legs nearly gave way beneath her. But still, she somehow managed to run over to the ministry men who'd sent her up in the plane. Lane-Bannister followed behind, his stick beating a merry tattoo on the airstrip as he did.

'What a plane!' Sally exclaimed. 'I've never flown anything like her. And oh my goodness, I've missed flying like that. You wouldn't believe how much I have!'

'I'm a naval man by training, so the air is all rather mysterious to me,' Commander Seaton told her with a smile that brightened his sombre expression. 'But that was very impressive indeed.'

'Oh, it's like sailing, really!' Sally told him excitedly. 'We talk about knots, and rudders, and everything! You'd take to it like a duck to – well, not water, exactly, but... sorry, I ramble on so much when I get excited.'

'There's no feeling like being up there, Second Officer.' Chambers smiled. 'And you're one of the best I've ever seen.'

'Thank you, Group Captain,' Sally replied, and beamed at him. His praise meant a great deal to her. He was an amazing pilot himself and had flown with some very talented pilots.

She turned to Wyngate. She wasn't sure how he'd take it, but she wanted to thank him anyway. 'And Mr Wyngate, I don't know how often you've punched control panels on planes, but you saved me from a rather sticky landing! Thank you so much, really.'

'It was a toss-up between you punching the plane and me punching an engineer. A close-run thing.' Wyngate glanced at his watch, then shot his gaze towards Lane-Bannister.

Sally spotted the almost imperceptible nod the two men exchanged before Lane-Bannister said, 'Second Officer, we were really very impressed by that display. We'd like you to work with Maintenance Unit Zero here and serve as our test pilot until she's ready to go into service.'

Sally stopped halfway through taking off her gloves. She stared at Lane-Bannister in amazement. 'You're offering me a job as a test pilot,' she said, still trying to get her head around it. It was an honour as much as a huge surprise. 'I'd be dashed silly to turn that down. And I'd be working out here, every day? I wouldn't be working in the ATA any more?'

Lane-Bannister nodded. 'You'd still be officially in the ATA and your colleagues and family wouldn't know any different,' he explained. 'But your living at home rather than in barracks or shared digs makes that easier when it comes to the Attagirls asking questions. We need someone who can push the Spit to her limits, and we believe that means you or Flight Lieutenant Carr.'

'Who is *very* valuable to the Royal Air Force at this precise moment,' Wyngate added. 'He's got his job to do and you've got yours.'

Sally wanted to say, *he's valuable to me too.* But she held that thought back. They both had to do their bit. All the flying they'd done before the war was for fun, and now both Sally and Freddy were using those skills for the war effort.

'He's a splendid pilot,' she told them. 'One of the best. He'd love to fly this old girl. But if you want me to be her test pilot, then I will.'

'We can't take him away from active duty. He's simply too valuable a combat pilot,' Lane-Bannister explained. 'And you cannot discuss this with him, Second Officer, but I know you understand that. There would be a financial consideration for undertaking these extra duties, of course, and I can agree to a short period for you to consider our offer. Twenty-four hours, perhaps?'

Sally nodded as she took on board his words. Twenty-four

hours to decide. 'That's very kind of you, I'll definitely give it a lot of thought. I can't imagine my decision will change, though. And don't worry, I won't say a thing to Freddy. I dearly wish I could, but... it's all right, I won't tell a soul beyond this airfield.'

'Twenty-four hours. Leave word with Group Captain Chambers by sixteen hundred hours tomorrow,' Wyngate said. He gave a sharp nod, then, without another word, turned and strode away from the plane.

That seemed to signal the end of the visit and, as Chambers and Seaton took their leave, Lane-Bannister escorted Sally back to his waiting car. They had almost reached the vehicle when Engineer Officer Chabra called from the back door of the hangar, 'Thank you for bringing our girl to life, Second Officer Toussaint!'

Sally stopped and turned back to him. Even if Chabra didn't fly planes, he knew them. He understood them, and Sally decided that meant they were kindred spirits. 'It was a pleasure. An absolute pleasure. And I can't wait to fly her again!'

FIVE

Lane-Bannister dropped Sally in the lane near her home, but not so close that her parents would see her getting out of his car. She felt restless, still bristling with excitement, so she decided to wear it off by going for a walk.

She really was thrilled to bits that they'd asked her to be the secret Spitfire's test pilot. And not just because it meant she could fly all the stunt moves that she hadn't been allowed to do since war broke out. It was a huge responsibility, and she was proud that all those important people believed in her, trusted her, to take the plane through its paces and bring it home safely.

So what if the landing gear had failed? She'd fixed it with a thump, hadn't she, thanks to Wyngate.

Chambers believed in her, and that meant a huge amount to Sally. He was such a skilled pilot himself and had been through so much. She couldn't imagine how awful it must've been for him when... when—

Sally stopped walking. Her vision was suddenly blurred with tears and from somewhere – she had no idea where – she was racked with sobs.

She wiped her eyes on her sleeve and dug through her pockets for her handkerchief.

Why am I crying? This is ridiculous. I could do this job in my sleep.

But so much had changed, for all of them. So, the tears fell and Sally dabbed at her eyes.

She heard the rumble of a motorbike engine in the lane and hoped that whoever was riding it didn't notice her. But this was Bramble Heath, where everyone knew each other. The motorbike engine cut out.

'Sally?' a voice called.

Sally looked up and saw Annie, only a few feet away from her, on her motorbike. She kicked down the stand and came over to Sally.

'Goodness me, what's happened?' Annie said kindly, touching Sally's arm.

Does she think I've had bad news? Sally shook her head. 'Nothing,' she said through her tears. 'Nothing's wrong. I'm just being daft.'

'I'll listen,' Annie told her. 'You don't need to worry.'

Sally looked at Annie's gentle expression, and wondered what was going through her mind. Did she think something had happened to Freddy? Or was she wondering if Sally had got in the family way? Annie wouldn't gossip, Sally knew that, but there was something in the other woman's manner that made Sally open up.

'Just had a bit of a shock at work, that's all,' she explained. 'I'm all right, really. Just needed to have a cry.'

It had been a lot, to fly that amazing plane and perform all those moves that she'd missed. And yet it was top secret and she had to keep it all to herself. Then there was the landing gear; even though it'd worked out in the end, she had come very close to ditching the plane.

Annie rubbed Sally's shoulder. She knew the dangers of the

air more than most, being Chambers' fiancée, and regularly visiting the pilots in sickbay at the airbase. 'You poor thing. You weren't hurt at all, were you? Was anyone else?'

'No. All in one piece,' Sally replied, trying to sound chipper as she dabbed away more tears. She knew Annie would understand that she couldn't give any details. 'It's just sometimes it gets a bit too close for comfort.'

'I can imagine,' Annie said sympathetically. 'You're so brave, Sally. But it's all right to cry when you need to. In fact, it's rather brave to cry, do you know that?'

Sally looked at Annie rather doubtfully. 'I was just going for a walk, and... and suddenly...' She gestured to her sodden handkerchief.

'You'll feel better afterwards,' Annie assured her. 'We're all under a lot of strain. Some of us more than others – brave women like you, doing a job I wouldn't even know how to do.'

'I couldn't do yours either. I can't even tie a sling,' Sally told her with a smile. She was starting to feel better, but it wasn't the tears. It was Annie and the warmth of her kindness that was helping her. 'I'm keeping you from your patients. Thank you, Annie. I really appreciate it.'

'It's really all right,' Annie replied. 'Our feelings can hurt just as much as a cut or a bruise. More so, sometimes. If you ever need a chat, you know where to find me, don't you?'

Sally nodded. They said their goodbyes, and Annie got back on her motorbike. She waved to Sally as she set off along the lane.

Sally stood there for a few moments, her tears gone. She only now realised how much she'd needed to cry. The past few hours had been so overwhelming. But she knew what she had to do. She wouldn't turn down the job that had been offered to her. Despite the risks, despite the secrecy, she knew she had to take it on.

SIX

The next morning, in the cottage that Sally and her parents now called home, she sat through breakfast trying to keep her excitement bottled up. She was no longer anxious about what had happened the day before and the offer of the top-secret job was beyond thrilling; but, of course, she couldn't breathe a word to her mother and father.

As soon as Sally arrived at the airbase, she collected her chits as she always did – the notes that told her what she was flying that day – and realised she was being packed onto a transport plane.

She and the other ATA girls would be collecting Spitfires from a factory, delivering them wherever they needed to go. As the girls had talked about how, despite the dangers they faced, *they* had the best war job a woman could have, Sally had bitten her lip.

No, no, I'll have the best job, because I'll be test-flying the secret Spitfire!

Once the transport plane had landed, Sally and the girls got on a bus to the factory. The seats were scarred with cigarette burns, and someone had written rude limericks on the backs of the chairs. As if you'd ever find anything like *that* in Lane-Bannister's elegant ministry car.

'D'you see that London fella at the base yesterday?' Sylvia asked, blowing out a smoke ring as she gestured with her cigarette like a film star. 'Bloody wedding ring... haven't they all?'

Lane-Bannister!

'Oh, him,' Sally said casually. 'Yes, I saw him. Don't know what he was at Brambles for.'

'Big fancy car,' Mabel told them. She glanced around disdainfully at the shabby bus. 'I wouldn't mind having *his* job.'

'I wouldn't mind having your old house neither, Sal!' Sylvia laughed. 'Big place in the country, good-looking London gent on my arm. And no bloody bombs dropping!'

'I'd quite like my old house too!' Sally replied, chuckling, hoping the girls would change the subject. 'Although... I don't know, maybe it would feel odd living there again once all this is over.'

Enid gave her a gentle pat on the shoulder then suggested brightly, 'Anyway, you and Freddy will be married and have your own home!' She bit her lip like an excited schoolgirl. 'And flying all over the world again. Maybe you'll live in Hollywood!'

'Hollywood?' Sally laughed. 'Cricklewood, more like! Besides, we're not engaged yet. I keep hoping Freddy will ask. If he takes much longer, I might have to do the asking myself!'

Sally kept smiling, even though a shadow had fallen over her. She was sure Freddy was waiting for the war to be over before he proposed, hoping that Hitler would be defeated. Freddy didn't know how to be anything other than optimistic, but Sally couldn't shake her fear.

What if something happened to Freddy?

'Tie a banner to the next plane they give you?' Sylvia

suggested. She dropped her cigarette butt on the floor and ground it out with the toe of her boot as she ran her hand through the air to illustrate the headline. '*Fancy tying the knot, Freddy-boy?*'

Everyone laughed, and Sally did her best to bury her worries and join in with the gang of Attagirls.

Once they arrived at the factory, Sally was given another Spitfire to deliver to Bramble Heath. The planes were waiting outside, ready for their pilots, and they had to get into them and take them up in the air as quickly as they could. Rows of shiny new Spitfires were a temptation for enemy planes.

Sally got airborne as soon as she could. She always felt relieved once she'd got the plane off the ground; it was one less stationary plane for the Luftwaffe to target. As she flew, looking out for anything suspicious in the sky, her thoughts kept drifting back to the amazing plane she'd flown the day before.

And she'd been offered the job of test pilot.

She knew she should think it over earnestly, because being a test pilot could be dangerous, as she'd witnessed for herself on her first test flight. But so could working in the ATA. She'd lost her friend Amy in severe winter weather, and she'd had colleagues who'd been shot at by enemy planes while delivering unarmed aircraft. If that wasn't dangerous, she didn't know what was.

Of course, there would be a lot of secrets to keep if she took the job, but it would be easy to do. Sally already kept plenty of secrets working in the ATA. She was certain that a few more wouldn't make the slightest difference.

As Sally neared Bramble Heath, seeing the village nestled down below, she spotted another Spitfire in the sky. It was alone, and she suspected it wasn't heading out to, or coming back from, a mission.

The Spitfire's wing dipped in an acknowledgment and Sally's heart skipped as she recognised one of Freddy's moves. It was his airborne salute, honouring a brother – or sister – in arms.

Freddy!

When on earth had Sally last been in the air at the same time as Freddy? There was no radio yet on the Spitfire she was delivering, so she couldn't tell him she was there. So instead, she echoed his salute. She hoped he'd notice that her plane was unarmed, a sure sign it was being delivered by the ATA, and quite possibly by her.

She remembered the hundreds of displays they'd flown together all over the world in peacetime and how they'd practise in these very skies, challenging and celebrating each other as they jousted in the clouds. One day they'd do it again, but there were no tricks and aerobatics allowed at the moment. Sally didn't mind though. It was enough to be up in the sky with Freddy again.

He was flying towards her – or Sally towards him – and she continued on her path, ensuring they wouldn't collide, but close enough that she could see him in his cockpit and the words MY GAL SAL painted in white on the nose of the fighter. Sally raised one hand from the stick and waved to Freddy, the biggest wave she could manage in the confines of the plane. Then she blew him a kiss as best she could given her oxygen mask.

As Freddy banked his plane up and over Sally, she saw him return the kiss with his gauntlet-clad hand. Then his Spitfire soared overhead, clearing the way for her to land first.

Ever chivalrous, that was her Freddy.

Sally circled the village to get in position for her final approach, before landing the plane as neatly and carefully as she could. Then she taxied it away from the runway, glancing up to see Freddy make his landing. It was always a treat to see him behind the controls of a plane.

As Sally watched the plane descend from the clouds, Wilbur galloped across the grass from her old home to welcome his pa back. He circled Sally's feet, barking merrily and wagging his tail. The little dog had arrived here in Bramble Heath just a few months before the war broke out, riding as a passenger in Freddy's Tiger Moth on their return from a display over Hyde Park. Freddy and Sally had found the sorry little pup as a stray outside their digs, unclaimed and unwanted.

Except by Freddy. As soon as their landlady told the couple that the dog had been hanging around for weeks, there was no question that he wouldn't be joining Toussaint and Carr as an unofficial lucky mascot. As befitted a mascot, he returned home in triumph, making the trip in Freddy's plane, travelling in a wicker travelling basket purchased at Harrods just for the occasion.

Sally scooped up Wilbur and fussed him as he watched Freddy. It never ceased to amaze her how he could know which plane Freddy was in.

Freddy's plane landed with all the grace of a ballet dancer, barely kicking up any dust from the runway. From the mess she heard a round of teasing applause from the boys who flew with him, and who never tired of ribbing the celebrity in their midst.

Shame he's not allowed to fly a couple of stunts to keep the boys entertained!

Sally waved Wilbur's paw at Freddy. 'Bravo! Nicely done. Now get back up there and show us some aerobatics!' She was teasing, of course.

'I don't want to show you up!' Freddy laughed as he climbed down from the plane and strolled towards her. 'And I don't want to be late for dinner. What would your folks say if I rolled up in time for pudding?'

Sally walked towards him and slipped her arm round him, Wilbur between them. She kissed Freddy's cheek. 'You know how fond they are of you. They wouldn't mind at all!'

She glanced at her watch. She still had time before four

o'clock, when her decision was expected. But she'd already made up her mind.

'Sweetie, I just need to nip indoors and deliver a message to someone. I won't be two ticks,' she told Freddy, trying to sound as casual as she could. As she gently passed Wilbur over to him, the cheery sound of a bicycle bell rang in the afternoon air.

'Don't be late home you two!' It was Sally's father on his bicycle, heading for home after a day spent tending the planes of the British and Polish squadrons that flew from Bramble Heath. Freddy's father would likely be heading to his own home soon too, both men having enthusiastically given their aviation expertise to the ground crews from the first moments of the conflict. It still humbled Sally that her parents had handed over their home without a grumble, moving out to the village so Heath Place could house the brave boys who were fighting for freedom.

'I'm all set once I change, François,' Freddy said, beaming. 'It's your daughter who's holding *me* up!'

'Women, eh?' laughed François, as he pedalled on his way.

Sally gave Freddy another kiss on the cheek, then went to the ATA mess to change out of her flight gear. Once she had changed and had pointlessly run a comb through her unruly hair, she went into her old home. Even though it was full of people in RAF blue, all her memories were still there. She remembered decking the corridor with paper chains at Christmas, and playing hide-and-seek when she was a child.

And when she was older, how many times had she run along the very same corridor with Freddy, heading for adventures in the sky? But now she was on the verge of *another* adventure. One Freddy couldn't know about.

Without Gladys there to introduce her, Sally went up to Group Captain Chambers' office door and knocked. 'Group Captain Chambers, it's me, Sally Toussaint!' she called.

'Come in,' came Chambers' reply. Sally's heart was in her

mouth, the image of the Spitfire waiting in its isolated hangar bright in her mind. What an opportunity she had been given.

Fizzing with excitement, Sally went in, then swiftly closed the door behind her. She covered the space to Chambers' desk in two steps, then gripped its edge.

'I've made my decision, Group Captain,' she told him excitedly. 'I'll do it.'

SEVEN

Sally and Freddy walked hand-in-hand through the lanes from Heath Place into the village, Wilbur trotting alongside. A farm wagon lumbered by, drawn by a beautiful bay Shire horse. Holding the reins was Nicola, and beside her was Frances, two of the Land Girls from the Goslings' farm. The girls waved enthusiastically as they passed by, and Sally and Freddy waved back, before the wagon rounded the corner and was gone.

'I knew it was you in the plane,' Sally told him. She could talk about *that* at least. 'It was when you dipped your wing. I knew straight away.'

'That old smooth move,' he said and laughed. 'Dad'd been running some repairs on her and asked me to take her up for a few minutes, just to be sure she was all set. And of course, what could I say but yes? Any excuse to get into the sky!'

'I don't blame you.' Sally grinned at him as they walked through the dappled sunlight that fell through the trees above them. 'Just flying for fun. How wonderful that we flew together again, even if it was only for a little while. It's been so long, Freddy. *Too* long.'

Freddy pecked a kiss to Sally's cheek and gave her hand a squeeze.

'Thank goodness they don't let you girls in the RAF,' he said. 'Because you'd leave us all standing!'

Sally couldn't reply at once. Her mind was full of her flight only the day before in the secret Spitfire. She knew that if she could've told Freddy what she had just signed up to, he'd have been terribly impressed. But she couldn't say a word.

'Imagine, girls in the RAF!' she said after a moment. 'At least we can be in the ATA. If they'd insisted I had to be a Land Girl instead, I would've been out in the fields watching the planes overhead and feeling desperately jealous.'

'I'll tell you who I'm jealous of: that chap from the Air Ministry who's always around Brambles these days,' Freddy said. 'Whizzing around in that fancy motor as though there's petrol on tap!'

He's talking about Mr Lane-Bannister.

'Oh, *him*,' Sally replied, trying to sound casual even though she was on her guard. She couldn't let on that she was now working for the man from the Air Ministry, could she? 'I doubt he's driving about for fun, though,' she went on. 'Must be something important going on for him to be at Brambles. But then, there's a war on, so *everything* is important.'

Sally shrugged, laughing, but she felt so awkward inside. Because she knew very well what Lane-Bannister's business was at Bramble Heath.

'Ginge was saying in the mess that our cosmopolitan chum's always in and out of the Attagirls' depot.'

Sally knew the pilots could be as gossipy as the elderly village ladies who clustered around a table at the tea rooms to discuss who was intriguing in Bramble Heath. There was no harm in it, but this time there was no fun in it for her either. 'Maybe he's got his eye on one of you!' Freddy went on.

'I doubt that.' Sally shook her head, laughing awkwardly

again as panic brewed inside her. 'I'm sure it's just to talk about the different jobs we have. You know we're sent all over the place – he must be speaking to Antonia about super-secret things.'

Antonia, the depot head, assigned jobs to the Attagirls, handing out their chits each morning.

Freddy dotted a kiss to her cheek. 'We've got to talk about something in between chasing down Jerry,' he said, and gave Sally's hand a tender squeeze. 'Good luck to the lad, because the best girl in Brambles is very definitely spoken for!'

Sally's panic melted away. Thank goodness Freddy had been put off the scent. Of course, she knew that Lane-Bannister *was* interested in her, but only as far as her flying was concerned.

But then she was lanced with guilt again, because she couldn't tell Freddy what was really going on.

'You've got nothing to worry about,' she promised him. 'I adore you, Freddy Carr. I wouldn't be without you. I'm on the arm of the best pilot in the RAF. And not only that, but the most handsome one too!'

He gave a jokey shrug and said, 'I should deny it... but it's all true!'

Sally heard the sound of laughter up ahead, coming from a cottage she knew very well. Freddy's home, where his family had moved to when the Toussaints surrendered Heath Place to the Air Ministry. Sunlight twinkled on the little panes in the cottage's window, and out in the front garden Freddy's brother, Peter, was playing with his friends.

'I'm glad he's too young for any of this,' Freddy admitted in a whisper. 'I wouldn't be able to fly straight if that little chap was over in Europe or heaven knows where.' He lifted their joined hands and kissed them. 'That's another reason I wouldn't want you in the RAF. I want to know you're safe here at home.'

Sally did her best to keep smiling. She wasn't going to be in the RAF for her mission test-flying the secret plane, and she wasn't going to be all that far from Bramble Heath. She'd still go to sleep in the same bed every night. The only difference was that she wouldn't be delivering planes for a while. She'd just be flying *one* plane in particular.

Besides, none of it mattered at that moment, because what Freddy had just said was so sweet, so affectionate, that Sally's heart filled with love. She tightened her fingers round his.

'I'm safe and sound, and so's Peter,' she told him. 'You don't need to worry about us. Just concentrate on getting yourself home in one piece. That's all I'm worried about.'

'Don't you worry about me.' Freddy gave her a playful wink. 'Charmed life.'

As they passed Freddy's cottage, Peter's head popped up over the top of the hedge.

'Hope you're not canoodling!' The boy laughed. 'We had two Spits over not long ago. One of them was ours!'

Freddy pointed to himself with his thumb. 'One of them was me. The handsome one.' Then he nodded towards Sally. 'And the very English but also a little bit French one was this miss!'

Peter's eyes lit up as he exclaimed, 'Toussaint and Carr, together again!'

'Amazing!' gasped Peter's friend Sam, who was now peering at them over the top of the hedge too. 'You should've done a barrel roll!'

'I'm so glad you saw us flying, boys,' Sally replied, pleased to see how excited Peter was. 'Let's hope it won't be long before you see us perform our old tricks together again.'

'And we'll be training you up to fly with us,' Freddy told his brother. 'Or, knowing you, wielding a spanner on the ground with Dad.'

'That's where you'll find me,' Peter said, beaming, and exchanged a nod with Sam. 'Tinkering with my feet on the floor! I sorted out the brakes on Sam's bike today, gave them a fine tune.'

'He did too.' Sam nodded enthusiastically. 'They always stuck – they were rubbish. Then Peter got out his toolbox and, quick as a flash, they're like new!'

Sally wasn't surprised. Peter had spent his whole young life in a house where bits of aeroplanes littered the dining table. She pictured the hangar where the secret Spitfire was waiting for her. Peter would've loved it there.

'Bravo, Peter!' she said, giving him a round of applause. 'You're a handy chap to know.'

Freddy narrowed his eyes and told the two boys, 'I see what you're up to, stealing my girl.' Then he laughed and scrubbed his brother's unruly hair. 'Ma Toussaint's feeding me up tonight, so we'd better be on our merry way!'

Then he took off his uniform cap and set it rakishly atop Peter's head.

Sam chuckled, and Peter's other friends, who had joined them standing by the hedge, were laughing too.

'He'll have all the girls after him now, won't 'e?' said Bill, a boy who'd been evacuated early in the war and had lived in Bramble Heath ever since. He'd become firm friends with Peter and Sam.

'*Girls?*' Peter grimaced. 'No thanks!'

Freddy let his mouth fall open in a pantomime of shock before he asked, 'What about my Sally?'

'She's not a girl,' Peter assured him. 'She's a pilot!'

It was Sally's turn to laugh now. 'It *is* possible to be a pilot *and* a girl, you know. What would all my Attagirl chums say if they heard that?'

Peter shrugged and replied, 'They'd be happy because they're pilots!'

Still laughing at Peter's words, Sally and Freddy continued on their way to Sally's new home. She still called it that, even though it'd been nearly two years since she and her family had left Heath Place.

Bramble Cottage stood a little way back from the road, with a large front garden full of vegetable plots and beanpoles. The thatched cottage was older than Heath Place, and there was something about the way it wore its years that made Sally hopeful. It had stood here through wars and plagues, yet it was still here. It had survived.

François' bicycle was leaning against the wall, and one of the windows downstairs was open. Jaunty music playing from the wireless drifted out into the garden.

Home. As long as I have my family, home is wherever we live.

With a pang, Sally suddenly thought of her family in France; of sitting on her grandmother Mémé's knee as she sang to her in French; of climbing trees with her cousins; and of sitting around an enormous table together to eat.

Living in an old cottage really wasn't a hardship. It was nothing like what her family would be living through on the other side of the Channel. There would be no enormous family feasts now – and where were her cousins? Were they all safe? They were no longer climbing trees, that was for sure. Had they gone to Germany, to the factories, as Sally feared? And Mémé, dear Mémé, would she survive another war?

Sally couldn't change what was happening over there, other than doing her bit for the war effort. She didn't tell Freddy what was on her mind. She didn't want to worry him when he had enough to deal with every day in the air.

She led the way down the garden path to the kitchen door, where her mother, Emily, was busy at the hob.

'Come in, you two!' Emily said.

'Hello, Ma Em!' Freddy beamed. She was as good as family to him, thanks to the happy years the Toussaint and Carr families had spent sharing Heath Place when the aerodrome and flight school had filled the air above Bramble Heath with planes. Heath Place was too big for just Sally and her parents, so the Carrs had moved in too. They had been one big family. 'Whatever dinner is, it smells fantastic!'

It always seemed miraculous to Sally what Emily could cook despite rationing and shortages. She went up to her and kissed her cheek.

Emily returned Sally's kiss. 'There's leeks in here that are fresh from the garden only an hour ago,' she told them, then returned to stirring the pot. 'They've come up huge, so none of us'll go hungry.'

As Emily started to dish up the stew she'd made, Sally kept thinking of the decision she'd made that day, which she couldn't tell her family about. There she was, sitting in the familiar kitchen in Bramble Cottage with Freddy and her parents, as if nothing had changed at all.

As they tucked in to dinner, they might've forgotten there was a war on at all; but the tape on the windows and the heavy blackout curtains brought everybody back to reality if they needed a reminder. Still, the conversation was merry and the food was good, thanks to Emily's finely tuned skill. Here in Bramble Heath, they didn't do too badly. Even Wilbur had his own dish of stewed meat and gravy to enjoy beneath Freddy's chair.

'Today, when I saw Sally and Freddy follow each other in, my heart almost burst,' François admitted with an affectionate smile. 'My little girl and Arthur's boy flying together again. I stood at the hangar with your father, Freddy, and we watched you both in.'

'Just like the old days,' Emily said, smiling at everyone sitting round the table.

'I'll be honest, it was so much fun to be flying with Freddy again.' Sally reached for Freddy's hand across the table. 'Even though we couldn't do any aerobatics. But once things are back to normal, Toussaint and Carr will take to the skies again.'

'I'll drink to that!' beamed François as he raised his glass. 'À votre santé!'

Once they had eaten, it was time for Sally to say goodbye to Freddy. He was on standby, and Sally knew he could end up being scrambled.

They went out into the garden and along the path to the gate, Wilbur pattering alongside them. The garden had come alive again after sleeping through the winter. The branches were dotted with fresh, green buds, and the blossom on the apple tree was as fluffy as a cloud.

'Take care, darling,' Sally said, the words weighted with uncomfortable meaning when Freddy might have to fly at any moment.

'I always do,' he assured her with his usual carefree smile as Wilbur weaved around their feet, the little dog's tail batting happily back and forth. 'Because I've got you to come home to.'

Sally danced her fingertips against his cheek. 'I'll be waiting right here for you. I love you, Freddy.'

'Love you too.' Freddy caught her hand and turned it over to kiss the palm. 'And I'll always see you tomorrow. You sleep tight, mademoiselle. Dream of me?'

'Every night,' she told him, as she brushed her lips against his cheek. 'Goodnight, Freddy.'

EIGHT

There wasn't any time to lose. Now that Sally had agreed to be the secret Spitfire's test pilot, she was at work on it the very next day. While everyone, apart from a tiny circle of people, thought she was still delivering planes with the ATA, Sally left the house and headed out to the barn. Chambers had made arrangements; Antonia, the ATA depot head, wasn't expecting to see Sally that day.

Sally sometimes rode her bicycle to the Bramble Heath airbase, and today she pedalled away from the village, taking a shortcut she knew through the fields and woods to keep her journey as secret as she could. Finally, she cycled up the bumpy, unmade track to the top-secret hangar in a forgotten field.

Sally's heart raced with excitement as soon as she saw the humble building up ahead. Flying an amazing plane was such a treat, and she felt as proud as anything to have been personally selected for this mission.

Sally arrived at the barn, which looked just as ordinary as it had done two days before. But she knew better.

She had been given a secret signal by Chambers the day before, so the ground crew in the barn knew it was safe to open the door to her. It was wonderful fun, like the time she and Freddy, as children, had commandeered a shed on the grounds of Heath Place and wouldn't let anyone in unless they said *Winifred Spooner*, the name of Sally's aviation heroine.

What a marvellous adventure!

Sally knocked firmly once, then twice, then she called, 'Hello, does anyone know the way to Bluebell Woods?'

From inside the hangar she could hear approaching footsteps, then Chabra's voice replied, 'You're almost on the path,' and a bolt slid back. As soon as the door opened she could smell the metal and oil and machines. And there was Chabra, the man in charge of Maintenance Unit Zero, greeting her with a bright smile. 'I knew you'd say yes!'

Sally laughed, and reached out her hand to shake Chabra's. 'How could I possibly resist?' She glanced at the plane waiting in the hangar and sighed happily. 'I hope she's had a good rest after I took her out.'

One of the women on the ground crew was rubbing a cloth over the plane propellers. She grinned at Sally. 'She did. And she's raring to go again. I'm Esther, by the way. We're all really looking forward to working with you.' Esther gestured towards the other ground crew, who were busily at work.

'And I'm Viraj,' Chabra said as he pressed his hand to his chest. 'Come and meet the family.'

Sally received a very warm welcome from the ground crew. They'd all heard of Toussaint and Carr, and they were full of astonished praise for Sally's flight two days prior. It reminded her of the old days, when she and Freddy had met their fans after landing at airshows. Except, of course, Freddy couldn't be there with her today, or even know where she was or what she was doing.

Sally was shown around the hangar, seeing the workbenches and the stores, and given a quick talk through the blueprint of the plane hanging on the wall. It wasn't long before she had her own tin mug and a locker where she could leave her things, and she started to feel at home.

What a lovely, friendly bunch I'm working with. I'm so glad I said yes.

'I can't wait to get her up in the air again,' she said out loud, bouncing on her toes with excitement as she took in the wonderful aircraft that dominated the space. Despite her excitement, there was still one very important question to ask. 'But the landing gear – that *is* working properly now, isn't it?'

'We stripped it back to the bones and found nothing,' Viraj said, which didn't fill Sally with confidence. 'But we've had that gear up and down and every which way to Sunday and we haven't been able to replicate the problem. In something like a thousand tests, it's worked like a dream every time.'

Sally knew planes well enough to know that sometimes, for no reason that anyone could put their finger on, glitches happened. It'd been fairly nerve-wracking at the time, but she'd coped. If she hadn't taken up Wyngate's no-nonsense suggestion to punch the control panel, she could still have ditched her safely, Sally was sure.

'I'm sure it was a one-off,' she replied. 'You couldn't have done anything more.'

'I don't like leaving a question mark over it,' Viraj admitted, nodding towards the corner of the hangar with the lockers. It was their version of a mess, with a tea urn and biscuit tin and a sofa that had seen better days. 'Let's have a cuppa and I'll talk you through what we're doing here.'

Sally went over to the mess and filled her mug with tea, before dropping down onto the sofa. She gripped her mug. 'So... I suppose I'm not going to be putting on aerobatics displays every day, am I?'

'I'm afraid not,' he said with a chuckle, settling onto the sofa. 'What we're doing here is really giving the Spit a real taste of sherbet. Not just a little improvement, but a real step up... like swapping a horse and cart for one of Mr Lane-Bannister's motor racers.'

Sally stared at him, wide-eyed. 'Gosh! Spitfires are already fantastic machines, but making it even better...' She thought back to her first flight and said, 'She handled so well. I have to say, I've never been allowed to fly any fully loaded Spits before the other day, but I've heard all about them from Freddy, when he's flown in combat. And really, this one will do boys like Freddy proud. I could really feel the power in the engine, and she didn't struggle at all. I didn't once feel as if I was pushing her too hard. If anything, I wasn't pushing her hard enough!'

Viraj beamed like a proud father. 'She'll have twice the manoeuvrability and twice the range, and will be able to carry far superior weapons,' he assured her. 'Jerry won't be able to keep up with this one, never mind take her out of the sky.'

Sally looked over at the plane again. She thought of Freddy, and the very idea that one day he could be flying a plane that he'd never be shot down from filled her heart with hope. So much fear had crept into it since the war had begun, but just that little glimmer made a difference.

'That really is remarkable,' she said. 'And it's just what we need. You know, every time I deliver a Spit somewhere, I just... I just hope it's not replacing one that...' She glanced down at her mug, before summoning the strength to say, 'One that didn't make it home.'

Viraj nodded sympathetically. 'I understand, I worry too. My brother's just been seconded out to number 1 Squadron,' he said. 'He'll be flying with the Indian Air Force.'

'That's wonderful.' Sally companionably patted Viraj's arm. He'd be just as worried for his brother as she was for Freddy, even if neither of them put it into words. 'A love of flight must run in your family. And just think, maybe *he'll* be flying the secret Spit one day!'

'I'll be a lot happier when he is,' he admitted. 'Once we've got her signed off, we can start overhauling the existing planes and building new Spits to this blueprint. I like to think Mr Mitchell would've been proud of what we're doing.'

'He was a very talented man,' Sally replied, thinking of the genius who'd designed the Supermarine Spitfire. But Mitchell had died two years before the war started, and had never seen how his invention had become key to the country's defence. And now, Sally was test pilot for a new version of Mitchell's plane. A plane that could outmanoeuvre the Luftwaffe and defend the free world. A plane that had to be kept secret or their advantage would be lost. 'I wish he could've lived to see what his plane's achieved. But of course, he's passed the baton to people like you.'

Viraj lifted his mug in a silent toast to the man who'd invented the Spitfire. Then he told her, 'So, Mr Lane-Bannister has asked me to explain how your new job works.' He settled back on the sofa. 'You'll be performing all your usual duties on the days we're not test-flying. On the days we need you, we'll send word and you'll spend the day with us instead. It's important that nobody notices you're suddenly not delivering planes any more.'

Sally nodded. 'I had wondered that. Even though us Atta-girls fly all over the place, if I vanished from the airbase, but they saw me in the village, they'd wonder what was going on. It sounds like a good solution.' And she rather liked that idea, too, because she could sit among the girls fully aware of her secret while they knew nothing about it at all. 'Will I need to look out for a signal?'

'It'll be on your chit,' he explained. '*Bluebell Woods*.'

What fun!

Sally grinned at Viraj and tapped the side of her nose. 'Excellent. Bluebell Woods it is.'

And with that, Sally got to work.

The ground crew prepared the plane, and, instead of

performing all of her much-missed aerobatics again, this time
Sally had to go through a list of manoeuvres, making specific
checks. But it was still fun, and she was thrilled to be part of the
highly secret process that would make Spitfires even more
phenomenal than they already were. And this time when she
came in to land, she flicked the switch and the landing gear
lowered without any problem at all.

Her life had changed in a very short space of time, and yet
only a handful of people knew.

The next morning, she cycled to the airbase, hoping so
much that the chits she'd be given would carry those two words
that filled her with such exhilaration. *Bluebell Woods.* She had
to stifle her smile when she saw that they did and, after the
other girls were up in the air, she got back onto her bicycle and
headed for the secret Spitfire.

Sally easily fell into her new routine. She had never gone into
detail with her parents about where she'd been delivering
planes to, as her ATA work was secret in its way. And that
meant she could be just as vague about what she had been
doing on the days she was at the barn as on the days when she
was flying between factories and airbases. The girls in the ATA
hadn't noticed that she wasn't delivering planes every day. It
was an easy secret to hide, as no two days in the ATA were the
same.

The only person who *did* like to know what Sally was up to
on her days in the air was Freddy, who never tired of plane talk.
Yet he knew just as well as she did that careless talk wasn't a
good idea, so he never pressed her too much. It was enough for
him to know that his girl was still flying and still in her element,
up there with the clouds. He was the one person Sally knew
who would dearly love to hear all about her new adventures, but
she couldn't tell him. Besides, if the work of Maintenance Unit

Zero went to plan she wouldn't need to, because he'd be flying the Spit himself one day.

But Sally didn't feel isolated in her secret work. After all, she was part of the team up at the barn, and she quickly got to know everyone. Among the ground crew were Robert and Joe, who had been on the Spitfire development team right from the start – Joe had even worked with Mitchell, which made him a legend in the team. There was dependable Gus, who knew his way around the plane almost better than anyone, and Frank, who had an endless stream of puns.

Lane-Bannister visited when he could, keen to discuss the team's work and their progress with the Spitfire. He would stay to watch Sally fly, which always made her feel proud, and, if it was raining, he'd give her and her bicycle a lift home in his car.

It didn't take Sally long to make friends in the team. There was Esther, with her tales of the strict typing pool in London that she'd escaped by joining the WAAF. Then there was Connie, who'd grown up tinkering with the engines on her father's fishing boats.

And they all shared the same secret, one that could turn the tide of the war.

NINE

TWO WEEKS LATER

Sally couldn't help grumbling to herself as she left the ATA depot on her bicycle. The rain was bucketing down, and she had to get to the secret barn that morning. As exciting as it was to be summoned for a test flight again, the journey there would not be fun.

I'll be soaked! Or drowned, most likely, in this dreadful weather.

She could hear a car approaching through the downpour, and hoped against hope that it wouldn't pass so close that she ended up even more drenched than she already was. Instead, the driver chose to toot the car's horn, no doubt so she would clear out of the way into the muddy roadside.

Annoyed, Sally turned her head, ready to protest. But instead she smiled, because she knew that car. It was Mr Lane-Bannister from the Air Ministry, who'd given her a lift home from the secret barn once or twice before.

Sally climbed off her bicycle and walked it over to the car.

'Mr Lane-Bannister to the rescue!' she said to the driver, who had opened his window. She smiled at the ministry man in the back seat. 'I don't suppose you could give me a lift?'

'Why on earth do you think we stopped?' asked Mr Lane-Bannister as he climbed out of the vehicle. 'Jump in! You can laugh at us trying to wedge a wet bicycle into a government motor.'

'Thank you so much, you can't imagine how grateful I am!' Sally told him.

The driver climbed out too, and took charge of the bicycle. Sally got into the back seat, glad to be out of the rain, but worrying about the trail of water she was leaving all over the upholstery. She turned to watch the two men as they opened the boot and wrestled with her bicycle.

'To me, sir, just a bit,' the driver said. 'Watch out for that wheel.'

'Why is the bicycle suddenly so much bigger in the rain?' laughed Lane-Bannister in his plummy way, as they finally closed the boot as though trying to fasten an overstuffed suitcase. 'I'm sure it fit perfectly in dry weather.'

Sally laughed. 'What a hoot! Well, at least you got it in there in the end, that's the main thing. Now you two need to get into the dry!'

'Even the rain is cleaner in the countryside. I'd happily pass the war in our country pile if I could,' said Lane-Bannister as he climbed back into the car and set his stick against his leg. Sally had the impression that it wouldn't be in a little cottage like the one she now lived in, nor in a rambling house like Heath Place, which had hosted a flight school and aerodrome just to earn its keep. The Lane-Bannister country pile would certainly be rambling, but it wouldn't be a business. She wondered if it had been requisitioned too, or if his family still lived there.

'Is it like Bramble Heath, where you're from?' Sally asked him as the driver started the car again and steered them through the rain. 'I've lived here all my life, you know. In fact, I lived in Heath Place all my life – until your chaps decided it was a handy place for an airbase. Can't say I blame them, really.

Although... it always feels so strange going inside. Part of my brain still expects it to look exactly as it did when we all lived there, and I'm always surprised that it doesn't any more.'

'We're out in the middle of the Cornish wilds,' he explained. 'I am dashed sorry about your house. We promise not to keep it for ever. Flight school, wasn't it?'

Sally nodded. 'It was. Not much use for a flight school now, though, is there, seeing as the RAF have their own. But I do understand, really I do. The war effort has to come first, and I feel so proud of what my home has become. It's not a big sacrifice, is it? Other people have given – or lost – much more.'

As soon as the words were out of her mouth, Sally regretted saying them. Her gaze fell on Lane-Bannister's black armband, and she quickly looked away.

Oh, I'm a fool. That was so thoughtless of me.

'My people are in motor racing,' he said, deftly changing the subject. 'That's how I ended up with this.' And he gave a sharp rap on his lower limb.

He's got a fake leg!

Sally stared at him in amazement. 'I... I hadn't realised you've got a wooden leg. You poor chap, that must've been quite a smash-up. Gosh, I suppose your family and mine would get on famously, yours on the racetrack and mine in the sky. Put a fast engine in a machine, and the Toussaints and Lane-Bannisters are there!'

He nodded keenly. 'And my little brother's a Spitfire ace, so you and he would have lots to chat about!'

Sally laughed. 'We most certainly would. He'd get on famously with Freddy, too.' As soon as she said Freddy's name, Sally felt a stab of guilt. Here she was, being driven in an Air Ministry car, laughing with Lane-Bannister, and yet she couldn't tell Freddy. It had seemed so easy to begin with, just a few more secrets on top of the others, but...

'Mr Churchill was right. Never was so much owed by so

many to so few,' her companion said solemnly. 'And we count ladies like you in that. The boys might do the fighting, but they need the planes to do it.'

As if on cue, the heavy sound of a bomber engine could be heard humming overhead and, through the rain-lashed sky, Sally saw the huge shape of an Avro Manchester soaring between the clouds. It might be one of her own friends, delivering it to the men who would fly it into combat one day soon.

'Out here in the countryside, one can almost forget the war. And then... well, there's a Lanc instead of a tractor.' Lane-Bannister sighed. 'In London, one can't forget. But that's what we're fighting for, isn't it? This country of ours – and the loved ones we've lost.'

As he said that, Mr Lane-Bannister linked his hands and absent-mindedly turned the gold wedding band he wore.

Where is Mrs Lane-Bannister?

Sally wouldn't have been surprised to learn that she was safely tucked away in Cornwall with Lane-Bannister's mother. He must really miss her. And yet, the black armband... Sally had thought it was for a brother lost in the Battle of Britain, but he sounded very much alive.

Had Lane-Bannister lost his wife?

'I'm so sorry,' Sally told him, the words escaping before she could stop herself from saying them. 'I'm so sorry for your loss. Your-your armband. I'm so sorry.'

'The Blitz, you know,' he said carefully. And Sally knew precisely what he meant; there was no need to say more. Then he took a deep breath and said, 'But this won't last for ever.'

He lost his wife in the Blitz. Poor man.

'It won't,' Sally assured him, her heart filling with sympathy for the man from the ministry. 'There'll be peace again one day.'

'We'll kick them right in the pants, as my little nephew is fond of saying – not that he really *should*.' The car glided to a halt outside the hangar and Mr Lane-Bannister clapped his hands together. 'We'll see how she handles in this sort of weather today, Second Officer Toussaint. Confident?'

Sally nodded. The ATA flew in all sorts of weather, and, if it hadn't been for that fact, well... her friend Amy would still be alive. It had only been a few short months ago, back in January, that Amy had been lost in the Thames Estuary in a snowstorm, delivering an Airspeed Oxford. It didn't matter that Amy Johnson had been a household name, she had still made the ultimate sacrifice for the war effort.

'Oh, very confident,' Sally said with a grin as the rain hammered against the car roof, because she knew Amy would've agreed. 'It's only a little bit of rain, after all!'

TEN

Sally dried off while the ground crew prepared the secret Spitfire for its flight. The rain was very heavy, but it wasn't anything she hadn't experienced before. It was only that it was a first for this particular plane, and the thought sent a wave of worry through her.

Don't be silly. It's just a formality. They have to tick a box to say they've flown her in heavy rain. It's nothing!

Once Sally was in her flight gear, she left the hangar. The secret Spitfire was on the runway, chocks under her wheels as her engine turned. Spitfires needed time to warm up, but not too long, otherwise they overheated. Sally hurried over, even though running in cumbersome flight gear with her parachute bumping against her legs was never easy, and climbed up onto the wing. It was slippery in the rain and she nearly lost her balance, but Gus, who was already on the wing preparing the plane, caught her.

The canopy was pulled back and rain spattered the seat. Gus pulled down the flap, and he and Esther, who was standing on the other wing, guided Sally down onto the seat and buckled her in. It was exactly as ground crew worked at the airbase, and it was important to follow the procedures that would be in place once the secret Spitfire went into action.

Sally closed the canopy, and Gus and Esther jumped off the wings, then Frank and Joe pulled away the chocks. Sally plugged herself into the radio. The windscreen was fairly clear, despite the rain, as the rush of air from the propeller blasted it away. And yet the rain still beat a tattoo against the canopy.

Sally watched for the signal from Viraj, then she was off, heading down the runway at speed. Her heart leapt into her throat as she realised the wheels were slippery. Of course they would be in the rain, but it still took her by surprise. But it was only seconds before she pushed the throttle and the stick forwards, lifting the secret plane into the sky.

'She'll need better tyres!' she said over the radio.

Sally took the plane higher and higher, until it was just below the rainclouds, and flew straight. She pulled back the canopy and as usual got a blast of cold air, but it was so exhilarating she didn't care one bit. Besides, the propeller stopped the rain from pelting her, so it was surprisingly comfortable despite the chill.

Sally went through the manoeuvres she'd agreed on with Viraj, banking, turning, climbing. The plane handled it well. There didn't seem to be any risk of the heavy rain damaging the engine, and Sally suspected that the water had helped to stop it from overheating on the ground.

She went into a loop – one of her favourite things about being a test pilot – and it was all going well until she came out of it. The plane sagged a little to one side, and Sally had to pull to the other side to get her even again.

'Did you see that? It could've gone better!' she told them back on the ground. It wasn't a huge problem, and could be easily fixed by the pilot, but everything had to be reported back. Even a tiny issue could herald something bad.

Once Sally had taken the plane through her paces, it was time to land. She descended from the heights, and saw the runway getting nearer. As she went through the landing procedure, she flicked the switch to lower the undercarriage. She should've heard the reassuring cranking sound of the wheels lowering, followed by a click as they locked into place. But all she heard was a metallic clunk.

Oh, not again. I mustn't panic. I mustn't. It just needs a thump.

So Sally clenched her fist and confidently gave the control panel a thump.

But this time, nothing happened. Not a sound. Her heart leapt into her throat.

'The undercarriage is stuck again. I've thumped it, just like last time, but it's not budging,' she told them, her voice trembling with fear. She was scared. What if she couldn't get the wheels down this time? She could ditch it, as she had suggested before, but the weather wouldn't make it an easy job at all. 'I'm aborting the landing. I'm going back up again.'

Sally was only just in time. She was almost skimming the tops of the trees that surrounded the secret runway, and she pulled up, gaining altitude again.

'Take her round and come in again when you're ready,' Viraj said, with measured calm, but Sally didn't doubt that everyone was muttering a silent prayer.

'Will do,' she replied, her voice tight with panic. She had to get the wheels down. She had to. If she ditched it, especially in the rain, the plane could be damaged. And if she baled, it was even worse – the plane would crash and be reduced to wreckage. Aside from the fact that she might be injured in the process, it'd ruin the prototype and they'd have to start all over again. It could cost weeks, months; it would delay the secret Spitfire being rolled out.

I'm a fool. I'm a bloody fool. Why did I ever agree to do this?

I should've stuck with my job delivering planes. Oh, Freddy, I'm so sorry. I've got into such a pickle.

As Sally climbed, she flicked the switch again, which would lift the landing gear. She could hear the cranking sound, and for a moment she thought she was saved. But it only lasted a couple of seconds, and all she could hear was the wind whistling past her and the roar of the Spitfire's engine.

'How does she feel?' That was Lane-Bannister, his voice tight. 'Any change?'

There was no sign of the humour she'd heard in his voice as he'd wrestled her bicycle into his boot.

Maybe I should've stayed on the ground, on two wheels.

'I could hear the mechanism just then, but now... nothing,' Sally replied, trying to sound level-headed even though she wanted to cry.

On the runway below she could see her friends from the crew race out into the rain to begin scattering a carpet of straw on the ground, but that wouldn't do anything to arrest the Spitfire if she brought it down without its landing gear. It was like trying to stop a Lancaster bomber with an elastic band.

'Take her round again,' Lane-Bannister said with urgency. 'Viraj is working on it.'

It struck Sally then that they didn't know what to do. They were preparing for the worst.

Up in the sky, the boffins and engineers might as well be a thousand miles away.

ELEVEN

'I'll keep going,' Sally told Lane-Bannister. 'Never fear. I'll leave off flicking the switch again until I hear back. I don't want to make it any worse. By the way, Mr Lane-Bannister? Just wanted to say thanks ever so for giving me a lift this morning. You're a gentleman.'

'And we'll give you a lift home too,' he assured her.

'Brilliant,' Sally replied, then she added, 'I'm sorry your plane's a bit broken.'

How long would it be until she could take up Lane-Bannister's offer? How long would she have to wait for someone on the ground to work out what to do? They'd be poring over blueprints and scratching their heads, while she was stuck in the sky, in the rain. She could wait for hours and they might not come up with anything that'd work. She desperately didn't want to damage the plane, but it was already too late. The landing gear was stuck, and Sally was stuck in the air until it came down.

There had to be something she could do.

'Look, chaps, I'm going to have another go,' she told them on the ground, her voice suddenly edged with steel. 'I'm flicking the switch to lower the undercarriage, and I'm going to get the blessed thing down. Maybe it just needs the equivalent of a good thump. Don't worry, I know what I'm doing!'

Sally flicked the switch. She heard the *thunk* again.

'We're working on it,' Viraj assured her, but she heard his urgency in his usually so relaxed manner. 'But we trust you. Do whatever you think you need to do.'

'Righty-ho,' Sally replied. And with that, she took the plane into a roll, and rolled, and rolled, one roll after another. She hoped that each time she went from being upside down to the right way round again, gravity would work on the stuck undercarriage and eventually pull it down. She strained her ears for any sounds from the landing gear and, after her tenth roll, she heard it.

It was cranking.

'It's coming down!' Sally called. 'It's worked!'

But no sooner had she announced it than the cranking stopped again. It hadn't been running long enough for the undercarriage to have fully lowered.

What am I going to do?

If only she could get under the plane and pull it down. But there was no way *that* was going to happen.

She looked down at the trees passing below, the fields, the hills...

The trees.

'Chaps, I think I've got it,' Sally told them. 'The undercarriage is partially down now – can you see it? It just needs a little nudge, then I'm home and dry. Well, home, at least!' And she chuckled. Being wet through really was the least of her worries at that moment.

'We can see it!' Lane-Bannister assured her. 'You've nearly got it!'

'Phew!' Sally replied. But what she was about to attempt was not in any way easy.

She descended again, but she wasn't aiming for the runway

but the trees surrounding it. If she could get the height just right – low enough for the highest branches to catch on the landing gear, high enough not to get tangled or crash into the trees – she could get the landing gear down.

She tried a first pass, just to get an idea of the altitude she needed. The treetops were very close, but not quite close enough. So Sally tried again, her heart in her mouth as this time she heard the wet branches scrape against the bottom of the plane, and – *thank heavens!* – there was that cranking sound again. Was it enough?

She didn't want to try again, in case the landing gear ended up with damage from the branches. She flew past the hangar where her team was anxiously watching.

'Can you see if the undercarriage has lowered?' Sally asked over the radio. 'Have I brought half a tree with me too?'

'You've done it!' Lane-Bannister exclaimed. 'Now get her down straight away, not that I need to tell you that!'

'Here I come!' Sally cheered, and she brought the plane round for her landing. Despite the rain, the members of the ground crew were all out on the runway watching her – with the exception of Viraj and Lane-Bannister; whatever conversation they were having, Sally couldn't imagine it was an easy one.

Normally, Sally never enjoyed landings because it meant the end of her flight. But today she felt very differently. All she wanted was to feel firm ground under her feet.

She descended, and, as she felt the tyres bounce against the runway, she felt an enormous wave of relief wash through her. She taxied to the hangar, the controls struggling with the damaged undercarriage. But it could be fixed, again. If she'd hit the runway without any landing gear at all, it would've been a very different story.

And not one I want to think about right now.

.   .   .

The crew chased after her, applauding despite their pale complexions. They had been just as worried as Sally, but they'd had the good fortune to be on the ground at the time.

'Get out of there!' Connie told her, running to stand at the wing. 'That was— Are you all right?'

'Yes, yes,' Sally replied as she pulled off her oxygen mask. She was surprised at how out of breath she sounded. 'I'm fine. It's fine. Everything's fine! I'm in one piece, and the plane *almost* is. That's what we're all about, isn't it?'

Sally plucked at her buckles and freed herself, then she took Connie's hand and climbed out of the plane.

'My legs would be like jelly!' Connie helped Sally down onto solid ground, then gave her an unexpected hug. 'I'm just glad you're back here with us. That was horrible to watch.'

Sally, so pleased to be hugged, held on to Connie for a moment. She couldn't tell anyone beyond this secret place what she'd just been through. She needed to hang on to Connie's hug for as long as she could.

'It was pretty terrifying when the thumping didn't work,' she admitted. 'But I just got on with the business of landing the plane. Somehow. Never had this sort of problem on my Tiger Moth – the undercarriage doesn't go up and down, it's always just *there*!'

'Chief engineers debrief *now*!' Sally was surprised to hear Wyngate's voice echoing across the hangar. 'Why is our *secret* plane turning somersaults over the Home Counties with its landing gear stuck in its bloody ear? I don't start tearing off heads if it happens once, but when it happens twice, I am *very* unhappy!'

'Glad I'm not a chief anything.' Connie winced. 'Come and sit down, take a moment.'

Sally went into the hangar with Connie and they headed for the mess and the tired-looking sofa. Sally gratefully sank onto it, but she couldn't help but whisper to Connie, 'What's Wyngate doing here?'

Sally could see that Connie wasn't a fan of his either. Could anyone be, when the man was so rude?

'I don't know, but whenever he is I feel like I'm about to get in trouble,' Connie said with a chuckle as she headed to the tea urn and picked up Sally's mug. When she spoke again, her tone was grave: 'But I wouldn't want to be in Viraj's shoes now. He's a really good man and he knows what he's doing, but what just happened – and after we supposedly fixed the problem... We're all so sorry, Sal.'

'Make that all the engineers!' As Wyngate bellowed that, Connie grimaced and handed Sally her tea. So she wasn't off the hook. 'Now! I don't want a hat-trick!'

'Sorry,' Sally whispered to Connie. Did Wyngate really not understand how test flights in prototype planes worked? If the plane was perfect, Sally would never have been hired to fly it. Surely it was better they knew about the problem with the landing gear when there weren't any enemy planes on the Spitfire's tail, ready to shoot it out of the sky.

Connie shrugged and told her, 'It's okay. I guess he has a lot on his plate, huh? But he's right, we've really messed up.' Then she touched Sally's shoulder gently and hurried away to join her colleagues.

Sally sipped her tea, alone. She could hear Wyngate's irate voice, but she didn't try to listen to what he was saying.

I'm in one piece. And that's all that matters. And I can't tell Freddy or Mum and Dad or anyone else, but I know what happened. I—

The air raid siren suddenly screamed, and Sally was on her feet in a moment.

'What a day...' she sighed to herself.

Robert and Joe ran to collect up the secret Spitfire's blueprints, and Sally followed everyone out of the barn to the shelter, which was hidden just inside the trees a few feet from the barn.

'I bet they've got some trouble over at Bramble Heath,' Gus told Sally as they took their places in the metal and concrete shelter.

It was hardly a comforting thought, but Sally had known worse during the Battle of Britain, when the airbase had come under frequent attack.

Here in the shelter, though, it appeared to be business as usual. The ground crew were explaining to Wyngate exactly what they believed had gone wrong twice now, with plenty of apologies for Sally, and details of how they intended to fix it once and for all. He listened to their explanations in stony silence, occasionally giving a curt nod, but it was better than the furious temper he'd unleashed in the hangar. As planes could be heard passing overhead, the members of the Spitfire's crew got down to the business of their debrief, with Sally called in to explain in painstaking detail exactly what had just happened.

She tried to keep her mind on the job, but it kept wandering to Bramble Heath, where her friends and family would be sheltering just like this. Or rather, some of them would. Freddy and Ginge and Mateusz and the other boys would be up there in the sky, ready to meet the Luftwaffe in the storm.

But Sally couldn't let herself think about that now, because she had her own part to play. If they could get the secret Spitfire perfect, it could change everything.

She glanced towards Lane-Bannister, wondering if he was thinking about his wife as the planes hummed high above them. He met her gaze and offered her a smile, then said, 'I'd like to just thank Second Officer Toussaint. Her clear thinking and bravery got us out of a very tight spot indeed.'

Connie nodded, then added, 'The tightest spot of all, Mr Lane-Bannister.'

Wyngate shot Connie a very stern look and for a moment

Sally thought he was going to give her a telling-off. The moment passed though and he nodded, curt as ever.

'It was very impressive,' Wyngate told Sally. 'Another good job, Second Officer.'

'Thank you,' Sally replied, aware that praise from Wyngate was a rare thing indeed. 'Just wanted to bring her down safely. If I'd landed her on her belly, it would've set everything back, wouldn't it? Couldn't have that.'

She thought of her mug of tea, cooling in the mess. She really could've done with it after a landing like that, but at least she was on the ground again and in the safety of the shelter. She shouldn't grumble. Right now, in the rainy skies above Bramble Heath, Freddy and the other boys from the airbase were fighting off enemy planes. Flying a Spitfire was one thing; flying it while being shot at was something else entirely.

Come home safely, Freddy, please, that's all I ask. I hope the luck I've had today will smile on you as well.

TWELVE

After the all-clear sounded and it was safe to leave the shelter, Viraj and his ground crew needed to get to work, fixing the undercarriage mechanism. Sally had little to do, other than tidy away her things. She wasn't an engineer. What could she do to help?

The rain was still lashing down, so hard that it bounced from the sodden straw that still coated the runway so impotently. If Sally had bellyflopped onto that unforgiving surface, she might not be standing here now. And the plane would have been in bad shape.

But her job was done for the day and she was back on solid ground. Now her mind was on Bramble Heath and the friends she had there. Most of all, though, it was on the man she loved.

Ever since Freddy's first combat flight, Sally had gone through the extremes of fear and hope each time he went up. She knew he was a brilliant pilot, but it was the actions of the enemy, not Freddy's flying, that worried her. Over time her fear had almost been conquered by hope, but it was still there, every time.

The fear that he might not make it home.

'Mr Lane-Bannister?' Sally asked the man from the ministry, while everyone else was gathered over the blueprints. 'I suppose I'm not needed for the rest of the day now?'

He glanced up from the papers he was reading and gave her a smile. Wyngate had left, taking his temper with him, and a calm had descended over the hangar despite the drama of earlier.

'Why don't you go over and join them?' he suggested. 'You got yourself out of a bind and you're the only one who actually flies the bally thing. You're a big part of this team.' Then Lane-Bannister glanced at his watch. 'Unless you'd prefer to get back? I would understand, Second Officer.'

Sally glanced over at the radio, which connected the secret barn with RAF Bramble Heath.

Freddy.

But then, he might still be flying, if they were chasing the enemy planes, trying to stop them from reaching London.

Freddy's always fine. They can't shoot him *down.*

'If I can help, then of course,' she replied. 'The sooner this undercarriage business is fixed, the sooner Freddy and your brother, and Viraj's brother, and everyone else will be zipping about in an unstoppable Spit. We'd all be a lot happier then, wouldn't we?'

'And a good many millions of people who will never know anything about it,' he told her. 'Go and slip your two-penn'orth in.'

So Sally joined the ground crew around the blueprints. She had worried that she wouldn't know what they were talking about, but she found that she could in fact follow them. Everything hinged on one question: was the issue mechanical or electrical, or both? The members of Maintenance Unit Zero hadn't been able to replicate the problem, but the problem had replicated itself and could've cost Sally her life. It had to be solved.

With the team's expertise, and Sally's explanation of what

had happened, the team gained a better idea of the problem and how to fix it. It seemed that the problem was caused by the switch. Sally was able to tame her frightening experience and transform it into something good.

Robert went over to the plane and climbed in. All they could see of him was a pair of legs sticking out of the cockpit as he levered off the instrument panel to look inside.

They heard a muffled cheer, then he reappeared and slid down from the wings.

'The switch shorted out,' Robert told them. He sounded very happy, but Sally knew he was just relieved that they'd got to the bottom of the problem. 'It must've got too warm the first time, but this time it just shorted. We'll need to look at the instrument panel again – the wire was too close to some others and I suspect it all got too hot in there and the casing on the wire melted, then the wire shorted. Sorry about that, Sally.'

'It's one of those things.' Sally shrugged.

Viraj nodded, but Sally could see from his expression that he was as angry at himself as Wyngate had been at the team.

'I'm sorry,' he said. 'We should've seen that.'

'The plane's a prototype, and it needs to be tested to find things out like that,' Sally assured him. 'It can be fixed now, can't it?'

Joe nodded as he unrolled another blueprint, showing the complicated wiring behind the instrument panel. Sally tried to understand it, but she had to admit she was lost.

'It definitely can,' Joe told her. 'You won't have any more flights like that, I promise you.'

'That's a shame,' Sally said, chuckling. 'No, honestly, let's get it fixed. I love performing rolls in the air, but only for fun!'

'That's why we need a pilot like you,' said Lane-Bannister. 'A flier who keeps a cool head and gets out of trouble. It's a shame we couldn't put you in a squadron!'

Sally had to laugh. It was something she'd discussed with

Freddy before. Why couldn't she fly in combat when she had the experience and skills? Why did being a woman make the slightest bit of difference?

'At least I've been able to do *something* with my pilot's licence,' she said. 'Even if I can't fly with the boys.'

Half an hour later Sally was in Lane-Bannister's car, driving away from the unassuming barn into the rain. When she and Freddy were flying together, after a close shave like that they'd head to the pub and share a drink, talking through what had happened until they could consign it to the past. She couldn't do that tonight though, because as far as anybody knew she'd been delivering planes just like every other day. It was just part of her new job, albeit a difficult one.

At least she'd been able to focus the experience onto something positive and help to solve the mystery of what had happened in the air. But what she really wanted was to tell Freddy and hug him, because that way she knew everything would be all right.

Sally watched the raindrops chase each other across the window of the car. Then she turned to Lane-Bannister. 'How do you do it, Mr Lane-Bannister? Keep secrets, I mean?'

A man from the ministry would know better than most, surely.

'I think about the Blitz, and losing my wife,' he said after a very long moment had passed. 'And I remember what's at stake for all of us.'

'I'm so sorry you lost her like that. What an awful thing to happen to you,' Sally said gently. She thought of her family here and in France. Keeping secrets would keep them safe too. 'You're right, of course you're right. There can't be a better reason to keep secrets, can there? I was just thinking about what used to happen back when Freddy and I were Toussaint and Carr. If one of us came a cropper – well, we'd sit down and thrash it out. But I won't say a thing about what happened today, I promise.'

'Perhaps one day,' Lane-Bannister replied. 'Somebody has to fly that bird into combat, after all. We'll see.'

Sally smiled. Knowing that it might not be a secret for ever, at least from Freddy, made her feel better.

'I can't think of anyone better than Freddy to fly the secret Spit in battle, you know,' Sally said, before teasing, 'Although perhaps you'd recommend your brother!'

Lane-Bannister gave a rather sorry smile, as though torn between recommending him and wishing that he didn't have to.

'Once the prototype's proven, it won't be an only child for long,' he said. 'We can put it into serious production as soon as we've got all this signed and sealed.'

Sally clasped her hands. 'Thank goodness. I can't wait, you know. I'll feel so proud when they're in the air. I can't tell you how wonderful it is to be part of all of this. You know, part of *making* a new plane!'

'Few people ever get to see it.'

And it was a privilege, Sally knew that.

'And we're very grateful to have you on our team.'

The car drove through the village and towards the airbase. The heavy rain had made for a dismal day. Not many people were in the street, and the few braving the rain with their umbrellas were unsmiling.

Dratted weather.

But there was something else, something Sally couldn't shake. Almost as though the air itself was heavy with feeling. She'd experienced this before, she was certain, and it bothered her. She searched through her mind, trying to find it, and she travelled back to the autumn before.

Those were painful, difficult memories that she didn't care to revisit. Who would want to recall those days of the Battle of

Britain, when the boys at the airbase were worn thin, and when they had lost so many friends?

The planes had been scrambled earlier, Sally was certain of it. And this mood in the village, this heavy, sad mood, it could only mean... *oh, no.*

She glanced at Lane-Bannister, wondering if he'd noticed it too.

The man from the ministry was chewing on his thumbnail, watching the village streets as they passed. His face was drawn, his eyes moving back and forth as he took in the scene.

'Would you like us to take you back to Heath Place?' he asked quietly.

Sally nodded. 'Yes, please.' If it *was* Freddy, God forbid, she wanted to know as soon as possible. She didn't want to blunder into his parents' home unprepared. '*We* were safe, but...'

The gates of Heath Place always stood open these days, but someone had already tied a bunch of daffodils to them despite the rain. Sally felt desperate, half wanting to run towards the house and half away from it. Whoever had perished – and she knew somebody had – she would've known them. Whether one of the British squadron or the Polish, it was one of the impromptu family that had been thrown together by fate at Brambles.

The driver took them through the gates and up the drive-way. Second by second, Sally was closer to knowing who it was who'd died. She gripped the handle above the door, her knuckles white. She didn't look at Lane-Bannister. What could he say? And besides, having lost his wife, what awful memories might be forced to emerge from his mind at the knowledge that someone – someone Sally knew, perhaps even loved, if it was Freddy – had been killed?

I was safe in the shelter. But the boys weren't. The boys were in the air. They can't run and hide.

The usually short journey up the drive seemed to take for

ever, but finally the car pulled up outside Sally's old home. She
let go of the strap just as the driver got out and opened the back
doors for her and Lane-Bannister. He climbed out first, then
turned to offer Sally his hand.

This, this was more terrifying than what had happened
earlier to her in the sky. Sally's legs were like wet string. She lost
her footing and stumbled into Lane-Bannister.

'I'm so sorry,' she gasped.

'It's all right, we're all allowed a little stumble,' he assured
her gently as he caught her about the waist and righted her. A
pall hung in the air itself, heavy and mournful. 'We'll get your
bike out and leave it by the ops room. Good work again today,
Second Officer.'

'I do my best,' Sally said, blushing at his kind words. But this
awful atmosphere... She'd know soon, very soon, who had been
killed. There was sadness in every breath of air. 'I better go
and... find out.'

She wished it wasn't Freddy, but then that felt selfish,
because it meant that someone else would have lost their
loved one.

Then Sally heard barking, and she lifted her head. *Wilbur.*

She followed the sound and, there, leaning against the door
of the mess, she saw Freddy. Wilbur was tucked neatly beneath
one elbow, and Freddy was holding a pint in the other hand.
Sally blinked, but she wasn't imagining it. It really *was* him.

'Freddy!' she called.

She glanced back at Lane-Bannister with a smile to tell him
it was all right, that Freddy was right there, then she ran over to
her boyfriend. She was so happy, so relieved, and yet the bleak
atmosphere of the airbase took the shine off her joy. She threw
her arms round Freddy, Wilbur, the pint and all.

'Busy day?' Freddy asked, his voice flat and heavy. 'Travelling in style these days.'

Sally went on holding him. She wished she could tell him

about her day. But he was alive, that was the most important thing.

She did have a ready excuse for her arrival in Lane-Bannister's car, though.

'You know how it is in the ATA,' she reminded Freddy. 'If I'm not catching a lift in a bomber, I'm flagging down men from the ministry. Darling, what's happened? Has someone...?'

She lifted her head to look up at Freddy. His expression was stony.

'Was he taking liberties?' he asked, his eyes boring into Lane-Bannister and the driver as they wrestled Sally's bicycle out of the car. Her boyfriend, usually so light and carefree, was ashen, his bright eyes dull and bloodshot. 'Did he have his arm round you?'

Sally shook her head, astonished at Freddy. *What on earth...?*

'No, of course he wasn't taking liberties! I stumbled, that's all,' she protested. She went to cup Freddy's face, but his cold accusation held her back. 'Freddy, you look ill. Darling, what is it?'

Freddy bit his lip and shook his head as Wilbur nuzzled lovingly against his jaw. He said nothing for a moment, which stretched until he whispered, 'They got Ginge.'

Ginge?

One of Freddy's closest friends at the airbase. They were always gossiping together, always laughing and joking.

And to think he...

'They got him?' Sally closed her eyes for a moment, before asking with all the hope she could muster, 'Did he— Is he in sickbay?'

Maybe he wasn't dead. Maybe it was all right. Maybe he'd got a few cuts and scratches, but he'd survive.

Freddy shook his head and swallowed hard, his throat bobbing. Sally saw a muscle tighten in his jaw and he managed to tell her, 'He's in the mortuary.' Then he rested his forehead atop Wilbur's head and drew in a very deep breath.

Freddy blurred in front of Sally as tears rose in her eyes. She held him tighter. Freddy's manner, and the atmosphere in the village and the airbase, made sense now. Everyone had known Ginge. No one had ever had a bad word to say about him. And now he was dead.

'I'm so sorry, Freddy,' Sally whispered. 'You poor chap. It's awful.'

'Ginge was a one-off,' Freddy said as he lifted his head and took another deep breath. 'That bastard came out of nowhere and put one straight through the canopy. Ginge didn't even know what hit him.'

'He was a lovely boy. We should all feel fortunate to have known him,' Sally said gently. 'And... Ginge loved flying. He died doing what he loved. But we can all wish he hadn't been taken so soon.'

Freddy nodded, but he still didn't meet Sally's gaze. It wasn't like him; even at these horrible, horrible moments when they lost one of their own, Freddy was usually still Freddy.

Sally took a step back from him. She fussed Wilbur, then summoned the courage to ask Freddy, 'Darling, what is it?'

Although she had a feeling that she already knew, after that remark about Lane-Bannister.

What on earth can I tell Freddy?

'I took Wilbur over the fields this morning for a run – rain doesn't bother a Tiger Moth pilot, after all.' He took a long drink from his glass of beer, then raised the pint to the departing ministry car. 'And I saw my girl getting into Prince Charming's car.'

Sally blinked rapidly, her thoughts in tumult. *What can I say? What the heck can I say?* But she couldn't tell him, could she? Even if he thought the worst of her, she couldn't say a thing.

'He's not a Prince Charming,' Sally replied. She decided to skirt around Freddy's accusation, and said quickly, 'He's Mr Lane-Bannister, he's only from the Air Ministry. His family are in motor racing. Do you know, now I come to think of it, I'm sure I've heard the name before. His brother's a Spitfire pilot too, you know.'

'Oh, I know who he is,' Freddy assured her. 'Evander Lane-Bannister... son of the duke of so-and-so. I saw him drive a few times when we were kids. And now he's making eyes at my girl.'

The door behind Freddy opened and Mateusz emerged. He gave the couple a sombre nod, then painted on a smile for Sally.

'Come in and drink to Ginge?' he asked them.

'I'm sorry for your loss, Mateusz. I'd love to raise a glass to Ginge,' Sally replied. Then she said to Freddy, 'It's not like that. He's just involved with the ATA, that's all.'

Freddy turned to hand Mateusz his empty glass as he said, 'I need to clear my head, mate, and Wilbur wants to go for a run.' Then he offered Sally a nod and told her, 'I don't blame you, you know. We Spitfire boys might not even be here tomorrow.'

'Freddy, don't say that,' Sally said urgently, but in her heart she knew he was half right. Freddy and his comrades lived a precarious life. But she'd never give up on him. 'I'm *your* girl. I always will be. We're Toussaint and Carr, remember?'

Or at least we were, *before the war changed everything.*

Freddy answered with a silent nod, then, Wilbur trotting ahead of him, he walked away into the rain.

THIRTEEN

The next morning, Sally sat at the breakfast table slowly eating her porridge. It didn't have any flavour. Nothing did. All she kept thinking of was Freddy and his cold anger. She tried to tell herself it was grief because he'd just lost his friend, but she knew that her secretiveness made everything worse.

He thinks he's lost me too.

But he hadn't. Yet there was no way Sally could explain everything without breaking the agreement she'd signed. Who knew what they'd do to her if she did?

Her mother patted her hand, like she used to do when Sally was a child. 'I'm sorry, love. Ginge was such a nice boy.'

'He's going home to Brighton today,' François said. 'We're all going to see him off at home— The base.' He shook his head at the all-too-easy mistake. 'Why don't you come along? Freddy'd be glad of it.'

Freddy.

Sally kept her face as still as she could, trying not to show her worry.

'I'll come,' Emily said, and nodded. 'That poor Freddy. Losing his friends, and every time he takes off, he—' She stopped herself and patted Sally's hand again. 'It's a lot to carry, darling, we know. You must be worried all the time.'

'Yes, it's true, I do worry about him,' Sally replied.

In more ways than I can tell you.

Emily went off to change into her black dress, and once she was ready Sally and her parents headed to the airbase that had taken over their old home. Sally brought her bicycle with her, and all it did, as she recalled Freddy watching Lane-Bannister take it from the back of his car, was remind her of Freddy's accusations the day before. As they reached the gates, where more flowers had appeared for Ginge, Sally was wiping away tears. For Ginge, for Freddy, and for the home that was no longer theirs.

'I'm sorry,' she said, as she folded away her handkerchief. Then she and her parents were off again, heading up the driveway. She thought of the vanload of their possessions that had bumped this way, leaving the house, when they moved into the cottage. But that was nothing compared to what Ginge had lost yesterday.

I'm still alive. We're still here. Giving up the house is nothing, really. And what about my family in France? They'd laugh at me for being silly while they live through horrors.

As they reached the top of the drive, Sally saw what looked like most of the airbase and half of the village standing in the carriage circle outside the front of the house; RAF pilots and ground crew, sickbay staff and their patients who could make it outside, the Goslings and the Land Girls who worked on their farm, Rose from the tea rooms, Ewa and Zofia, Reverend Ellis and Constable Russell with his wife, Betty and her mother from the post office. Sally's fellow ATA pilots were gathered around too. But there was no sign of Freddy, and that worried her.

But he won't do anything silly, will he? Not good old Freds.

Sally spotted Peter, with Wilbur at his feet, and his friends Sam and Bill. There was Jamie Farthing from the village, who had lost his pilot brother almost a year before, and other boys who idolised the brave men who flew from Brambles. Among them were evacuees, and Sally was sure they realised that the pilots were risking their lives to save the homes the children had left behind. Wilbur suddenly noticed her and ran across to her side, so she crouched down to pick him up.

Lane-Bannister was there, too, beside Group Captain Chambers, who was with Annie, his sweetheart.

Sally went over to stand next to Annie, who fussed Wilbur as Sally whispered, 'I'm so glad to see all these people here.'

'Everyone was very fond of him,' Annie replied sadly. 'Doesn't matter how many boys we lose, they're all remembered.'

Sally fell silent, her thoughts on Ginge and the other pilots who'd never made it home, the boys in the RAF, her friend in the ATA. Everyone was solemn, their sadness a leaden weight like the grey clouds overhead.

At Group Captain Chambers' signal, a bugler started to play the 'Last Post'. Sally turned to look at the entrance to her old home, and the double doors slowly opened. She saw, crossing the threshold, some of Ginge's fellow pilots, their faces grey and drawn, acting as his pallbearers.

And right at the front was Freddy, carrying his friend's coffin.

Ginge wouldn't take his final journey home in a polished hearse, but in an army truck that was likely carrying plenty of other cargo alongside the young pilot who had never stopped laughing. It waited for him there on the driveway and beside it stood its uniformed driver, his head bowed low in a show of respect.

On top of the simple coffin stood Ginge's cap, a simple gesture to honour a man who had never thought too much about bravery. None of these men believed themselves heroes, they were just doing a job.

Sally's tears rose again. She suddenly felt cold. Because it could've been Freddy inside that box. And with a sense of horror, she realised she could've died yesterday too.

If I hadn't got the landing gear down. If I'd crashed, or if I'd baled and the parachute hadn't opened.

Sally held Wilbur tight. She glanced across at Freddy, trying to catch his eye to give him a sympathetic smile. Instead, Freddy's gaze was fixed on the truck and Sally could see even from where she stood that his jaw was held tight, even as his eyes swam with unspilled tears. A few years ago he hadn't even known Ginge, but they'd become the firmest of friends, wingmen in every sense.

Sally thought again of her friend Amy, who she'd lost only a few months before. She knew how Freddy felt. Losing a comrade was so painful; inevitably there would be guilt wrapped around their grief, because the loss could so easily have been the other way round. It could have been Ginge carrying Freddy in his coffin.

But fate had decided otherwise.

Freddy and the other pallbearers placed Ginge's coffin in the truck with all the solemnity of a monarch's final journey. Then they stepped back and, as the driver closed the doors, took off their caps and bowed their heads. With a glance to Group Captain Chambers, the driver climbed into his cab and closed the door. Only then did Chambers step forward and salute, still as a statue as he held the rigid gesture. A second later, the others joined him.

Finally the truck started off, and Ginge was carried away, down the driveway and under its arch of trees that were beginning to open into new, green life.

The bugler had stopped playing, and nothing stirred the silence until Chambers dismissed everyone. Heads bowed, the pilots began to make their way to the mess, while Emily and the boys went back to the village, and the sickbay staff and their patients returned to their makeshift hospital. François joined the other ground crew, and Lane-Bannister went into the house with Chambers.

But Freddy was still there in the carriage circle, as Sally held Wilbur. A large model of a Tiger Moth had once stood in the circle, but it went when the house was requisitioned. There was only neatly kept grass there now.

'He had a good send-off,' Sally said to Freddy as she approached him, taking each footstep as carefully as if she was walking over glass.

'He was nearly home,' Freddy told her, every word measured to keep his emotions in check. 'Five more minutes and he'd have been down safe.'

Sally held Wilbur out to him. 'I'm so sorry,' she said gently. 'Five minutes can make all the difference, can't it?'

He took the little dog and kissed the top of Wilbur's head. 'Five seconds sometimes.'

'We know more than anyone how dangerous it can get up there,' Sally said, hoping that reminding him of Toussaint and Carr would reconnect them somehow. 'Yet we still fly. There's something about being up in the sky, isn't there?'

Freddy shook his head and replied, 'We fly because we don't have a choice. If we don't, they'll flatten us.'

Sally couldn't reply at first. Everything felt so bleak. She glanced at the carriage circle again, and thought of the model plane. The war had taken that away, just as it had robbed Freddy of his passion for the air.

'But you do it because you're bloody good, too,' Sally reminded him, hoping against hope that she could bring back the old Freddy she'd known. 'You're the best pilot I know.'

'Oi-oi lovebirds!' Enid called merrily as she bounced down the steps from Heath Place. 'Break it up, break it up!'

Sally tried her best to smile at Enid, but she couldn't feel the other woman's normally infectious happiness. Not today.

'Hello, Enid,' she said. 'I'll come by presently and pick up my chit.'

'No chits today, Sal!' Enid clearly suddenly realised that her permanent cheer was terribly out of place here, and tried to arrange her face into something more sombre. 'Sorry about your pal, Freds.'

Freddy nodded and assured her, 'It's all right to smile, you know.'

So Enid smiled again, perhaps a little less brightly though.

'No chits,' she said again. 'We're all off to Southampton today. Must be a big delivery, eh?'

Sally couldn't bring herself to look at Freddy. Whoever flew a Spitfire back to Brambles would be replacing the plane that Ginge had been killed in only the day before. And how many other planes were replacements for others that young men had been flying, only never to land them?

'Must be,' she said, nodding. She forced herself to turn to Freddy. 'Darling, I've got to go. Take care, won't you?'

'You too.' He gave the two women a sorry ghost of a smile, but Sally could feel the distance between them even now. When Freddy glanced towards the house as Lane-Bannister and Chambers made their way down the steps, though, his expression hardened again. 'Come home safe.'

Sally swallowed. If only she could tell him.

'I promise,' she said, then she followed Enid to the house.

Bluebell Woods.

There it was on Sally's chit. It had taken a few days, but surely this meant that the secret Spitfire was fixed now. With Freddy avoiding her, always busy with his friends at the airbase or walking Wilbur alone, she couldn't wait to get back into the air in the secret Spitfire to clear her head. He was so distant that there seemed no way to bridge the gap that had opened up between them.

He needed time to grieve, Sally knew, but she wished he'd let her in so that she could help him through it. They'd both lost friends in this war and before, when they had, they'd turned to each other. That had changed.

She was proud to be part of the secret Spitfire project, even if it had contributed to her problems with Freddy. Once the plane was ready and the project signed off, her life would go back to normal – or at least, as normal as the war allowed – and then she and Freddy could go back to how things had been before.

Yet there was still the fact that something had gone wrong,

twice, while she'd been in the cockpit, and it had dented her confidence.

'We've fixed it, once and for all,' Gus explained, as Sally stood on the runway looking up at the plane. She clutched her mug of tea, hoping the ground crew wouldn't see the tremble in her hand. 'It's taken a few late nights, I can tell you, but we didn't want this to delay the project. The instrument panel's been rewired, and we've got some special insulation around the wiring now as well. That switch won't short out ever again.'

'I guarantee you she's perfect,' Viraj said as he joined them on the runway. 'It was unforgivable. It won't happen a third time.'

'I-it's fine, really,' Sally told them, trying to keep her voice steady. 'I trust you to have fixed it. It's funny actually... well, maybe not *that* funny. Back when I was flying with Toussaint and Carr, I came in to land over at Heath Place, and one of the legs snapped under the plane when I landed. Everything suddenly went sideways, and the wing tip scraped along the runway and really tore it up. It all happened so fast, I didn't have time to be scared. Only afterwards I realised what a close scrape that was, and it took me a good month or two to get back up in the air without shaking like a leaf! But we don't have months, do we? I *have* to trust you. And I *do*.'

'You have our word.' Viraj pressed his hand to his breast. 'There isn't a more capable plane in the Air Force than this one. Or a more capable and cool-headed pilot.'

'Well, there's only one way to find out, isn't there?' Sally patted the plane's nose. Her nerves were starting to turn into excitement. 'Let's take her up again!'

Sally got into her flight gear while the ground crew prepared the plane. By the time she climbed into the cockpit with Gus and Esther's help, the plane was warmed up and ready to fly, just as it would be for combat.

Sally plugged herself into the radio and clipped on her

harness, Gus and Esther pulled away the chocks, and she was ready to go.

She looked over to Viraj for the signal. As she did, she saw three tall figures in the mouth of the hangar, watching the preparations. One was Wyngate, his no doubt grave expression concealed by the brim of his hat, and the other was Lane-Bannister, who gave her a cheery thumbs-up. From Group Captain Chambers, she received a nod, one pilot showing respect to another.

Their presence was a reminder of just how important this was.

'Come on, plane,' Sally said to the Spitfire. 'You can do it this time, can't you?'

And with that, Sally thundered down the runway and into the air again. As soon as she was airborne, her fears evaporated. The plane handled wonderfully, so responsive it was like dancing in the air. And as for the undercarriage, she flicked the switch and it rose up without a hitch. Lowering it would be the biggest test, of course, but right now there were no problems at all. Just Sally and the secret Spitfire, flying over the early summer countryside.

She went through the manoeuvres she'd been tasked to carry out, without any problems at all.

'I'm so glad to be flying her again,' she told them down at the hangar, over the radio. 'She's a very special plane!'

'You're very lucky,' Chambers told her. 'I'd love to be sitting in that seat.'

'The team have made a few more refinements in weaponry, but you won't see that side of it. She'll be fully loaded when she goes into combat, but not on a test flight over home turf,' Lane-Bannister replied. 'The handling's probably as tight as it's ever going to be. Show us what she can do.'

Sally chuckled. Why had she been scared? *This* was what she loved.

She flew in loops, she went into a roll, she flew upside down. Everything she wasn't supposed to do when delivering planes in the ATA. The plane seemed to be enjoying it, so Sally climbed sharply, then turned and zoomed down, almost skimming the trees, before shooting back up into the air.

'We should be selling tickets!' she joked over the radio.

And as she flew, she read off the dials and meters in front of her, letting the ground crew know the secret Spitfire's speeds and climb rates. All the details they needed that told them this plane was exceptional.

'It's just incredible!' Sally told them, as she climbed again. 'She's so quick. Look at her go!'

'Bring her in, Second Officer.' That was Wyngate, sounding as unimpressed as ever. 'I'll see you on the landing strip with your orders.'

Sally rolled her eyes. It was just as well they only had radio contact up in the air rather than a camera as well.

'On my way,' she replied.

This was the test, now, to see if the landing gear would come down. Sally aimed for the runway and, at the usual height, she flicked the switch. Her heart was in her mouth until she heard the familiar cranking sound.

It's working! Hurrah!

'Landing gear lowered,' she reported to everyone on the ground. 'I'm coming in to land.'

And seconds later, the plane was bouncing along the runway. Sally had brought the secret Spitfire safely home, without a hitch. She taxied the plane back to the hangar, where the entire ground crew were waiting for her, relief clear on their faces. At least, everyone looked relieved apart from Wyngate, who never seemed to look anything other than annoyed.

As Sally climbed down, the audience greeted her with a round of applause. Even Wyngate gave a couple of grudging claps, though it looked as though such a gesture was entirely alien to him.

'You've all still got a job,' he told the ground crew. 'And I've still got a plane that Jerry won't be able to catch.'

'And a dashed talented test pilot,' Lane-Bannister added, rolling his eyes at his colleague's manner.

'Thanks, everyone,' Sally said, as she pulled off her oxygen mask and her helmet. 'To be honest, it felt like she flew better than ever today. Maybe whatever it was you had to do with the instrument panel has done more than just fix the landing gear switch.'

The ground crew all looked very pleased about that, even if Wyngate looked as unimpressed as ever.

'This afternoon you'll be working with the crew on test data and ground readings,' Wyngate barked. 'At sundown, we want to see her fly by night. We need to do it as soon as darkness falls and keep it short for the obvious reasons.' He lit a cigarette and took a draw on it. 'We'll even feed you.'

'A night flight?' Sally gasped with excitement, even though she knew it wasn't without its risks. 'Fantastic! Oh, I can't wait. That's just wonderful!'

Sally knew it'd be a while before darkness fell, but her parents were used to her keeping odd hours with the ATA, when she battled to get home after a day flying here, there and everywhere. It wasn't unusual for her to find a late train home, only to discover it was so packed that she would end up sitting on her parachute in the corridor and fall asleep.

But this time, she wasn't at some far-flung airbase, but flying in the dark. She only ever did that in the ATA in the winter, when the short days would have curtailed the number of planes they could move if they didn't fly after sunset. It was dangerous. If the Luftwaffe were going to be around, it was usually at night, and a plane flying on its own was easy prey for them.

Especially a plane that didn't have any guns.

But there was plenty to do at the hangar to keep everyone occupied before sunset. Robert and Joe drew up charts and graphs using the statistics Sally had relayed from the plane. Everyone could see that the ongoing tweaks they'd been making to the plane since Sally had been test-flying it were having a significant impact on the plane's performance. Another line ran through all the charts, showing the current standard model of Spitfire. The secret plane outshone it.

Later that afternoon, as the setting sun bathed the sky in a red glow, Maintenance Unit Zero lined up for the vast pan of strong-smelling stew and wedges of bread that had appeared from heaven knew where. Sally knew she was lucky to be part of this and to be there in the queue laughing with Connie and Esther, alongside the stern-faced man from the ministry and the *duke's son*, if Lane-Bannister really was such a thing. They all came from such different places to be united here. Each one of them had been hand-picked for the project.

The atmosphere at the hangar was electric; the plane was nearly ready and everyone knew that this was it. They were within touching distance of the finish line. All they had to do was this one faultless night flight, and the secret Spitfire would be signed off and ready for action.

When they'd all eaten, darkness had fallen outside. The lights in the hangar were turned off and the ground crew worked only by muted torchlight.

Sally took a moment and went outside. She wanted to take a few breaths of fresh air to calm her rising nerves, and to accustom her eyes to the darkness. Even though the countryside had never had much light at night, the blackout still made a difference even here. There was nothing but the stars blinking through the scraps of moonlit cloud far above her.

She had to be brave – a night fight was dangerous; but Freddy did it all the time, after all, heading straight into danger. What Sally had to do was nothing compared to that.

Oh, Freddy, I miss you.

She smelt tobacco smoke and saw a dark shape a couple of feet away.

'Who's there?' she whispered. It had to be one of the ground crew, but she knew they all had to be watchful. It was a top-secret project they were working on, after all.

Sally saw the brief flare of a cigarette from beneath the shadow of a hat brim before Wyngate held out an opened packet of cigarettes to her.

'You're a bloody good pilot, Second Officer.' To Sally's surprise, she even heard a smile in Wyngate's voice when he added, 'Have you thought about doing it for a living?'

'Very funny,' she replied with a chuckle. 'And *merci* for offering, but I don't smoke, Mr Wyngate. I don't suppose you ever saw Toussaint and Carr fly? Before the war, I mean?'

She couldn't imagine Wyngate at an airshow, looking bored in the excited crowd.

'Now and then,' he replied. Sally was stunned to hear him answer in fast, fluent French. 'I was in Paris, 1938. Now *that* was a display. It feels like a long time ago.'

'Doesn't it just?' she replied, speaking in French too. She always loved the opportunity to slip into the language her father had taught her from her cradle. 'That airshow in Paris was fantastic. You know, I loved flying in France. Le Touquet, Deauville... I didn't get to go very often, but just being in the country where I was born feels rather magical, and I'd get to meet my family too. And now... well, just the thought of all the terrible things happening there – my cousins, my aunts, my uncles, Mémé, they're still there. And I could've been, too, if Papa hadn't moved us to England when I was small.'

Sally never spoke about it. She kept those thoughts tightly packed away. Life was hard enough in England, but, if she spared a moment to think of what her family were facing in

France, it overwhelmed her. She felt helpless, and she felt selfish, too.

Moving out of Heath Place really was nothing compared to what they're living through.

'We'll run the rats to ground, whatever it takes.' Wyngate flicked the remains of his cigarette away. 'Better get up in the air, Second Officer. We can't waste time.'

The ground crew had prepared the Spitfire again, and this time Frank and Connie helped Sally into the cockpit. Frank wasn't cracking jokes for once – he must've realised that Sally wasn't the right audience for his humour at the moment, as she was facing so many risks in the dark sky.

'Fifteen minutes and bring her in,' Lane-Bannister called to Sally. 'Good flying, Second Officer Toussaint.'

Fifteen minutes wasn't long at all, but Sally knew it could feel like for ever if something went wrong again.

She sped off along the runway. The trees around it swallowed what light there was, and she fretted for a moment that she wouldn't clear their branches in time.

But she needn't have worried. In seconds, she was soaring above the trees and into the night sky. The gauges and dials were all backlit, designed to be brighter, as an improvement on the standard instrument panel. Sally read off the numbers to the ground crew below.

'The instruments are showing clear?' Viraj asked. 'You can read everything by the new lights?'

'I can read them perfectly,' she replied. 'They're really clear.' So that was one night-flight test passed.

Sally kept going, climbing higher as if she was chasing the sunset. The plane coped perfectly, as she always did. She performed her manoeuvres and they all went swimmingly. As she flew over a farm, she hoped the people inside wouldn't feel afraid as they heard the plane go over.

Maybe it's going to be a quiet night. Thank goodness for that!

Sally glanced at the clock on her instrument panel. She'd been in the air for nearly ten minutes. Not long to go now and she'd have completed the night flight without a hitch.

'I think—' Wyngate fell suddenly silent and, through the crackle of the night airwaves, Sally heard the unmistakable wail of the air raid siren. She didn't have to panic though; it wasn't as if the Luftwaffe were about to drop out of the sky. 'Bring her into the hangar, Second Officer, I'll be here.' Then he told the team with an air of unflappable calm, 'If I don't need you, get to the shelter.'

And that was when the Messerschmitt 109 hurtled out of the clouds.

FIFTEEN

'Wyngate! There's a plane right in front of me! A 109!' Sally gasped.

She couldn't believe what she was seeing. She was faced with her worst nightmare. The Messerschmitt's pilot must've seen her, and he must, she knew, be wondering why on earth the Spitfire in front of him wasn't firing at his plane.

And that could only mean that he was seconds from firing at her.

Sally quickly climbed, going into a large loop so that she'd come back down well behind the Messerschmitt, away from its guns. She could only hope it wouldn't follow her.

'You can outfly him,' Wyngate assured her tightly. 'Don't let him get behind you, Second Officer.'

Sally didn't need telling twice. She'd had a brief glimpse of the moonlit swastika on the Messerschmitt's tail and the row upon row of neat lines painted there, each one symbolising a kill. This wasn't a novice, a lad out on his first mission. Whoever was in the cockpit of the plane was an ace several times over.

He's not adding me to his tally!

Sally came down from her loop, descending so she'd be

behind and below the enemy plane. But she couldn't guarantee she'd escaped.

'He's a fighter ace, Wyngate,' she told him, her voice tight with fear. But she couldn't be afraid. She had to focus. She had to get out of there.

'Head towards Heath Place,' Wyngate told her. 'He's lost his formation. He won't follow.'

But it suddenly seemed like a long, long way to Heath Place, and, as the Messerschmitt began to bank, Sally got the distinct impression that he would follow. He had her in his sights and would be looking for another marker to paint beside that swastika.

The fighter was still banking into a turn and Sally realised that he was taking his time, because he believed the Spitfire was easy pickings. But just as the clouds had concealed the Messerschmitt, it seemed they had another surprise in store too. Behind the German plane, another screamed down into the fight, and there on its nose, in a shaft of moonlight, Sally saw three words.

My Gal Sal.

Then the night was split by gunfire and the Messerschmitt, so graceful and smooth mere moments before, was spiralling down towards the trees below. A thick plume of black smoke trailed from the stricken aircraft, flames lapping at the darkness. It was by the light of those flames that Freddy gave Sally his characteristic wing dip, as though to say, *don't mention it*. Then he pulled the Spit up and over Sally's plane, no doubt heading back to join the boys from Bramble Heath in pursuit of the other members of the German's squadron.

'Bring her in!' Wyngate barked. 'Now!'

Sally was so stunned that she merely flew along aimlessly for a few moments. 'Did you see that? *Could* you see that? Freddy just appeared out of nowhere like my guardian angel.

And he took the ace out. Shot him out of the sky, just like *that*. Freddy...'

And Freddy could have had no idea that *his gal Sal* was in the plane he'd just saved.

'Straight into the hangar!' was all Wyngate said. 'Come on!'

Sally looked for the runway lights, which she now saw glowing below her. She knew they couldn't be left on for too long, in case another enemy plane was in the area and discovered the secret runway. As she brought the plane down, she saw the flicker of flames in the trees behind the hangar where the Messerschmitt had crashed. Fortunately, she realised with relief, it was some way from the shelter where the ground crew were waiting out the siren.

Once she was down safely, Sally taxied the secret Spitfire to the hangar. In the near-darkness, she saw the figures of the few ground crew who hadn't gone to the shelter as they hurried along the runway, extinguishing the lights.

'Bad night for someone!' Wyngate said as he strode to the Spitfire to help Sally down. 'Very good job, Second Officer, and that friend of yours too.'

'Thank you,' Sally said, trying to control the shuddering that was suddenly rushing through her. 'Close shave, wasn't it?'

Somehow, she got to the mess and changed out of her flight suit, the Messerschmitt's last few moments repeating and repeating in her mind like a film that had got stuck. After the all-clear sounded, Lane-Bannister took her home with her bicycle. There was no question of her riding home on her own, not when her teeth were chattering and she couldn't stop her hands shaking from the shock of what had just happened.

When Sally let herself in at the kitchen door, she realised her parents were in bed. She was alone. She robotically poured herself a glass of water and went up to her bedroom, trying to forget the images that were replaying in her mind's eye. She climbed into bed, still shaking, and bundled herself up in her blankets.

There it was again, the Messerschmitt coming after her unarmed plane like a cat after a mouse. Until a Spitfire had burst from the clouds, coming to Sally's rescue.

Freddy.

Freddy had saved Sally's life. And she could never, ever tell him.

SIXTEEN

Despite Sally's sleep being disturbed by nightmares of the Messerschmitt, she still had to go to the airbase the next morning. She couldn't remember the nightmares in much detail, but the impression of terror lingered.

After breakfast, and the strongest cup of tea she could make with her ration, Sally got on her bicycle. Instead of going straight to the airbase, she cycled towards the main street of the village. She wanted to see life, and people. She wanted to see something that wasn't that hell-machine dropping from the clouds and coming after her like a shark.

Sally'd had too many close scrapes lately, and it did her good as she reached the main street to see the children – locals and evacuees alike – heading for the village school, laughing with their friends and fooling about. Just as she and Freddy had done once when they were small. Jamie Farthing nodded a hello as she rode by, and she acknowledged him with a salute.

This was what she was risking herself for up in the sky – what *everyone* was risking themselves for. Life, and happiness, and friends. Peace.

Sally rang her bell, saying hello to Bramble Heath's post-man, who'd come out of retirement to work his rounds again when their regular postman joined up. Mrs Gosling was laughing with Mrs Hubbard as they walked along the pavement together, while Laura, the local vet, put an envelope in the letterbox. Annie was chatting to Betty Farthing as she opened the post office, and Rose was polishing the windows of the tea rooms, while Reverend Ellis strode by heading for his church. Constable Russell, Annie's father, had stopped to talk to Ewa outside the butcher's shop as Ernie leaned out of the door to wave hello.

Sally saw Peter, Freddy's brother, riding to school, his satchel bouncing against him as he pedalled. Sally stopped, and called, 'Peter, good morning! How are you?'

His brother might be avoiding her, but it didn't mean Sally couldn't say hello.

Peter skidded his bike to a halt alongside her and said, 'Freddy cracked another ace last night!' He held up five fingers. 'And today we're getting loads of new evacuees at school, so wait until they hear all about that!'

All over again, Sally saw Freddy's Spitfire flying out of the clouds, her unwitting guardian angel. She tried to look surprised.

'Oh, did he? Bravo, Freddy. Will you tell him congratula-tions from me? In case I don't get to see him today,' she said. 'And how lovely there's more children coming to the village. You'll have *lots* of new friends!'

'What do you think you'll be flying today?' Peter asked excitedly.

'I have no idea!' Sally said truthfully. After all, she could be going back to the secret Spitfire, or she could be sent off to deliver a plane somewhere. 'It could be anything. I never know from one day to the next! I have a rather fun job, don't you think?'

Fun. It certainly hadn't been last night but, to a boy like Peter, flying planes all day for a job must've sounded like fun – even though she knew he preferred staying on the ground and tinkering with the engines.

'You've got a brilliant job,' the boy said, beaming. 'And because you're so good at it, I know I'll be on a good wage when I'm working on the crew for Toussaint and Carr!' He was every inch Freddy's brother, from his cheeky comment to the even cheekier smile. Then Peter gave his bike bell a ring and set off towards the village school. 'Have a good fly, Sally!'

Sally saluted him. 'Thank you, Peter, I will!'

She was determined to. She wasn't going to let the memories of what had happened yesterday overwhelm her. She had a job to do.

She headed for the airbase, the breeze rushing past her as she pedalled. She headed up the driveway, only thinking of what she would do today – *my bit, that's what I'll do, whatever I'm called on to do.*

Parked outside the house she saw two familiar vehicles: Lane-Bannister's shiny black car from the ministry and, beside it, Wyngate's dark blue sporty car. Puzzled, she wondered what they were doing at the airbase. The secret Spitfire project was nearly over – perhaps Group Captain Chambers needed to sign it off?

Or perhaps it was another secret project, one that she would never know anything about.

Here's hoping. I'm all done for secret projects.

As Sally got off her bicycle outside the ATA depot, she saw Gladys, Chambers' secretary, coming towards her. And she knew then exactly why Lane-Bannister and Wyngate were at the airbase – it did involve the secret Spitfire after all.

'Would you mind stepping inside to see Group Captain Chambers?' Gladys asked, as if Sally had a choice.

'Not at all,' she replied, and she and Gladys headed for

Sally's old home. She surreptitiously glanced left and right, wondering if anyone – the other Attagirls, or RAF pilots or ground crew – had seen. But everyone looked too busy, involved in their own tasks, to notice. It wasn't usual for an Attagirl to be summoned by the RAF, and she started to feel paranoid.

Oh heck, is it about that Messerschmitt?

She didn't want to have to give *that* any more space in her head. Instead, she contented herself remembering playing blind man's buff in the corridor at a birthday party, and Freddy coming out as the winner. It made her smile.

Gladys knocked on the door. 'Group Captain Chambers, it's Second Officer Toussaint to see you.'

'Come on in, Second Officer.' Chambers smiled as he opened the office door. 'I'm sorry to call you from your duties.'

'That's quite all right, Group Captain,' Sally said to him as she entered his office. 'What can I do for you?'

For a moment – a horrible moment – seeing Chambers' scars from the burns he'd suffered in his plane crash reminded her of the flames from the downed Messerschmitt. But she pushed the thought away. Her experience had given her a whole new respect for men like William Chambers, deep in her heart.

Life could – life *did* – go on.

'Please, have a seat,' he said, clearly doing his best to put her at ease. Chambers had that air of urbane calm that made him able to do that, unlike the barking, stern-faced Wyngate. Even when Wyngate spoke fluent French, when his manner softened slightly.

'Would you like tea?' he said, gesturing to the tray set ready on his desk.

'I'd love one, please,' Sally said as she took a seat at Chambers' desk. She wondered if he had noticed the dark circles under her eyes, which she'd done her best to conceal with a smear of the little make-up she had left.

Chambers picked up the teapot and poured, casual as anything when he said, 'Mr Lane-Bannister told me what happened last night. He tells me you flew that Spit like an ace.' He settled his gaze on Sally and she was reminded of the weeks just before Christmas when he'd barely left Heath Place at all, afraid to show his scars to the village. Those days, happily, were gone. 'I hope I'm not speaking out of turn, but I wanted to ask whether you were all right. Usually when we have our first encounter with Jerry, we're not flying without cannons. I just wish I'd been up there in a Spit to help you out.'

Sally blinked at Chambers, taken aback. She'd thought she'd just have to get on with it, put up with the nightmares and hope they'd eventually fade. But here was a man who had literally come through an inferno, asking her if she was all right.

'Thank you for asking, I can't tell you how much that means to me,' she replied. She wondered how on earth to put her feelings into words; but Chambers would understand, she thought, however she phrased it. 'I-I was in shock afterwards. I kept shaking. My teeth were chattering. And all night, over and over again, I had nightmares. Terrifying nightmares, though I couldn't tell you exactly what they were. That plane just appeared out of nowhere and came at me. I thought – I just had to get out of the way. I'm sure he knew I was unarmed, and he was enjoying it, I'm certain of it. He was enjoying the thought of how terrified I was. I was so alone up there, until Freddy— And moments later...'

She didn't need to tell Chambers what had happened next.

'You kept a cool head when the landing gear let you down. And not only once! But to come up against Jerry on your first night flight...' Chambers held Sally's teacup out to her and said gently, 'Every single one of us – and I dare say we can count Jerry in that number – has felt that terror.' He resumed his seat before the window, bathed in the spring sunshine. 'But none of us had signed a piece of paper promising not to talk about it.

That's why I wanted to see you today, because I can't imagine having to keep such a frightening thing to myself.' With a smile he added, 'Happily, I've signed a similar piece of paper, so you *can* talk to me.'

Sally sipped her tea, then told him, 'I so desperately wanted to tell my parents this morning, but of course I couldn't. You're so kind, Group Captain. It's just... it's come a week after the landing gear getting stuck again, and that was pretty terrifying too. But I'm not grumbling, you know. I have to keep reminding myself I'm doing my bit. And if I do my bit, I'm a tiny cog in a massive machine, and we'll end this dreadful war one day. It means Freddy can fly for fun again, and my family over in France will be free. Isn't that a wonderful thought?'

Chambers nodded. 'We're all small cogs,' he admitted. 'Except Mr Wyngate. I don't think he'd like to be called a cog.'

Sally chuckled. 'I imagine he wouldn't! But I should say – because I don't know if Wyngate would tell you – he stayed on the radio last night. He made almost everyone go to the shelter when the sirens sounded, and he stayed on that radio while I was in the air. He didn't abandon me.'

'I'm surprised he didn't make you sign an agreement not to tell anyone *that*.' There was mischief in Chambers' eyes when he said that. 'A little hidden spark of humanity, eh?'

'Oh, yes, he's not as fearsome as you might expect,' Sally replied, amused. She sipped her tea, reflecting for a moment, before saying, 'When I said I was alone up there, I wasn't entirely, was I? Because Wyngate was there, on the ground, trying to get me back in one piece. And in a sense, everyone who'd worked on that plane was there with me too.'

And that made Sally feel a little better.

'I know it's difficult to believe and I'm not sure you'll feel any better,' Chambers said, 'but the chap last night likely didn't give a thought to the person in the hot seat. As far as he was concerned, he was about to score an easy point by taking down one more Spit. The machine, not the person inside it... I don't think many pilots could bring themselves to go into combat otherwise.' He drew in a breath and shook his head. 'We're all relieved when we see a parachute, believe me.'

Sally mused over his words. A plane, not a pilot. She had to remember that. It was what Chambers had told himself and what Freddy must've done too. Not that Freddy ever talked about shooting down planes.

'It's easy to take it personally, isn't it, when they're coming straight for you,' she observed. 'I dread to say it, but I didn't see a parachute last night. He might've survived it, though. Please don't tell me if he didn't.'

Sally knew the pilot couldn't have survived, and yet... if she could tell herself he had, then it might be easier for her to bear.

Chambers nodded and assured her, 'You're not alone, Second Officer. I'm always here to listen.'

'Thank you,' she said as she put her empty teacup on its saucer on Chambers' desk. 'It would be lovely to have another cup of tea with you one day, and, now we're working together, I'm sure we will. I'm so grateful to you for giving up your time. Talking to you has helped, I really think it has.'

'I'm not just a pretty face,' he teased. 'Though if my Annie heard me say that, she'd give me a jolly stern telling-off.'

'I bet she would!' Sally chuckled. Chambers' and Annie's romance was the talk of the village, Bramble Heath's much-loved nurse and her dashing RAF beau. Although Sally felt a pang as she thought about Freddy... They were barely a couple at all at the moment.

There was a quick rap at the door, the two knocks barely sounding before the door opened and Wyngate swept in. He took in the scene before him as Lane-Bannister followed, looking rather apologetic at the intrusion.

'Second Officer, you're booked for the day,' Wyngate instructed. 'We need you at Bluebell Woods to brief the pilot who'll be flying our new plane in combat.'

And there in the doorway, virtually bouncing on his toes like a little boy on Christmas Eve, was Freddy.

SEVENTEEN

Sally stood on the secret Spitfire's wing, leaning in to show Freddy the plane's instrument panel as he sat in the cockpit. He looked like he'd just been given a new toy – which, in fact, was exactly what had happened.

And he was smiling. Sally had missed that smile so much, and now it was back.

While the ground crew were busy, Sally leaned closer to Freddy and whispered, 'I'm so glad you know about this plane now. You can't imagine how hard it's been keeping this a secret from you.'

'I behaved very badly. And I'm sorry,' Freddy admitted, looking suddenly ashamed. 'I couldn't imagine what you saw in him. Now what you saw in *this*... I'd dump me for *this*!'

Sally chuckled. How typically Freddy. 'It's a wonder-machine. Just you wait until you're up in the air, Freds, you won't believe how smooth she is. I've done all sorts of things – the ATA's hair would stand on end if they knew how I've flown this plane!' She rested her hand against his shoulder. 'But really, Freddy, I understand. You lost your friend, and you thought you were losing me. I'm not surprised you were upset. But you know I'll always love you, darling, don't you?'

She glanced over her shoulder. They had been left to it by the ground crew, so she chanced a kiss on Freddy's cheek.

'I love you.' Freddy didn't seem to care about duty then, as he kissed her. It wasn't exactly a chaste peck on the cheek, but there was nobody there to complain.

'A kiss from a handsome pilot,' Sally whispered, beaming at him, as they broke from the kiss. 'Aren't I a lucky girl? And just think – you saved my life last night. Imagine that!'

'If you'd been armed, you'd have got the bugger,' Freddy assured her. 'Him getting split from his formation and spotting you – that was rotten luck for you, Sal.' He gave a casual shrug. 'Worse for him. But... you're my girl. I keep thinking about what could've happened.'

'We're all relieved when we see a parachute,' Group Commander Chambers had said. Only there hadn't been one last night. Freddy had taken a life to protect whoever it was in the other Spitfire. He'd had no idea it had been his girlfriend in the cockpit.

'It was terrible luck,' Sally agreed. 'But then I had wonderful *good* luck, because you appeared. You're my guardian angel, Freds.'

He kissed her cheek and said, 'You've always been mine.' Then he asked, 'Will you miss flying her?'

Sally sighed. 'It's true, I really will. It's been such a lot of fun over the past few weeks, flying this plane like I used to fly before the war. Only better because she's just incredible, Freds. But *you'll* get to enjoy flying her now.'

But Freddy would fly her in combat, facing men like the one she had encountered last night, time and again.

'They're going to put her into production once she's done a few runs in the field,' Freddy replied. 'But you'll always be the one who made her what she is.'

'Thanks,' Sally said, blushing at his praise. 'I wouldn't have got anywhere without the ground crew, though. They've been brilliant. I'd love to work on another project like this, but I know I'm really lucky to have been in on this one. And I'll know you're going to be safer in the skies now, because you'll be in this truly amazing plane.'

She'd only had a tiny taste of what Freddy faced on every scramble. How he could face that sort of life-or-death danger, day after day, week after week, and still smile, she didn't know.

'What matters is making everyone on the ground safer,' he admitted. 'And she'll do that. She's faster, more agile... the armaments are going to make all the difference.'

Sally glanced across at the wing. The secret Spitfire had now been fitted with her guns. They were an innovation too, lighter than the ones on standard Spitfires, and they could shoot faster.

'They've thought of everything in this plane,' she said with a smile. 'It's all very clever. We just have to fly them!'

She was being flippant, of course. It was never a case of *just flying*, especially not in a war.

Freddy nodded. 'So I've already got the most gorgeous gal in Bramble Heath and now the Air Ministry's handed me the keys to the second best too,' he said, his voice alive with enthusiasm. 'The boys are going to be green with envy.'

Sally had a wonderful day working with Freddy. It reminded her of the old days before the war, when they used to work together on their planes in the hangar at Heath Place. And she knew from the joy in Freddy's expression that he was thinking the same thing. As long as she didn't think about the reality of what Freddy would be doing in the secret Spitfire, facing down Luftwaffe fighter aces, she felt happier than she had in some time.

A burden shared is a burden halved. That was the saying, wasn't it?

When Sally watched Freddy thunder down the runway in the secret Spitfire and take to the skies, she had never felt more proud. As far as she was concerned, her brave, skilled boyfriend was the best pilot in the RAF, and the perfect man to sit behind the secret Spitfire's controls.

'We always intended to give him the plane,' Wyngate told her as he strolled across the airstrip. 'But we needed the *very* best when it came to the test flights.'

Sally was taken aback not by Wyngate's words, but by the fact that the stone-faced ministry man had made a joke. A stone-faced joke, but a joke all the same.

She laughed and replied in French. 'Very funny, Mr Wyngate. You're full of surprises. First of all, you speak fluent French, and now you're telling jokes! And... you're very brave. You didn't abandon me last night. That meant a lot, you know.'

Wyngate lit a cigarette and blew out a breath of smoke. Only then did he deadpan in her native language, 'I couldn't risk losing the Spit, First Officer.' But there was the slightest hint, barely there at all, of a smile.

First Officer?

Sally blinked at him. 'Did you just call me First Officer, Mr Wyngate? I'm Second Officer, you know!'

'That can't be the case, because it would mean I was wrong,' Wyngate replied. 'So you must be First Officer Toussaint, First Officer Toussaint. Congratulations.'

'You've just promoted me!' Sally exclaimed. First Officer at last! She'd longed to be promoted, and now that she had been, she couldn't quite believe it. Wouldn't her parents be proud? Wouldn't Freddy be too? She held her hand out to shake his. 'Thank you, Mr Wyngate! Back to the ATA with a feather in my cap, eh?'

'Well earned.' He took her hand and shook it. 'And if I

could put you in the RAF, I would. But some things, even I can't do.'

'I don't think I'd suit a moustache!' Sally replied, although she would always think it was jolly unfair she wasn't allowed to fly in the RAF.

Freddy zoomed overhead and she shielded her eyes with her hand to watch him. 'There's my Freddy. Just look at him go!'

And the more planes like this there were in the sky, the stronger they would be against Germany. The Battle of Britain had already sent them running, but they kept on coming back even now. Every time the sirens wailed and sent people running for shelter, the people of Britain were reminded that the war was not over yet. But there was so much that they could do with the technology Maintenance Unit Zero were working on, and Sally knew these were just the first steps. It wouldn't stop at Spitfires, not now.

Sally had never seen the secret Spitfire fly other than from the cockpit. Feeling how different the plane was as the pilot was different from actually *seeing* the plane in flight. It really was incredible to watch as it rolled and banked, looped and climbed, and Sally knew Freddy would be flying with an enormous smile on his face.

He didn't stop grinning even when he was back on solid ground, and, when he and Sally joined the boffins and ministry men for an afternoon of technical talk and debriefing, he was still as bouncy as ever. It was the Freddy Sally had known all her life, her best friend and the man she loved, and when he said, 'Ginge would've given his eye-teeth to fly this kite,' she couldn't help but smile too. Freddy had lost his wingman, but his name wouldn't ever be forgotten.

Once their day at the secret hangar was over, Sally and Freddy turned down Lane-Bannister's offer of a lift back to Bramble Heath. Instead, they walked hand-in-hand through the lanes to the village. Sally was so relieved that everything was fixed between them, and she wanted to enjoy every moment she had with Freddy; life had been so lousy without him.

'Aren't you pleased that you're dating a First Officer now?' Sally said happily as she swung their joined hands to and fro.

'You'll be running the Air Force next,' Freddy laughed. 'Give me a raise if you do, eh?'

'Of course I would!' Sally replied. 'And a special stipend for Wilbur, too, so he's never short of dog biscuits. And I'd let you do as many loop-the-loops as you like, whether they're necessary or not!'

She thought back to their days flying before the war, and she glanced at Freddy. Was he remembering them too?

'We'll be Toussaint and Carr again one day, Freds,' Sally told him, her words full of hope.

'Up in the air with the girl I love.' He dashed a kiss to her cheek. 'And the whole world'll turn out to see us!'

And how much they loved each other.

Freddy left Sally at the door, promising to return after tea to take her along to the pub for a quick drink before the blackout. His kiss was polite, in deference to François, who was changing his bicycle tyre on the garden path. As Sally went into the house she could hear the two men chatting merrily, as though they were father and son. But Sally's and Freddy's fathers had been friends for decades, the friendship that had seen them launch their flight school together at Heath Place.

And she knew how very proud François would be if he only knew about the secret Spitfire.

After tea, Sally put on a pretty dress she'd bought in Paris, at the last airshow they'd flown in France. She was in such a happy mood. For the first time in a long time, she was optimistic that the war could be won by Britain and her allies, and that her dear Freddy wouldn't be flying in combat much longer.

One day I'll be back in France again, and I'll see my family, and I'll buy an even prettier dress than this one.

When Freddy and Wilbur knocked at the front door to collect Sally, her heart sang. They strolled arm-in-arm through the village with the little dog trotting ahead in the dappled sunlight as Freddy said, 'You're a bombshell in that dress, Sal. The Paris frock!'

'I keep it for special occasions,' Sally told him, swishing the silky skirt with its print of pink roses. 'I felt like celebrating. I don't get promoted every day, do I?'

And she knew Freddy would realise she was talking about the secret Spitfire too. And the fact that they were together again.

'Congratulations!' He gave a whooping cheer as they pottered along past the post office, earning an indulgent smile from Ewa and Zofia as they strolled past pushing Zofia's little girl in a pram. Freddy knew both of their husbands, of course, one a pilot and one a translator in the Polish section at Heath Place. 'Say hello to Air Chief Marshal Sal, ladies,' he called out, 'my girl's been promoted!'

Ewa nodded and both women said, 'Congratulations,' then Zofia gave Sally a beaming smile.

'Shall we sit out in the garden?' Freddy asked as they reached the George and Dragon.

'Oh, why not?' Sally replied. 'I do look like a giant flower in this dress, after all! But it's so nice to wear something all floaty and fun for a change. I wouldn't expect you to agree – gents don't really have the same options. You always look very dashing though, darling, whether you're in your uniform or civvies.'

Freddy did look very handsome in his open-necked shirt and slacks, wearing the polka dot cravat Sally had given him one Christmas.

There were green-painted picnic tables in the George and Dragon's garden, mostly occupied by Land Girls, WAAFs and pilots of the RAF and the ATA, who were all engaged in drinking and flirting. The hanging baskets that used to be full of geraniums now contained tomatoes and herbs, and a sign on the wall of the pub pointed to the air raid shelter in the cellar. But it didn't dent the customers' fun.

Freddy and Sally waved to their friends as they made for an empty table off to one side, where it was quieter. After all, they were party to a secret project. And they had some time to make up.

Sally settled herself on the bench and Wilbur jumped up beside her, his tail wagging happily. Freddy left her with a kiss to her cheek and turned away, before suddenly spinning on his heel and slapping his hand to his forehead. 'Oh dash, I almost forgot!' He dropped down to one knee on the grass. 'Will you marry me?'

Sally gasped in surprise. She was vaguely aware that the chatter at the other tables had stopped and that she and Freddy suddenly had an audience. But all she cared about was Freddy, kneeling on the grass in front of her, his eyes twinkling as he smiled up at her.

Marry Freddy?

'Oh, Freddy, of course I will!' she replied. 'I love you, Freddy!'

'We Carrs don't have many country houses or heirlooms,' he murmured as he took a little box out of his pocket and opened it. 'But this is one of them. Nana Win's ring, which I *hope* is going to fit because I really do love you, Sal. I want to spend every bit of my life with you, however long I've got.'

Sally stared down at the glittering diamond set on a gold ring. It wasn't a huge diamond, but she didn't care. She knew how much Freddy had adored his Nana Win, and to be given her ring overwhelmed Sally.

'Oh, it's beautiful,' she murmured, taken aback. 'Freddy, you're so sweet! Slip it on my finger, let's see if it fits!'

Freddy took Sally's hand in his and tenderly slid the ring

onto her finger with such ease it might've been made just for her to wear. As he did, the garden erupted in cheers and applause.

'How's that?' he whispered.

'It's just perfect!' Sally replied, her voice hushed with emotion. 'Freddy, I adore you!'

And she flung her arms round him and held him tight.

'Well, I'm glad to hear it.' He put his arms round her waist. 'Because I'm not going anywhere.'

EIGHTEEN

For the next couple of days, Sally felt as if she was floating on air. Who could blame her? She was going to marry her sweetheart, and she'd just been promoted. The news of Sally and Freddy's engagement quickly spread through the village, and congratulations poured in. She was the luckiest girl alive.

She still had her work to do in the ATA and, although it wasn't as fun as being the test pilot of the incredible secret Spitfire, she delivered the planes knowing that she had been part of something amazing.

Freddy was busy too, of course, and it made Sally so relieved to think he would be flying that special plane.

They still managed to see each other, even if it was only briefly at the airbase. One day Sally flew in with another Spitfire delivery, she spotted Freddy sitting on the grass beside the runway with his friends. Her heart rushed with love at the sight of him.

After she had taxied the plane and climbed out, she bounded over the grass towards her fiancé.

'Freddy!' she called, as Wilbur appeared and started running laps around her.

'Hello, First Officer!' Freddy beamed, catching his arms round Sally's waist and drawing her into his embrace. He turned to his friends and told them, 'Have you met the girl I'm going to marry? Oh you *have*? Well, here she is again!'

'Here I am!' Sally giggled, and waved to Freddy's friends. Then she looped her arms round his neck and kissed him on his lips. 'Aren't we naughty? But why not!'

Freddy returned the kiss and murmured, 'We're allowed to rehearse for married life, after all.' Then he added, 'We've had a busy day too... Ginge's sign's gone up!'

Sally wondered what he meant, until she turned to follow his gaze. There in front of the mess, someone had painted a sign. THE GINGE AND DRAGON, it proudly said.

'That's wonderful!' Sally told him. 'He would've loved that, I'm sure of it! And he won't be forgotten. Not for a moment.'

'Would you join my pals and me for a swift drink before you hasten home to Ma and Pa?' asked Freddy playfully, mimicking the sort of upper-crust character found in the pages of P.G. Wodehouse. 'Champers on the lawn, Miss Toussaint? Or bitter, at least.'

'Half a pint of bitter would be fine!' Sally replied, and, with her arm linked through Freddy's, they headed to the mess.

They had a wonderful time that evening, uninterrupted by any raids or other duties, and all the RAF and ATA pilots congratulated them on Freddy finally proposing. Sally could think of nothing but the happiness before them now.

She eventually headed home, floating on a cloud of hope and joy. As she wished Freddy goodnight at the garden gate, all she could think of was that once they were married they wouldn't say goodnight and part to sleep in separate beds. Her heart was full as she drifted off to sleep, dreaming of Freddy and the life together that awaited them.

· · ·

A couple of days later, she was humming cheerfully to herself as she got ready for work, combing her hair in the mirror by the front door. Another day of delivering planes awaited her and, if she was lucky, she'd bump into her dear Freddy again at the airbase.

It wasn't a bad life at all.

She heard a knock, and heaved open the heavy oak door. She was surprised to see Group Captain Chambers standing there.

Why on earth has he come to see me?

'Good morning,' she said, noticing at once that something was off.

'Good morning, First Officer.' Chambers took off his cap and put it under his arm. 'I hope you don't mind me calling in person. I wonder if we could speak?'

'Well... I suppose so, yes,' Sally replied, still wondering what was up.

Maybe they've got another secret project for me to work on?

When Chambers spoke again, however, a cold dart of fear shot through her blood.

'Perhaps your mother or father could join us?'

He wouldn't want her parents to hear about any secret projects.

'It's Freddy, isn't it?' Sally said, the words tumbling out. 'Something's happened to Freddy, hasn't it?'

Emily appeared from the kitchen. 'Sorry, I couldn't help but hear that we have a guest. Group Captain Chambers, would you like to come this way, please, into the parlour?'

Emily gently took Sally's arm and guided her. It was just as well her mother had appeared, as Sally couldn't have walked a step. It felt as though every limb of her body had seized up.

Emily opened the door, and gestured for Chambers to go in. The parlour was just the same as always, filled with as much of the furniture from Heath Place as they'd been able to take with them. An elegant silk-covered chaise longue stood under the window, and a portrait of a lady in a white powdered wig hung on the chimney breast above an ornate clock. There were antique armchairs and a walnut cabinet. But Sally didn't see any of it.

Group Captain Chambers went into the room first, and stood politely as he waited for the two women to sit. Only when they had did he settle onto one of the chairs and clear his throat to break what Sally already feared would be bad news.

Emily clasped Sally's hand, while Sally stared straight at Chambers. Her head was swimming.

'Please tell me,' Sally said, her voice trembling, the words struggling to come out.

Something had happened to Freddy. She knew it, she could see it in Chambers' face. Her fiancé, her love, the handsome, happy-go-lucky man who she adored more than anything. They were going to be married, and, after the war, they'd fly together again. She couldn't lose him. She couldn't. Not Freddy. What future would there be for Sally without him? But she had to know. Even if it would be agony to hear, she had to know.

'What's happened to Freddy?' she asked, a tremor in her voice.

'I'm afraid his plane was lost over occupied France last night,' Chambers said. 'We've received no word since. I wanted to speak to you myself before you heard from someone else.'

The clock stopped ticking.

Sally stared at Chambers, not wanting to believe him. Hoping that at any moment she'd wake up and find out it was just some horrible nightmare that she would soon forget. But his words repeated again and again in her head as tears rose in her eyes.

Lost over occupied France. Lost over occupied France. Lost over...

That's why he proposed. He knew he was going on a

dangerous mission. He knew he might not come back. But he has to. He has to come back, because we're going to get married.

'H-he can't be lost,' Sally insisted. 'Mummy, isn't that right? He can't be! Freddy's the best pilot in the RAF, he can't be lost! He's on his way home, right now. Any second now, he'll knock at the door, and I'll go to the airbase with him. Isn't that right, Mummy?'

Emily didn't reply. She put her arms round Sally and held her. And Sally, suddenly a child again, burst into tears.

'There's every chance we'll receive word of Flight Lieutenant Carr,' Chambers assured them. 'And as soon as we do, you'll know.'

Sally lifted her head to look at Chambers. 'Lost doesn't mean dead, does it?' *Dead.* The word was so heavy on her lips. 'Lost means that, right now, he can't tell you where exactly he is.'

But occupied France? Sally couldn't think of many places to be lost that were worse. And yet, she'd heard of men who'd crashed over France and had been helped to safety by the Resistance. There was a chance. There *had* to be.

'Lost doesn't mean dead,' he confirmed, his gaze kind. 'I've spoken to Mr and Mrs Carr this morning too. Once I receive news, I'll make sure you're properly updated.'

Sally nodded. Her mouth was dry with fear, but she somehow managed to say, 'Thank you, Group Captain. I really appreciate you coming to see me. We'll all hope for good news, won't we? All of us.'

Chambers nodded. 'All of us,' he said.

There was nothing in Sally's mind other than the memory of Freddy, her Freddy, down on his knee in front of her as he proposed. She wanted to hold on to that image, she couldn't let it fade. She couldn't lose him.

Where are you, Freddy? Please come home.

NINETEEN

Every day, when Sally woke up, the first few seconds were bliss. In those moments, she forgot that Freddy was missing. Then she would remember, and she'd feel the pain of his disappearance all over again.

But he's lost, he's not dead. They're not the same thing. They're not.

Then she'd get out of bed, suddenly awash with hope, because today, today would be the day they'd get the news that everyone wanted to hear. Today they'd know that Freddy was fine and was on his way home.

But every night, Sally would get back into bed without having heard a word about Freddy at all.

Freddy was still lost.

She wasn't going through it alone, at least. News had spread around Bramble Heath, and whenever Sally was out in the village she received sympathetic looks from everyone. All the locals had known Freddy his whole life. They had seen him grow up, from boy to man. He was part of Bramble Heath, the famous pilot who did the village proud. His disappearance cast a shadow over the village.

'Oh, love, is there still no news?' Mrs Farthing asked Sally when she went into the post office to buy stamps.

Sally shook her head. 'No, not today. But tomorrow... you never know.'

She was holding on to hope. She couldn't give up on Freddy. He wouldn't give up on her if she was lost. The least she could do for him was hope.

Sally felt a hand on her shoulder, and she turned to see Zofia, who had found sanctuary here after escaping Poland, with her little girl.

'I thought my Szymon was lost,' Zofia told Sally, her gaze full of sympathy. 'I thought, *I will never see my love again*. But he came back. God decided he would not part us. And he will bring Freddy back.' Zofia touched her crucifix and gave Sally a gentle smile.

'Thank you,' Sally told her. 'It means a lot to me, hearing you say that.' She knew what Zofia had been through, and to think that she still had faith touched Sally. Hope was a sort of faith, wasn't it?

When Sally left the post office, Annie came up to her. She smiled gently and said, 'We're all thinking of you. If you need anything, anything at all, you know where to find me, don't you?'

Sally nodded. So many doors were open to her and to Freddy's family. The whole village had rallied round them.

As she headed out to the airbase, she called in on Freddy's parents, as she did every morning now.

She knocked at the door of the Carrs' cottage. She could hear Wilbur inside, barking, as she did every morning. And every time, she wondered if Wilbur was thinking what they all were.

Is it Freddy?

This morning it was Peter who answered the door, his face pale and his eyes dark from too many late nights. The little boy who never seemed to stop smiling hardly ever smiled at all any more, even when Wilbur was circling his feet, just as he did now.

'Hello, Sal,' he said forlornly.

'Morning, Peter,' Sally said, trying her best to smile although she knew it wouldn't fool him. 'Just thought I'd pop round to say hello on my way in. How are you?'

'Trying to keep Mum and Dad smiling,' Peter said, forcing a sad smile onto his face for Sally's benefit. Her heart broke for him, the little boy who adored his big brother.

'They've made you a cup of tea.'

Sally heard the gate open and turned to see Jamie wheeling his bike onto the path. The teenager met them with a nod of greeting and said, 'I thought you and me could ride to school together if you like, Pete? D'you fancy it?'

Sally was heartened to see Jamie take Peter under his wing. Jamie could understand how Peter was feeling, as his own older brother had been shot down. Killed. Jamie hadn't coped at all well and had for some time caused a lot of trouble in the village with his gang. But he'd changed. His anger at losing his brother had gone. Instead, here he was helping Freddy's little brother.

'That's very kind of you, Jamie,' Sally told him.

Peter glanced up at her, as though wondering whether he should accept. Whatever he saw in her expression must have given him the answer he sought because he said, 'Yeah, if that's all right?'

Jamie beamed and replied, 'Definitely! And I'm going to help the Land Girls fix one of the tractors after school. You're the only other lad in the village who's nuts about mechanics like I am, so you can come and help if you like?'

And for the first time since Freddy was lost, Peter's eyes lit up. 'I'll have to ask Mum and Dad,' he said. 'Just a minute!'

And with that, he dashed away into the house, leaving Sally

on the doorstep. Wilbur didn't follow him, but instead settled at Sally's feet, wagging his tail as he peered up at her.

'I'm really sorry,' Jamie told Sally. 'It's horrible what's happened.'

Sally crouched down to fuss over the little dog. As she stood, a shaft of morning sunlight picked out the diamond on her engagement ring and it glittered. For a moment, she was taken back to that sunny day when Freddy had dropped down onto his knee to propose. A day full of hope for their future together.

'Thanks, Jamie, I appreciate it,' she replied. 'It's... it's very difficult. But I'm really glad to see you're being a good friend to Peter. You're one of the few who understand.'

'We've got to stick together, just like the lads at the base,' he said. 'Everywhere's really quiet without Freddy. The whole village is missing him.'

'I know,' Sally said, her voice gentle. She knew how much Freddy was missed, and that helped in a way. She didn't have to walk through the village looking in on everyone else's happy lives, because whenever anyone met her they were kind, supportive. *We're all thinking of Freddy and hoping he comes home soon.* 'There's always hope, isn't there? Until we have word he's not coming back...'

Sally thought of her friend Amy. No trace of her was ever found. But she'd crashed into the mouth of the Thames in a snowstorm. Some sailors had tried to rescue her, but she'd disappeared into the cold, dark water. Sally knew in her heart that Amy, brave, indomitable Amy, hadn't survived.

Not Freddy. He was in France somewhere. He was still alive. He *had* to be.

'Mum and Dad said yes!' Peter said as he ran back from the kitchen, with his and Freddy's mother, Elsie, following on behind. He dropped to his knees to give Wilbur a cuddle and kiss his head, then, to Sally's surprise, stood and hugged her too.

'Come and have a cup of tea, Sally.' Elsie was like all of them, trying to keep up her smile even as she spent every second fearing for her lost son. 'You have a good day, Peter. He'll chatter your head off, Jamie.'

But Jamie assured her, 'That doesn't bother me at all, Mrs Carr. We're just two mechanics on our way to school.' He waited for Peter to climb onto his own bike, then the two boys pedalled off together.

'I'd love a cup of tea, Elsie,' Sally said, and went into the cottage with her, Wilbur following behind. 'How are you all?'

Sally knew the answer. There was still no news; nothing had changed. And yet she always asked.

'You just missed Arthur by five minutes.' Elsie sighed, leading Sally into the kitchen. For a moment she fell silent, then her shoulders shook and a sob escaped her. 'Oh Sally, I don't know what I'll do if—'

Sally hugged her. There had been a lot of hugs lately, because words alone struggled to embrace what they were all feeling.

'I know, I know...' Sally whispered. 'But there's hope, Elsie. Until they tell us otherwise, there's hope.'

TWENTY

TWO WEEKS LATER

Sally was alone in the church, up by the altar, trying to arrange some flowers. She wasn't very good at it, and she knew that if Freddy could see her attempt he'd try very hard not to laugh.

But he wasn't there. No one had received any news, and Freddy had been made officially Missing in Action. The flowers were for him, picked from gardens and meadows across Bramble Heath by the villagers who missed him. Because, as much as Sally tried to be hopeful, each day that passed wore away at her optimism. Part of her – a small part – had given up and accepted the worst. She had no way to mark it other than ineptly arrange the flowers in Freddy's memory, because she had to find a way to turn her mounting grief into something that wasn't ugly and sad.

'You're a better pilot than florist,' said a voice in French as the sound of a striking match split the silence.

Sally knew who it was at once. She turned to see Wyngate, and replied in French. 'I might be a terrible florist, but I'd never smoke in a church!'

Her surprise at seeing Wyngate again faded, and now she was wondering instead what on earth he was doing there. He didn't seem like the sort of man who would pop into a church during the day for a few quiet words with the Almighty.

After a moment, she asked him, 'What are you doing here?'

'Looking for someone who can fly a plane, speak French and keep a secret.' He took a draw on his cigarette.

A thought was forming in Sally's mind. But no, it couldn't be *that*.

She laid down the cornflowers and the coppertips she'd been wrestling with. 'That sounds like me. Go on, what is it?'

'You should finish the flowers.' Wyngate strolled along the aisle towards her, his footsteps echoing. He seemed ridiculously out of place in this little country church, surrounded by the trappings of a simpler sort of life.

Corn dollies were arranged along one of the windowsills, and the stained glass of Jesus as the Good Shepherd surrounded by his sheep cast red and blue light across the old stone floor. The worn burial slabs of Sally's ancestors, long-gone residents of Bramble Heath, passed beneath Wyngate's immaculately shod feet as he approached.

Sally picked up the flowers again, but she felt foolish now that she had an audience, and they seemed to mock her – a memorial arrangement, instead of a bride's bouquet.

'I don't know why I ever thought this was a good idea.' She shrugged. 'I just wanted to do *something...*'

'If you start a job, you finish it.'

'Is that why you're here?' Sally asked him as she poked one of the cornflowers into the vase. 'You're back in Bramble Heath to finish a job?'

Wyngate took a seat on the front pew and reverted to French to tell her in a low voice, 'You're covered by the addendum you signed until you take your last breath. And even after that.' He took another drag on the cigarette. 'Sometimes, that means difficult choices.'

'So I don't have a choice,' Sally replied in French. Her heart sank. 'Ever since they made Freddy MIA, something's bothered me. If he was flying what I *think* he was flying, then... if something went wrong, I'm partly to blame, aren't I? I should've seen it during the tests.'

'We've found the plane,' was all Wyngate said.

So Freddy was flying the secret Spitfire.

Sally's heart was racing. Her hands were clammy. 'If you've found the plane, then you know... you know what's happened to Freddy. You *have* to tell me, Wyngate. You *must.*'

'Plane and pilot are both accounted for in northern France. A little battered, but aren't we all?'

Sally gasped, dropping the rest of the flowers. She stared at Wyngate. 'Oh... he's... Freddy's... oh, my word.'

She dropped down onto the pew. Suddenly everything seemed brighter.

Freddy's alive. He's alive.

'Shoulder injury coming down,' Wyngate told her. 'He'll recover, but not quick enough. That's why we need someone.'

'He can't fly it himself with an injury like that... So, you want me to go and get Freddy back, is that it?' Sally whispered excitedly. She couldn't wait to let everyone know that Freddy was alive and coming home. 'I'll do it. Of course I'll do it! Just name the date, and I'll do it!'

'We want our plane back, First Officer.' Wyngate blew out a breath of smoke and continued, 'There's technology on that Spit that can't fall into Nazi hands.'

'But it's only got one seat,' Sally pointed out. 'I can't fit Fr—'

'We want our plane back.' Not Freddy. *It's the plane that he's come here for.*

'You! You terrible man!' Sally glared at Wyngate. 'You come into a church, you light up a cigarette, you tell me my fiancé's still alive, and all you care about is getting your plane back!'

For a second Wyngate was silent, then the second stretched,

the silence deepening. He simply watched Sally, his expression as unreadable as ever.

'Freddy has to come back too,' Sally whispered, turning and turning her engagement ring round her finger.

Just how injured was he? Wyngate had said it was just a shoulder injury, but could she trust him?

'I need him. His family needs him. Please, Wyngate. I can't go over there, bring the plane back and just leave him behind.'

'My job is to get the plane back. The weapons technology *cannot* find its way to Berlin,' he said. 'Flight Lieutenant Carr is in good health other than the arm; he's being cared for by members of the underground. I'm speaking to some people about extracting him, but the plane comes first.'

Sally didn't reply at once. She slowly digested Wyngate's words. The secret Spitfire was an amazing plane, with some incredible modifications. She knew he was right – they couldn't possibly risk it falling into the wrong hands.

It pained Sally to acknowledge it, but this wasn't just about Freddy.

'I know that plane,' she said quietly. 'She knows me, even though it's a daft thing to say. I'm the only one who can bring her back, aren't I? The only pilot who knows that plane and can pass as French.'

'It's going to be a very challenging take-off; I don't think we've got many pilots who could pull it off.' He blinked, then matched Sally's gaze. 'This is the most dangerous thing you'll ever do. If it goes wrong, if you're discovered, there's no chance of rescue, First Officer.'

Every hair on Sally's body stood on end at those words. The air seemed to crackle around them.

'I might die,' Sally murmured. But then, hadn't she evaded death before? She'd stared it hard in the face and she had survived. And there was no one else who could do it. If she didn't, the plane might well be discovered by the enemy, and it would mean disaster for millions of people. 'But then again... I might not. I'll do it. Maybe I'm crazy to agree to this, but...'

Wyngate rose to his feet. 'I'll be in touch,' he said. 'It was a lightning strike, by the way. Nothing but bad luck.' Then he swept down the aisle, leaving Sally alone.

Nobody's fault. It was only lightning. It was only Mother Nature.

That was a reason to feel relieved. And Sally was relieved all over again, because she knew now what Freddy's fate was.

So long as Wyngate was telling the truth.

Freddy's alive.

But Sally couldn't tell Freddy's grieving family that, just like she couldn't tell her own that she had volunteered for a task that might mean she'd never see them again.

Yet she was determined that she *would* see Bramble Heath again. And Freddy would be there with her when she did.

TWENTY-ONE

The next day, Sally was supposed to be at work again. She hadn't slept much, as her dreams were haunted by Freddy. She reached her arms out towards him, trying to pull him to safety, but he slipped away, over and over again. And every time, she woke with a sob.

He's alive. But I can't save him.

Wyngate had said they would try to bring Freddy back, and Sally knew it was possible – she'd heard of crashed RAF pilots who'd got back home from occupied France. It was just hard, when he'd saved her life, knowing that she couldn't save his in return. And he was hurt. Was he being looked after? Could he see a doctor? Sally had no idea.

She went to the airbase via the Carrs' cottage, and as she witnessed Peter's sad, drawn face, and Elsie's tears, she wished she could tell them the truth. But she'd signed that addendum, and it apparently extended further than she'd ever imagined.

If only I could tell them that he's alive.

As she cycled to the airbase, Sally wondered at how ridiculous it was – she *should* be over the moon to discover that Freddy was alive. But all she felt was a lead weight in her heart.

. . .

At the ATA depot, she collected her chit.

Bluebell Woods, via Heath Place, was all it said.

She glanced over to Heath Place, and saw Wyngate's sporty car parked up. Maybe he'd changed his mind and didn't want her to have anything to do with rescuing the plane after all?

But as Sally headed towards her old home, she was surprised at how disappointed the thought made her feel.

I want to do it. And I'll tell him so.

She went through the door from the garden into the corridor at the back of the house where she'd ridden her tricycle on rainy days when she was small. She stopped and glanced around, wondering which of the shadows Wyngate was concealed by.

Where are you, Mr Wyngate?

'Read, digest, memorise.' Wyngate suddenly stepped round the corner right in front of her, a thick buff folder in his hand. 'Don't leave the Heath Place estate. When I'm ready for you, I'll find you.' He held out the folder and went on in French, 'Meet the new you.'

Sally took the folder. *Meet the new me? So I really am going to France.*

'You pop up like a jack-in-a-box,' she told him. 'All right, I'll squirrel myself away with this and memorise it.' Although she wasn't sure how easy that would be, given how thick the folder was.

'You have three hours and then I'll come and find you. If you pass today, we have three days.' He gave Sally a nod, then turned back round the corner.

If I pass what?

But she'd only find out by studying the contents of the folder. Intrigued, Sally headed off to read it. As she went through the garden, she saw Davey, one of Freddy's friends.

Oh, heck. I'll have to say hello. I can't just ignore the chap.

'Hello, Sally,' he said, in that strained attempt to be chipper that everyone adopted when they saw her or Freddy's family. Sally didn't blame any of the boys for it, because what else could they do? They were losing friends all the time, they couldn't give in to despair.

He nodded towards the mess. 'We were just wondering how you're getting on, what with everything.'

Sally held the file loosely at her side, hoping Davey wouldn't spot it and ask her what it was.

'I'm... I'm still hopeful,' she replied, deliberately avoiding a smile. She was lying to Davey's face, and that didn't sit well with her, but she had no choice. 'I have to be, really. I hope so much that he's still alive. It's not easy, though. But thank you, Davey. I really appreciate you asking after me.'

He nodded and assured her, 'There's no way anything's happened to Freddy. Charmed life, he always said it.' But the sadness in Davey's eyes told Sally that he believed something very different. 'We're all thinking of you both, and Fred's people too. It's quiet without that little dog of his. We miss the pair of them.'

I wish I could tell you the truth.

'I miss him too,' Sally replied. It wasn't a lie. She could be honest about that, at least. 'Thank you, for thinking of us. If we all keep Freddy in our thoughts, he's still with us, isn't he?'

'That's the ticket.' Davey smiled. 'You can't keep Freds down.' He gave her a nod. 'I'll leave you to get on, but we just wanted you to know that you're not on your own.'

'It means a lot,' Sally replied. Then, thinking of the fragile threads that they were all hanging from, she said, 'Take care, Davey. And the rest of the chaps. Bye for now.'

She continued on her way, heading for the old summerhouse. It was tucked away to the side of Heath Place, within the old walled garden, and hadn't been taken over by the RAF, although she was sure it was only a matter of time. The cigarette butts around it told her that the pilots were using it at least. It was a nice, sheltered spot, just the place to read a secret dossier.

Sally pulled open the creaky door and went across the cracked wooden floorboards, where the tendrils of plants were creeping through. She chose the least mildewed cushion from the few still piled up in the corner and settled down to read.

Top secret, it said on the first page.

Sally turned to the next page and saw a photograph of herself in civvies, wearing a blouse and a skirt. She remembered it being taken by her father – she was standing outside the hangar at Heath Place just before the war. To anyone else, it just looked like a farm building. She wondered how Wyngate had got hold of it, then recalled that her father had kept a photograph album of the flight school, and had left it behind when the house had been requisitioned.

Beside her photograph it said JOSETTE AUCLAIR.

A shiver ran through her. This was her new self. Sally Toussaint would soon cease to exist, and instead would be replaced by Josette Auclair.

Sally carefully read through the thin, typescript pages. Someone had constructed a whole life for Josette: the town she'd grown up in, the school she'd attended, her family, her friends. Sally even recognised La Roche-sur-Yon, Josette's hometown, because it wasn't all that far from where Sally had been born.

Someone had put a huge amount of work into compiling Josette's life. Sally read it, enthralled, because this really could have been her if her father hadn't decided to move his family to England.

As Sally reread all the details about the pretend life of the fictitious Josette, she thought of her family members still in France. She could pretend that Josette was friends with her cousin, that Josette had met her aunts and uncles. It hurt so much not to know what was happening to her family. And what pained her even more was that she would be in France but still unable to see them. She didn't need Wyngate to tell her that. She knew it would risk blowing her cover. She had to remember instead that she was going on this mission for *them* as much as she was for anyone else.

But to do that, she'd have to pass whatever it was that Wyngate had set up for her. She was starting to wonder if she could.

Hours passed as Sally immersed herself in someone else's life. *Her* life, at least for a little while... a life that Freddy's safety and the stricken Spitfire depended on. She barely noticed the passage of the morning as it ticked into the afternoon; she was too busy with the most important studies she'd ever been faced with.

After a while, Sally closed her eyes and pictured Josette and her life. She saw through Josette's eyes as she cycled through the countryside around La Roche-sur-Yon, and tasted the salty tang of the rolling Atlantic waves as Josette swam at Les Sables-d'Olonne. In her mind, Sally sat in a French cinema with Josette's friends, Marie and Sophie, watching Maurice Chevalier dance. She could taste the bread baked by Marie's father, and she saw Josette's father in his camionette van with PLOMBIER – plumber – painted along the side.

It was as if Sally wasn't in the summerhouse, or even in England, now at all. But the France she saw – because it was the France she had known – was not one that had been invaded by Nazis, bombed and battered. She tried to make the images in her mind dingier, the faces of Josette's family and friends sadder, more tired. And she swallowed down her tears as she sat there picturing them, and their faces began to turn into those of her own family in France.

Wyngate has to pass me, whatever test he's got for me. He just has to.

. . .

'When I speak French you're Auclair,' Wyngate announced in French as he pushed open the door and stepped inside. How he'd found her, Sally couldn't imagine. He reverted to English to add, 'In English, you're Toussaint. If you make it through today, you will *always* be Auclair when you're in training. Clear?'

'Yes,' Sally said, blinking at him as she wondered what this *training* would involve. Then she tapped the side of her head. 'I've memorised it all. I could sit an exam on this woman now.'

Wyngate gave her a rather narrow look. 'As fast as that?' Then he pushed open the door and held it open with his foot, only a jerk of his head indicating that she was being summoned. 'We'll see.'

TWENTY-TWO

Sally followed Wyngate back across the garden to the house. She only realised now how long she'd been sitting down to read through the file, as her limbs felt stiff. Once they arrived at the house, Wyngate led the way through the corridors and up the stairs, and Sally thought, as she usually did, how strange it was to be in her own home but not the mistress of it. She had no idea where Wyngate was taking her, but she hadn't expected the room they ended up in.

My old nursery.

Sally recognised it at once, with its low, child-height door handle that her father had put in when she was little. She hadn't been into the nursery since the house had been requisitioned. She still remembered it with a pink rug and brightly patterned curtains. Her toys had been all around the room, her mother's doll's house with its porcelain figures in pride of place.

I don't think it'll look like that now.

It had looked out over the aerodrome's landing strip, and Sally and Freddy had often stood by the window, watching the planes go by, and wishing more than anything that they would be pilots one day.

She couldn't have known then that their ambitions would bring her right back to the nursery, and for whatever awaited her behind its door.

Wyngate opened the door and stood back. 'After you, First Officer,' he said. Then he dropped his voice and told her, 'Keep a cool head.'

'Understood,' Sally whispered back, trying to be brave. *I suppose they can't just send anyone into occupied territory, can they?*

She stepped into the room. The toys were evidently long gone, as was the pink carpet and the patterned curtains. It was spartan, with bare floorboards, and plain blackout curtains at the windows.

A long table stood at the far end of the room, with three men sitting behind it. She recognised two of them – Commander Seaton, from that first day when she'd been taken to see the secret Spitfire, who rose to his feet as soon as she walked in, and Group Captain Chambers, who followed suit a moment later. There was a third man she didn't recognise, wearing an army uniform. He didn't stand at once, but looked at Sally over the file he'd been examining. After a moment he tutted, and finally stood.

A fourth chair sat vacant behind the table – for Wyngate, Sally supposed – and another stood empty in front of the table, for her.

'Good afternoon,' she said cheerfully. She instantly regretted it, because hadn't Wyngate told her to keep a cool head? Being chipper and smiley wasn't how to demonstrate a cool head, surely?

'You know Group Captain Chambers, of course, and Commander Seaton,' Wyngate said as he approached the table, lighting a cigarette as he went. The room was small and close, the windows shut tight, and the first billow of smoke hung in the air behind him. 'And this is Dr Cooper, the sort of medic who cures precisely *nothing*.'

'I am a psychiatrist,' Dr Cooper said, looking rather exasperated. Sally sensed that he and Wyngate did not get on. 'From the Royal Army Medical Corps. I'm on the panel, Miss Toussaint, along with these other gentlemen here, to assess you.'

Sally had never met a psychiatrist before, especially not one from the army. She wasn't sure she wanted an exasperated soldier peering inside her brain.

'Pleased to meet you, Dr Cooper,' Sally said, trying not to sound as nervous as she was beginning to feel. 'And it's nice to see you again, Commander Seaton and Group Captain.'

As Wyngate took his seat he leaned across to tell Cooper, 'It's *First Officer* Toussaint, Mr Cooper.'

'I'm *Dr* Cooper.' He narrowed his eyes at Wyngate and when he turned back to Sally, his gaze was even more hostile. 'My apologies, *First Officer* Toussaint.'

'Have a seat, First Officer,' Chambers said, gesturing to the chair in front of them. Sally decided that his eyes were welcoming, but he was otherwise poker-faced. It threw her off, as his manner was normally so warm.

At least Commander Seaton looked something close to benign. He offered her a nod of acknowledgement as Wyngate said, 'First Officer, I've no doubt you're up to the flying this mission will entail, but that's only one part of the job.' He knitted his hands atop the table. 'I'd usually have you halfway up a mountain knee-deep in mud and tears to get you ready for a job like this, but alas, time is short. I want my plane back before Adolf gets his claws into her.'

Halfway up a mountain? At least she would be spared that; but then again going into occupied France without the full training sounded risky. And besides, she now realised that another secret door had been opened to her. Behind it were men and women trained up and dropped into occupied Europe, doing who knew what. Sally certainly didn't know.

'I-I see,' she stammered. Then she added, 'I'm surprised, by the way, not nervous.'

Dr Cooper made a note in his file and looked rather smug about it. Then he sat there, his pen hovering over the page, waiting, Sally was sure, for her to slip up.

'Tell us about Josette,' Wyngate instructed, surprisingly benign himself. For now, at least.

'Well, Josette Auclair is my age, born in 1919 in La Roche-sur-Yon in the Vendée, near where I was born too,' Sally said. 'Her father's a plumber, her mother is a housewife, and Josette has two sisters – Lucie and Félicité. Lucie works in a grocer's, and Félicité is still at school. And... Josette's really quite an ordinary sort of girl, I think. She likes to go to the pictures with her friends Marie and Sophie, and they go for bike rides around the countryside, just like I do, actually, and they go to the cinema together. And... Josette has a great-aunt in Normandy, who's rather elderly. I shouldn't wonder if Josette is rather worried for her, being on her own. Her great-aunt's a spinster, you see.'

Sally had absorbed so much of Josette's life, even down to the essence of it, that she could feel something like Josette's worry. It mirrored her own for her family there.

And from there, Wyngate subjected Sally to the most rigorous test of her memory that she'd ever undergone. Fast as a machine gun he rattled off questions about Josette's past, from childhood holidays to the colour of her sisters' eyes and everything in between. It was like being caught in the glare of oncoming car after oncoming car, swerving each collision only to be faced by another set of headlamps coming straight at her.

But Sally knew all the facts. She could *see* all the facts, as she pictured Josette's life. It wasn't just a list of words, but actual people and places that she could visualise. She did her best to keep up with the speed of Wyngate's questioning, but even her method of seeing the facts was disorientating, as her mind had to move from one scene to the next with lightning speed – one moment, she was in Josette's classroom, where she was looking at a globe, because her favourite subject at school was geography. Then she was on the beach at Les Sables-d'Olonne, and... who was it Josette met there on the beach? Sally closed her eyes, and the figure appeared. A boy on holiday from Paris, that was it. They'd briefly dated, then he went back home and she didn't hear from him again.

But was she fast enough for Wyngate?

'Why are you here?' Wyngate asked suddenly, switching to French without giving her a moment to think. 'In Normandy?'

Sally's brain switched languages immediately. This sort of thing happened at home sometimes, when she could have two conversations at once, one in English with her mother, the other in French with her father.

'To visit my mother's aunt,' she replied in French, quick as a flash. That was why they'd included the information in the file on the elderly aunt, wasn't it?

'Why?' The word was sharp, like a whip-crack.

'She's ill,' Sally replied. The file had told her that Josette's Aunt Colette had been afflicted with a summer flu. 'And my mother couldn't leave La Roche to come to see her.'

Sally could feel Dr Cooper's gaze boring into her, but she didn't turn to look at him. Instead, her focus was on Wyngate.

'Is that true, Miss Toussaint?' But Wyngate asked the question in French and Sally remembered what he'd said earlier. If he was speaking French, she was Josette, not Sally.

'Miss Toussaint?' Sally shrugged dismissively, just like her father did sometimes. 'Never heard of her. I'm Mademoiselle Auclair.'

Something flashed across Wyngate's watchful gaze, something that looked almost like admiration. He rose from his seat and walked round the table so he could stand in front of her.

'You're lying,' he hissed.

Sally looked up at him, shaking her head. 'I'm not lying, I'm telling you the truth.' And she didn't elaborate any further.

And Wyngate launched into another staccato round of questions about her assumed life, all of them in French. The longer it went on the louder he got and the more aggressive his tone became, the questions turning and twisting on themselves in an effort to catch her out, the fiction peppered with occasional tripwires referring to Bramble Heath, the Toussaints or even Freddy himself.

Sally did her best to keep up, her answers becoming even shorter and less elaborate. She wanted to look away but, if she did, wouldn't that make her look evasive? But it was so difficult looking at this man, who in some ways she'd come to see as a friend, glowering at her and calling her a liar. He was the man who'd stayed on the radio while she had faced that Luftwaffe fighter ace alone, who she'd been cheeky to in French, just because she could. Sally was sure she knew Josette's story, but the more Wyngate shouted the less certain she became.

And if she didn't get it right, she wouldn't be able to go to France, and she wouldn't be able to see Freddy.

Except *Josette* didn't know who Freddy was.

What a bleak thought that is.

That was the last straw, and Sally began to cry. But in French, she still protested, 'I *am* Josette, I am, I am! I only came here to look after Aunt Colette. I want to go home.'

Dr Cooper's stare suddenly changed. Sally felt it, the moment it altered. He slouched a little in his chair, he coughed, and she realised he was hiding a chuckle.

Sally dabbed her eyes with a handkerchief. She'd blown it, hadn't she? The soldier didn't think she was tough enough because she had cracked under interrogation.

But Sally said it again anyway, even though her voice was

tired, because wouldn't the real Josette have done so? 'I am Josette Auclair...'

Then, slowly, Dr Cooper sat up again. 'Very interesting,' he observed, then fell silent again. Seaton was writing intently.

I've failed. Oh, heck, I've failed, and I've let everybody down.

But Wyngate reached out and laid his hand on her shoulder. Then he told her in French, his tone softer than she had ever heard it before, 'We're done. Good job. Very good job.'

Sally looked up at the blurry figure of Wyngate through the tears that were swimming in her eyes. She was still talking to him in French. '*Good* job? But... but I'm a mess.'

A good job, but not good enough, it would seem.

'Let's get some fresh air, First Officer,' Commander Seaton suggested as he rose to his feet. Wyngate stepped back to let Seaton approach Sally and offer her a pristine, folded white handkerchief. 'And perhaps a cup of tea.'

'I'd love one,' Sally replied, in English now, taking his handkerchief. 'Sorry, that's not very French, is it, wanting a cup of tea?'

'My French is dreadful,' Seaton said gently. At the table, Group Captain Chambers was in discussion with Dr Cooper. Wyngate was still watching Sally, his arms folded tight across his chest as he considered her fate. And Freddy's.

'Just as well,' Sally said with an awkward smile at the kind man. She rose to her feet. Her legs were still trembling, but she made for the door with Commander Seaton. She didn't want to be in that smoky, uncomfortable room another moment, facing her failure. It truly wasn't her old nursery any more.

A few minutes later, she and Seaton were stepping into the late afternoon sunshine outside Heath Place, each holding a tin mug full of strong, steaming-hot tea.

'How are you feeling?' he asked Sally as they strolled down onto the grass.

Seaton's gentle manner was like a balm after what had just

happened. Sally sipped her tea to give her strength and replied, 'Embarrassed. I thought I could do it, I really did, but... I obviously can't, can I?'

'I'm an observer in this,' Seaton admitted. 'But I wouldn't jump to any conclusions yet, First Officer.'

Sally glanced at him, curious. Was he being kind, or did he really mean it? Was there hope that Sally hadn't spoiled her chances after all?

'*Really?* Oh, but...' She sipped her tea, her thoughts suddenly whirring again. She'd kept it up right to the end, hadn't she? She'd refused to be anyone but Josette for as long as Wyngate had spoken to her in French. She'd burst into tears, just as the real Josette would've done if an interrogator had kept telling her she was lying about being Josette. 'You never know. Gosh, you must think it's ridiculous that I actually want to... y'know. But it means so much to me. I'm sure you know why.'

'We do mount rescue missions out of France. We have some planned very soon,' Seaton told her and, though Sally knew he was choosing his words carefully, she realised immediately the import of what he was saying. Wyngate had said he'd do what he could for Freddy, even though the official target of the mission was the salvage of the Spitfire. 'Mr Wyngate asked me to tell you that and no more. I think you'll understand.'

Good old Mr Wyngate!

Sally smiled. So Wyngate wanted her to know. And the fact that some rescue missions were planned soon... Freddy was coming home. Somehow, he was coming home.

'I *do* understand,' Sally replied in a whisper. 'And thank you, you can't imagine how relieved I'll be once he's safe. And I know it's...' She winked at him, trying to relay that she knew it was a secret. He returned the wink, then gave her a small smile.

'We'll give them five more minutes,' he said.

'That should give us time to finish our tea,' Sally said, her spirits buoyed up again. 'And for Mr Wyngate to smoke a cigarette!'

And somewhere on the other side of the Channel, Freddy was safe for now. Even if she had to carry the secret inside her like a lead weight, at least she knew. She knew and maybe, if Wyngate believed she had what it took, she'd soon be there to see him safely home.

Once they'd finished their tea, Sally and Seaton went back upstairs. As they went, she told him about the house, back in the days when she'd called it her home. The fancy visitors who came to learn to fly and see the planes, the locals who'd come for the airshows on the lawn. She felt a lot happier. He was such a sweet man, she wondered how he got on with someone like Wyngate. But then again, he probably didn't – they'd all just been flung together at random, thanks to the war.

As Sally saw the door to the old nursery again, she recalled how hostile and unpleasant it'd been. Her happiness drained away; she only went back inside again because she had no choice.

Chambers looked as benign and unflappable as ever, with a twinkle in his eye, but there were two spots of colour on Dr Cooper's cheeks, and he was staring out of the window as if he didn't want to be in the room any longer either. Wyngate, however, was leaning casually against the edge of the table reading the contents of a folder not unlike the one he had given Sally. He seemed, she sensed, rather pleased with himself.

The window was open and the room was fresh and airy, all trace of Wyngate's cigarette smoke carried away on the breeze. As she and Seaton entered, the taciturn man from the ministry glanced up from his folder at Sally and asked, 'You *are* para-chute-trained?'

Sally couldn't help it. She laughed. 'Me, parachute-trained? Yes, of course I am. I learned well before the dratted war started. We used to do parachute training here, at the aerodrome too. They trained me all over again, of course, when I joined the ATA, because they insisted. But... yes, that's one box you definitely *can* tick.'

Wyngate glanced towards Cooper as though to say, *I told you so.* Then he told Sally, 'We start our three days of training at seven o'clock tomorrow morning, First Officer. Welcome to my section.'

'I did it? *Really?*' Sally couldn't believe it. After sitting there, sobbing, she was going to France. She was going to need every ounce of bravery she had – she was going to rescue the secret Spitfire. She stilled her excitement enough to say, as steadily as she could, 'I won't let you down, I promise.'

TWENTY-THREE

Sally woke up before her parents did that morning, and left a note for them on the kitchen table.

Early call! I'll see you later. Could you say hello to Peter and everyone? I haven't time to see them this morning. Love Sally xxx

The message was far bouncier than she felt, and she wished she could've seen her parents before she left for her first day of training. She didn't want to entertain the thought that she might not have much time left with them, that she'd leave Bramble Heath in just a few days and might never come home again. But the thought was there, haunting the back of her mind like a shadow.

Maybe I'll be back in time to see Mum and Dad before they go to bed, she thought, as she pedalled her bike towards Heath Place through the morning mist. She would need to tell her parents, and Freddy's family too, her cover story before she left, as well. Just a simple lie – that the ATA was sending her to Scotland for a little while and, as communications weren't great, she'd be a bit quiet.

And if something went wrong, Sally supposed her parents would be told she'd crashed into a mountain. Or a loch.

But no, she couldn't entertain gloomy thoughts like that. Of course she'd come home to Bramble Heath. She *would*.

She rode past the Carrs' house, and felt a jab of guilt that because it was so early she couldn't stop to check in on them. But at least it would mean there was one morning when she wasn't holding back the truth from them about Freddy.

Perhaps it was for the best. She still wasn't sure about the shoulder injury that Wyngate had told her about. She'd have felt dreadful if she told Freddy's family he was still alive only to discover that his injuries were far worse, life-threatening even.

Sally winced, wishing she hadn't put that thought into her head. Freddy was alive, that much must be true. Wyngate wouldn't go that far. And that gave her hope.

The airbase never closed, and Sally was arriving just as pilots and ground crew who'd been on standby overnight were on their way home and the new shift were just arriving. She waved to them, because it was what she would've done ordinarily, and, until she started her training, she didn't want to be anything but her usual self. She only had a few precious moments left, and who knew what she would have to do today. They waved back, tired, but no doubt relieved that they hadn't been scrambled overnight.

Sally saw Wyngate's car parked up, and she wondered where he had his lodgings. But the man was full of mysteries, and that was just one of them.

He had told her to go up to the attic at the top of the house, via the back staircase, so she entered the house by the door that led to the kitchen. It no longer smelt of her mother's cooking, or her father's recipes that he made to remind him of France.

But that thought reminded Sally that she would be in

France very soon – and she wouldn't be able to tell her parents. And if it went wrong, if she made a mistake, or someone betrayed her, or any manner of things, she would never come back here again, to Heath Place or Bramble Heath.

She reached the back stairs and on trembling legs made her way upstairs. She could turn round now, she could go to the ATA office and wait to be allotted a flight.

But if I do that, the secret Spitfire will never come home. At least I have to try. Even if it's dangerous. I'm the only person who can do it.

Sally reached the attic, which ran the length and width of the house. She was all too aware of how quiet it was up here, how isolated. It was the perfect place for her training.

The dormer windows, thick with cobwebs, filtered the summer morning sunlight, but they were open to the soft, warm air. The attic was still full of furniture and crates, belongings of her family and the Carrs' that wouldn't fit into their new homes once the house had been requisitioned.

Wyngate was already there, standing by a window. He was waiting for her.

And he'd prepared. The memories stored in the attic had been pushed aside, clearing space for everything required to train Sally. Two chairs and a desk had been pulled out from under the dust sheets. A table with Thermoses and a couple of bottles stood to one side, and there were plates with tin covers no doubt concealing their lunch. A blackboard stood on an easel, and a couple of maps were pinned to one of the walls. There was a radio sitting on another table, with a thick book beside it, which rather worried Sally as she wasn't sure she'd be able to memorise all of *that*. There was a nondescript cardboard box on the desk, its lid partly open. Something metallic inside it caught the sunlight, and she nearly gasped.

Oh, heck, isn't that a gun?

But she had agreed to this, and, no matter how frightened

she was by the prospect of parachuting into occupied France, she *wanted* to go on the mission. She *had* to, because she was the only person who *could*.

'I'm here,' she announced in French. For the next few days during her training, French was all she would be speaking with Wyngate.

'Three days,' he told her. 'It's all we have.'

Three days? Only three days...

And with that, her training began.

TWENTY-FOUR

Sally's mind whirled as she took everything in. They started with the map of the local area that the secret Spitfire was in, around the village of St Aubert, which was famous for its orchards and cider.

Sally did her best to memorise the names of the villages and farms around St Aubert, and remember their position. As she recited the names, they became increasingly familiar, and she pictured them in her mind, thinking of them as if they were the towns and villages where her family lived. But she had to stop remembering the pre-war world. The France she knew had been swept away.

Then it was the radio. Wyngate was at pains to tell Sally that she shouldn't use the radio, but said that she needed to know the basics, just in case.

Just in case? What on earth could go wrong?

But Sally knew. If she couldn't get the secret Spitfire into the air, and she couldn't find someone better trained to get the message back, then she'd have to break the news on the radio. She did her best to listen to Wyngate's lesson, trying to ignore the shiver that ran through her at the thought.

Self-defence came next. Sally felt awkward to begin with. She'd never done anything like it before. She was supposed to run at Wyngate so he could show her how to deflect hostile moves, but she couldn't just raise her hand and try to hit him.

'I don't want to end up giving you a black eye,' she explained. 'I don't ordinarily go around hitting people, you see.'

Wyngate gave her a sideways glance as he asked, 'Is that a joke?' Was there just a hint of humour in his gaze? 'If you knock me out cold, First Officer, nobody will be more surprised than me.'

Sally backed away, giving herself a run-up. 'This feels very odd, you know. Right – here I come!'

She charged across the attic, fists raised, and swung her arm at Wyngate, aiming for his face.

She wasn't sure what happened next, but she found herself on her back on the mattress, blinking up at the ceiling of the attic. A moment later the man from the ministry was blinking down at her.

'That's why we all need training when we start out,' he said, offering his hand.

Sally took his hand and got to her feet. 'All right then, how on earth did you manage that?'

And as the training went on, she soon found out. She took tumble after tumble onto the mattress as she tried to learn each move; but eventually it was Wyngate who was falling rather than her.

Sally was feeling pleased with what she'd learned, and just a little bit braver than she had earlier. At least she wasn't being dropped behind enemy lines completely unprepared. But as she blocked Wyngate's fist for the twentieth time, she hoped like heck she'd never have to actually use any of the moves she was learning.

And after all that, it was more than time for a break. She

poured them both tea from the Thermos, and sat down in a chair.

'How am I doing?' she asked Wyngate.

He lit a cigarette as he considered the question. Eventually he said, 'You're doing all right, First Officer.' And from Wyngate, that felt like high praise indeed.

'Thank you,' Sally replied with a grin. She took a sip of her tea, before saying seriously, 'I'm glad, actually. I want to do the mission, and I want to do it well.'

'You shouldn't need any of this,' Wyngate explained. 'There's a Nazi presence in the region but nothing too close. They must know something special came down somewhere around there, because he led their planes a dance, but they've not been able to find it.' He picked up his mug of tea. 'We've got very good people on the ground.'

Sally nodded. That was reassuring, at least. Wyngate's *people on the ground* were keeping Freddy safe and somehow hiding the secret plane.

'I keep picturing the France I knew before the war,' she admitted, a little embarrassed. She sounded sentimental, she knew. 'It's silly, isn't it, because it's not how I knew it any more.'

'You'll recognise it,' he assured her. 'You won't be there long enough to see the sights.'

'Hopefully...' she replied, before finding her courage again and going on, 'I'll be there and back, quicker than you can blink.'

'A flying visit to Scotland,' Wyngate mused.

'Scotland...' Sally sighed at the reminder of her cover story. 'I do hope my parents won't be expecting me to bring them home a box of shortbread. I'll just have to tell them that I couldn't find any!'

Wyngate leaned one shoulder against the wall and took a drag on his cigarette.

'We'll need post-dated letters,' he explained. 'To send to

your family and any friends you'd usually write to. I imagine you'll want some for the Carr family too.'

'Oh!' Sally gasped. 'I hadn't thought of that. Yes, I suppose I ought to write some. Just very bland letters. *Nice to see a change of scenery. Keeping busy. Take care all*, that sort of thing. I suppose that's what the people who do this sort of thing always do? Even if they're not training in an attic?'

He took another sip of tea. 'Training in attics isn't how we generally do it. But we don't usually have a downed plane carrying experimental armaments in occupied territory either.'

'I suppose not.' Sally glanced around the attic, at the training equipment set up in front of a background of dust sheets. 'It's quicker this way. I understand that. And if I'm not going to be there for long... It'll be so odd going home tonight, after doing all this. Hardly a typical day's work for me. Or for most people.'

But for some people, like the man who was training her today, it was perfectly typical. In fact, there was something about Wyngate that suggested this was an easy day for him. Occupied France was probably familiar ground.

'I'll be parachuting in with you. We'll make contact with your liaison together and then I've got other work to do.' He drained the remains of his tea. 'Let's get on.'

Sally knew better than to ask Wyngate what his *other work* consisted of. She couldn't even guess. But she was glad she'd be parachuting in with him, and that he'd be taking her to her contact. She wasn't going to be alone.

Sally's training went on. More maps, more radio, more self-defence. She discovered what the clothes were for, as she searched through them for secret pockets. If she needed to, Sally could conceal things inside her clothes, so only the most thorough of searches would have a chance to find them. Of course, there was every chance she wouldn't need to hide anything, or be searched. But she was glad to know how.

She left Heath Place that evening tired, both physically and mentally. Her head was full of so many things. Having spoken in nothing but French all day, she found that she was thinking in French as well now. That, she realised, was a very subtle bit of training. She wouldn't be an English girl pretending to be French, she would be the French version of herself.

When she got home, her parents were listening to the radio in the kitchen. She nearly spoke in French, and felt the gears switch in her head as she forced herself to talk to her parents in English instead. As casually as she could, she told them that she was going to be working up in Scotland *for a bit, I don't know how long*. She tried to sound unconcerned. Her parents obviously knew they couldn't quiz her about it, but she could see something in their eyes, worry mixed with their pride. When she wished them goodnight and told them she loved them both, she meant it from the bottom of her heart.

The next day, Sally arrived for her training knowing that she could expect everything to be ramped up just a little – more intense mapwork, more signals on the radio, and her self-defence lesson now included tips on how to deal with an armed assailant. She felt no awkwardness now, gave Wyngate no warnings that she might give him a black eye. A new depth of seriousness possessed her. It was her penultimate day. She needed to get everything she could out of her training before it was too late.

Over lunch that day, Sally composed her letters. She frowned as she tried to say the same thing but in several different ways. At least, however, it meant her parents would receive *something* from her, even if Sally wasn't the person posting it.

Then it was back to the training; an afternoon of more maps, more radios, more ways to fend off an attack. It was hard work. Draining. But the more she learned now, the more chance she had of surviving.

When she got home, she hugged her parents extra tight before she went to bed. She really didn't have long now.

On the morning of her last day's training, Sally was so focused on what lay ahead of her that day that she barely remembered her bicycle ride to Heath Place. In the two days she'd spent with Wyngate, she'd absorbed his steely seriousness. Some of it, at least. Carefree Sally was temporarily on hiatus. When Wyngate told her that today she was learning how to use a gun, she didn't even flinch.

They got into Wyngate's sporty car – she didn't make a single quip about it – and he drove them over to the secret Spitfire's hangar. When they arrived at the hangar, Sally was astonished. All traces of the secret Spitfire were gone, as if it had never been there. It was back to being a barn stacked with straw bales, without blueprints or lockers, workbenches or oilcans. Without the team of engineers who had become Sally's friends.

But that had been another Sally. She was different now. She was on a mission. That Sally wouldn't have dreamed of learning how to use a firearm, but this Sally was as focused and attentive on that task as she had been on any other. And with every hour that passed, she was an hour closer to France.

As she learned how to load the gun, take aim, and shoot, Sally realised that she was ready. She was still afraid, but it was a different kind of fear now, muted, controlled somehow, because she was prepared. Or, at least, more prepared than she had been when she'd first walked up to the attic at Heath Place.

'Wyngate,' she asked, as she laid the gun down on a straw bale. 'Have you ever been scared?'

'No,' Wyngate replied, but he wasn't mocking her when he asked, 'Are you?'

She wasn't so sure that he was being honest. 'You must've been scared once or twice. Even just a little bit. But yes... Not as much as I was to begin with, since I've had all this training. But yes, I still am. That's not a bad thing, is it?'

He shook his head and said, 'I'd be worried for my plane if you'd said anything else.' And there was that ghost of humour again. 'Better scared than complacent. Some of the best people in my section are as scared now as they were the first time out. It keeps them on their toes.'

That made Sally feel better. 'It's good to hear that, you know. I'm clearly in good company. I could end up scared of being scared, if that makes sense, worried that I'm not supposed to be. Tomorrow. Tomorrow, I'll wake up and...'

Fate will take its course.

TWENTY-FIVE

When Sally got home from her last day of training, she headed upstairs to pack. Tomorrow, she would be going into France. It was inevitable now, and she was as prepared as she could be.

She could only take clothes with her that were French. If she was caught and someone realised she was wearing British clothes, the consequences would be dire. Her wardrobe contained some clothes she'd bought in France on trips there before the war, but she couldn't help taking the dress out of her wardrobe that she'd been wearing when Freddy had proposed.

For a moment, for just a second, Sally was in the sunshine again with Freddy.

But that warm image vanished, replaced with the risks that lay ahead.

She slipped the dress back into the wardrobe, and took out blouses, a simple dress, a skirt and trousers, all bought in France. Clothes she'd bought because she needed to wear practical clothes around the planes. Back in the days of Toussaint and Carr.

There was Freddy again, in her mind's eye, smiling as he climbed into his Tiger Moth. Sally was going to see him again.

She had almost given him up for lost, when all along he'd survived.

But that wasn't why she was being sent into France, was it? As she packed some toiletries – only French items would do, of course – she sternly reminded herself that she was going to collect the plane, and that the entire endeavour was fraught with risk. It wasn't a fun trip abroad to meet her fiancé.

For a moment her hands trembled on the clasps of her bag, but she soon stilled them. She'd been trained. She was as prepared as she could be for the task ahead of her. Whatever happened, she had done her best. And if she never came back again...

Sally hurried over to her dressing table and took a sheet of paper and a pen. She would write her parents a letter. Not one to be sent from Scotland as part of her cover story, but a letter for her parents to find if she never came back.

Without stopping to sit down, she wrote:

Dear Mummy and Papa,

I know you've always been proud of me. I want you to know that I was always determined to do my bit, whatever I would be called on to do. Some things are more dangerous than others, but I knew I had to serve, come what may.

Something has happened, and I won't be coming back. Please know that I've always loved you, and I always will. I did my bit – for our family, for everyone. Please be proud of me.

All my love,

Sally xxx

I hope they never have to read this, she thought as she folded the paper in two and slipped it into an envelope, before putting it into the drawer of her dressing table.

Now that she'd finished packing, Sally headed downstairs. She was surprised to hear several voices coming from the parlour. She walked through the open door to see her Attagirl friends Enid, Sylvia and Mabel, as well as Annie and Betty from the village. Her heart leapt at the sight of her friends.

'Evening,' she said, beaming, her joy at this unexpected gathering extinguishing her worries. For a little while, at least.

'We weren't going to let you go up to the Scottish wilderness without a send-off!' Sylvia announced. 'And we've still got your promotion to drink to!'

'First Officer Toussaint!' Mabel nodded enthusiastically as Emily passed around a tray of sherry glasses. 'We're all terribly impressed to know a first officer.'

'I've always wanted to go to Scotland,' Annie said, and Betty nodded in agreement. 'All those lochs and mountains. It's so different from Bramble Heath.'

In more ways than you can imagine.

'And we'll all be waiting for you when you get home,' Betty said kindly. 'You'll be back before you even know it.'

'A little drink to celebrate,' Emily said, and kissed her daughter's cheek.

'This is lovely,' Sally said as she took her glass. *Oh, heavens... this might be the last time we're all here together.* She didn't want to think of that, but it was the truth, lurking at the back of her mind. 'I'm so glad you could all come. I'll miss you all, and I'll miss Bramble Heath too.'

You have no idea how much I will.

'We know you'll be back before we have time to miss you, but—' Enid didn't have to finish her sentiment. There had been too many partings since the war began. She threw her arms round Sally and hugged her. 'Oh, please take care, Sally!'

'Sally's always been an adventurer,' her father said smilingly as he came into the room, proudly bearing one of his wife's cakes. It was amazing what Emily could do, even with rationing. 'Scotland's lucky to have her.'

Sally hugged Enid back. 'I'll take care. It's just the same as what we do down here, but with more mountains – which I will be *very* careful to avoid, don't you worry.'

It was easier said than done, of course. Who could've predicted that Amy Johnson, such a celebrated aviator, would lose her life on a routine ATA job, flying over the Thames? But it *had* happened. Working for the ATA came with dangers, but Sally's mission was even riskier still.

Seeing all her friends, part of Sally wanted to make everything stop. She could call it off, stay in Bramble Heath. She'd be fine.

But would she? If the Nazis found the downed Spitfire, then...

Before Sally could follow that thought any further, Annie told her, 'We all wish you the best of luck.' And she raised her sherry glass.

'Hear, hear!' Betty said, beaming, as the girls all raised a glass.

Sally tried her best to lose herself in the joy of the moment, the smiles of her friends and their well-wishes, but she was still haunted by what lay ahead. And what about Freddy? No one in this room, apart from her, knew that he was still alive, that his whereabouts weren't unknown, and that he was being brought home. And not even she knew the extent of his injuries. Perhaps, if her friends intuited Sally's fears, they would think it was down to that. The daily grinding despair of simply not knowing.

And her friends were trying so hard to buoy her up, just as they had since Freddy's plane had come down; she'd take their smiles and affection with her into France. All the training had prepared her for her short and hopefully simple mission, but the warmth of their friendship would provide something that all the training in the world never could.

Sally would miss them all, but she wouldn't be alone. Her friends would be there with her, in her heart.

Eventually the girls headed off, with lots of hugs and good luck for Sally. All of those hugs, she knew, could be the last.

Then there was a knock at the door, and she went to answer it, wondering if one of the girls had left something behind. But it was the Carrs.

Sally hid her surprise as best she could. She hadn't expected them to come. They had their own worries – for all they knew, they had lost their son for ever. And yet, they'd come to see Sally off. It meant more than she could say.

'It's so lovely to see you,' she said, hugging Peter first before she embraced his parents. A wave of guilt coursed through her. *I could take away your grief with only a few words. But I can't.*

Wilbur had trotted in with the family, and weaved around Sally's feet, demanding her attention. She saw him again as a puppy, sitting in his Harrods basket in Freddy's Tiger Moth, the one-time stray having got his very own happy ending. How the little dog must be missing Freddy. But he'd become Peter's shadow since the Spitfire came down.

'We couldn't let you go without seeing you off,' Elsie said. 'You've always been like a daughter to us.'

Sally crouched down and picked up Wilbur, fussing him. She couldn't imagine how difficult it was for them. They thought they had lost their son, and now Sally, who had become part of their family too, was leaving Bramble Heath.

'I'm so glad you have,' she told Elsie, her voice trembling. 'I'll miss you all terribly, you know.'

'And you'll only be gone a few days?' Elsie asked as she, Arthur and Peter went into the living room, where Sally's parents waited.

'Oh, yes, only a few days,' Sally promised. 'Not long at all. I'll be back before you know it.'

I hope.

Emily and François welcomed the Carrs with hugs, as well as sherry and cake.

'I'm so sorry I haven't been by to see you over the past couple of days,' Sally said, as the Carrs settled on the sofa. 'It's just the job – I've been so busy. I wouldn't want you to think that I was neglecting you.'

'You will come back, won't you?' Peter asked, looking at her with wide eyes. 'Please come back, Sal.'

Elsie and Arthur exchanged a look, then Arthur told his son, 'Don't you worry, Pete. Sal's only going to Scotland, then she's coming straight home.'

Sally smiled gently at Peter. The poor boy couldn't lose anyone else. 'Exactly. I'll be back here very soon. I'm not doing anything different from what I normally do. I'm just flying planes, that's all. I could do that in my sleep!'

Peter nodded keenly. 'And Freddy *will* come home too.' He looked from his mother to his father, as Sally tried to will away the pain in their gazes. 'Because he promised he always would. And he always keeps his promises.'

'Jamie's been like a brother to Pete since—' Elsie took a gulp of tea, unable to finish the sentence. 'He's turned into a good lad, that one. They go off to school together every morning.'

'A credit to his mother,' said Arthur. There was no need to say any more than that. Jamie's late father had been a brute, but his son had turned out to be everything he wasn't.

'That's good to hear,' Sally said. She really was pleased that Jamie had stepped up and taken Peter under his wing. After all, Jamie knew what the younger boy was going through. 'It's always good to have friends, isn't it?'

Peter smiled, then told her, 'And Freddy's pals from the base are always looking in. Aren't they, Mum?'

Elsie smiled sadly. 'Always, son.'

Sally was glad about that. People cared in Bramble Heath. She glanced at her parents, and an image came into her mind of her Attagirl friends coming to the cottage to see how they were, because Sally hadn't—

I'll come home. I have to.

'They're lovely boys at the airbase,' Sally told them, not that it would come as news to the Carrs. 'They're all very fond of Freddy. They all admire him—' She froze, realising that she was talking about Freddy in the present tense. But that wouldn't strike anyone as odd, surely?

Thankfully, Peter jumped in to tell them all, 'They'll have a real party when he gets home.'

And she saw the exchanged glances again. Elsie and Arthur were wondering whether Peter would ever accept that his brother was lost; perhaps they were wondering if they needed to tell him what Sally could see they'd come to believe. They were losing hope.

The most dangerous few days of Sally's life lay ahead of her. She knew she might not make it home, and, if that happened, she knew her parents would feel the pain and anguish that Elsie and Arthur were suffering.

Only she knew that Freddy was still alive. There was still hope, no matter how injured he was. She gave Freddy's parents a sympathetic smile. *If only I could tell you the truth.*

When it was time for the Carrs to go, Sally didn't wave from the front door, but walked with them up the garden path to the gate. The garden had blossomed into life, while the Carrs grieved for the son they thought they'd lost.

'You all take care,' Sally told them as she hugged them again. 'And Peter, I promise I'll go hunting for the Loch Ness Monster if I have time.'

'If you find him, tell him me and Wilbur said hello.' Peter

held up the little dog to Sally. In a gruff voice intended to be Wilbur's, he said, 'Have a brilliant time, Sal!'

'I will,' Sally replied, smiling at Peter's impression even though she was terrified of what lay ahead of her. 'Look after yourselves, won't you?' *Because I don't know if I'll be coming back.*

Elsie put her arms round Sally and hugged her tight.

'Freddy loved the bones of you,' she said, her voice thick with emotion. Arthur patted his wife's shoulder, hushing her softly. 'And we do too. So you'd better come home, Sally Toussaint.'

She thinks he's gone. Oh, Elsie...

Tears were rising in Sally's eyes as she hugged Elsie back. 'I'll do my best, don't you worry,' she promised. Because her best was all she could do.

TWENTY-SIX

Just pretend it's a normal day. That's all I have to do.

But it wasn't a normal day.

Sally kept telling herself the same thing, even as doubts buzzed around her like flies. Dressed in her ATA uniform once more, she kissed her parents goodbye, promising them she'd be back soon.

She had taken off her engagement ring and hidden it in a tin concealed beneath a loose floorboard in her bedroom. She didn't want anyone to know she'd gone away without it, but she couldn't take it with her. It pained her to have to do it; she hadn't given up on Freddy and they were still engaged. His photo still stood in a silver frame on her bedside table.

Sally left the house, slowly closing the front door to stretch out time. She headed down towards the gate, then she pushed it open and was in the street, walking away, leaving her life in Bramble Heath behind.

With each step, she was taking herself closer and closer to whatever lay ahead. Second by second, she was running out of chances to turn round and run for home. And yet, even though that thought kept visiting her, Sally wasn't paying it any heed. She wasn't backing out. She *couldn't*.

As she reached the gates of RAF Bramble Heath, she met the night shift heading home. 'Good luck in Scotland!' said Georgie, one of the ground crew, and Sally had to smile. Her cover story had spread fast.

She went up to the front of the house. She was instantly reminded of Ginge's farewell. He'd given his life in service, and if she did too—

She pushed the thought away.

Wyngate, dressed in an RAF uniform, was waiting for her in a Tilly – an RAF utility vehicle. It was like a van, with khaki tarpaulin over the back. A far cry from Wyngate's sporty car, but he could hardly drive around in that and look inconspicuous.

'Morning,' Sally greeted him as she opened the passenger door. She climbed in, putting her bag in the footwell. 'No suit today, I see.'

'Still beautifully cut though,' Wyngate deadpanned, glancing down at the RAF uniform he was wearing. She wondered if he was really Air Force or whether this was just one more cover story. He probably wasn't even called Wyngate.

'One of the night shift wished me luck in Scotland,' she told him. She thought he'd be pleased to know, even if he didn't show it. 'The cover story has done the rounds. I've promised Freddy's brother I'll hunt the Loch Ness Monster, but I don't think it has a cousin in Normandy.'

He glanced towards her, then started the rattling engine. As the sun rose over Bramble Heath, they drove away from Heath Place, the house that had been Sally's home for so long. But she'd see it again, she reminded herself, and Freddy would be with her when she did.

I hope so.

As he drove them through the lanes, she told him – all in

French – about the send-off she'd received last night, and as she did she wondered if anyone had put together a gathering for *him*. He struck Sally as a lonely sort of person.

They were heading for the coast, Sally realised, and her stomach tied itself in knots. The Channel was all that stood between the Sussex coast and Normandy. A strip of water between England and occupied France.

It's good to be scared, she reminded herself, thinking back to Wyngate's words from the last day of her training.

'Did you manage to sleep?' Wyngate asked eventually, English forgotten now it was just the two of them.

'Eventually,' Sally admitted. 'I just kept reminding myself of how lovely it was to see everyone, and that stopped me thinking about what I'm about to do. Did *you* sleep?'

She suspected he was one of those people who was either out like a light, or napped for half an hour, and nothing in between.

'In between cigarettes,' Wyngate replied. 'There'll be downtime to rest this afternoon.'

'That'll be good.' Sally nodded. 'I can't imagine I'll be sleeping much over the next few days.'

Eventually, they arrived at RAF Shoreham. Sally had delivered planes here occasionally, and she'd flown there with Freddy before the war, so it was familiar to her. It had an amazing art deco terminal building, but now that it was all RAF, with hangars and extra buildings everywhere, the glamour of the place had vanished.

Wyngate parked up outside a single-storey office building. They climbed out of the Tilly, and Sally took a deep breath of the sea air.

She glanced at the window of one of the offices, and saw a WAAF officer typing at a desk. There were filing cabinets and a typewriter, a map on the wall, and a man in RAF uniform talking on one of the two telephones on his desk. It all looked so normal, so busy.

To Sally's surprise, Wyngate took her bag from the Tilly. It seemed at odds with his very business-like attitude, but she reminded herself that she really knew very little about him. It was Wyngate who seemed to see all, who knew goodness knows what about Sally's life, but he was a mystery to her.

Another WAAF came striding out with bundles of buff-coloured folders in her arms. She looked over at Wyngate and Sally. 'The ATA office is that way,' she told them, with a nod towards the other end of the airbase.

Wyngate said nothing, but instead fixed the WAAF with a cool gaze. After a second had passed he said, 'Coffee for two. Briefing room B.' Then he told Sally, 'Keep up!' and strode into the building.

Sally followed him, the WAAF's words, 'But I—' vanishing as the door swung shut.

Telephones rang, typewriters clicked, and everywhere were people in RAF blue. They all had a job to do, and Sally was buffeted from side to side by staff hurrying here and there as she did her best to keep up with Wyngate. The bustle parted as he cut through it, striding along with Sally's bag as though he owned the place. Nobody so much as questioned their presence as they made their way along a corridor to the room he had indicated to the WAAF. Only then did he open the door to the meeting room and stand back, allowing her to go in first.

Sally stepped inside. The room was functional and dim, with a view through a narrow window to some parked-up Tillys. She took a seat at the table and looked across at a map pinned on the wall showing the south coast of England.

Wyngate quizzed her on her cover story again. She knew it all by heart. Then he explained what would happen once she'd met her contact in the Resistance. They'd take her to the village of St Aubert, which would be her home during her hopefully brief stay in France, and they'd also take her to the plane. The secret Spitfire. Sally felt as if she was going to visit an old friend.

And somewhere in St Aubert, Freddy was waiting to make his escape back to England.

The coffee arrived, of course, not that Wyngate seemed to notice. He was too busy running short, sharp questions in French, asking her the most minute details of her cover story.

But Sally knew she'd scored full marks on that particular test.

'Don't forget, the target is the plane. Not the pilot,' Wyngate reminded her as he sipped black coffee. 'But we have some naval extractions scheduled. I'll let you know where and when.' He lit a cigarette. 'If Flight Lieutenant Carr can get to the pick-up, they'll bring him home.'

'They *have* to bring him home,' Sally replied, her voice thick with emotion. 'His parents have given up, Wyngate. They think he's gone. But not Peter – Freddy's little brother. He still believes Freddy's alive, somewhere. I haven't said a thing to them, but... it's so hard keeping it from them.'

Wyngate's expression betrayed nothing, but he said, 'It's vital that you understand, First Officer, that the work we do is dangerous. If something goes wrong, nobody will be coming for you.'

Sally went cold. Her fear encased her. She was going to be alone out there. At least the Resistance might help her, but she was going into occupied territory. The dangers were enormous, and the chances of her getting out alive if their plan failed were tiny.

'Wouldn't I be able to get on one of these naval extractions?' she asked him; but he'd already told her, hadn't he?

'That's not what I mean by things going wrong,' he told her. 'The rest of the day's your own. If you need to rest, the base staff have a bunk for you; otherwise, treat this as home base for the day. We'll meet in the mess for supper at eighteen hundred hours.'

Sally spent the day mentally preparing. She had a French-language paperback of Colette's *Claudine in Paris*, so she read that, absorbing the story. Josette would be halfway through it when she arrived in St Aubert, and Sally wanted to make sure she had read the book too. The fact that it was in French helped her, as she felt herself more and more inside Josette's skin.

Every so often, Sally took breaks, just wandering outside near the offices and watching the planes. She knew that RAF Shoreham was a target just as much as RAF Bramble Heath was, and it was another reminder of just why she was laying her life on the line. So many others had, after all.

Six o'clock came, and Sally found her way to the mess for supper. As she took her place in the queue, she realised this would be her last meal in England.

'Special privilege.' Wyngate whispered the words in French against her ear before she even realised he was there. 'We don't wait in queues.'

And with a nod to summon her, he walked straight to the front of the line.

Sally could feel the eyes of the other staff boring into her, but she didn't care. There were far worse things for her to worry about than that. She was passed a plate of stew, then she sat down with Wyngate to eat. Nobody joined their table. Wyngate seemed to give off an aura that said, *leave us alone.*

Sally barely tasted her food. She was trying not to think of the enormity of what faced her, or the dangers. Instead, she tried to think of the small things, the steps she had to take.

Be Josette, meet the contact, go to St Aubert, see the plane, fly it home.

Put like that, her task was simple, as if she wasn't visiting a France that was crawling with Nazis.

Wyngate wasn't the sort of dinner companion who made small talk and, right now, Sally wasn't sorry. Only when the meal was finished did he turn and call to the woman behind the counter, 'Two glasses!' And, despite his extraordinary rudeness, she obeyed.

'Consider yourself privileged.' As Wyngate told Sally that, he reached into his tunic and took out a small silver hip flask. Sally watched as he unscrewed the cap and poured a generous measure of amber liquid into each glass. 'Let's drink to a successful mission, First Officer. I've no doubt you'll see home again.'

'I hope I will,' Sally told him as she picked up her glass. She took a sip and was moved to say, 'I don't know how often you hear this, Wyngate, but I hope you do too. Y-You're like the big brother I never had.'

He looked down at his glass, then back up at her.

'I don't hear it often at all, First Officer,' he admitted, clinking his glass against hers. 'Thank you.'

Sally smiled at him. 'I should let you know, though, that if – when – I get back, I won't be signing up for any more of this sort of work. I'd just be quite happy to go back to delivering planes, really.'

This time, there was a definite smile. 'Understood.' Wyngate drained his glass. 'It's time.'

TWENTY-SEVEN

Once Sally had changed into her flight suit, she handed her ATA uniform in for safe keeping.

Hope I see it again...

She was wearing a simple dress under the flight suit, so that as soon as they arrived in France she could transform into an ordinary French civilian, rather than a British woman on an extraordinary mission.

Sally had minutes before it would be too late to change her mind and go back. Once the plane's doors slammed shut behind her, that would be it. But she had already made up her mind. What lay ahead was dangerous and difficult, but she would go ahead regardless.

She went into the briefing room, where Wyngate was waiting for her with their parachutes. The sight of them made her chest tighten.

We're going to jump out of a plane over occupied territory. Are we mad?

She took a deep breath, calming her fears. 'I'm ready,' she told him, determinedly.

'Parachute checked and ready. I've just been on the radio

with Henri,' Wyngate told her. 'He's our host tonight; he's kindly provided the drop zone.' He dropped his cigarette into an empty coffee mug. 'Nice soft field, Mademoiselle Auclair.'

It was all very real now, Sally realised as she strapped on the parachute. She and Wyngate – *Guy*, once they landed on French soil – would spend tonight in Henri's home, then, when the sun rose tomorrow, she was on her own.

Sally's heart was hammering in her chest. She followed Wyngate from the room, the parachute heavy on her back and the rucksack of clothing dragging on her front. She was uncomfortable and the summer evening was sticky with heat. But comfort was the least of her worries.

As they reached the door of the building Wyngate glanced back at her, his unreadable expression granite as ever. Then he said, 'If you do change your mind when you get back, I might find a place in my section for you.'

When. Not if.

Then he pulled open the door and they walked out into the night.

The engine of a Whitley bomber throbbed, the noise so loud that Sally couldn't have replied to Wyngate even if she'd known what to say. But she clung to that word, *when*. He had faith in her, and that meant more than she could express.

She could see the pilot of the plane silhouetted through the canopy, and it reminded her that she and Wyngate weren't the only people taking risks tonight. The crew, taking the plane over the sea and into enemy airspace, were incredibly brave. They wouldn't have a clue what mission their temporary passengers were on, only that it had to be done.

And if they can do it, so can I.

As Sally climbed the ladder into the plane, she remembered the times she'd delivered Whitleys herself. It wasn't as agile a plane as a Spitfire but it was solid, dependable. Just the sort of plane Sally wanted to be in right now. But when she'd been flying Whitleys, no one had ever parachuted from them.

Oh, heck, I really do hope these chaps get back home in one piece.

She clipped the static line of her parachute to the rail, which would open her parachute automatically when she jumped. The metallic *click* was as final as the door of the plane closing. Then she sat down, leaning back against the fuselage. Her teeth chattered from the vibrations of the plane trembling through her.

Wyngate headed for the cockpit to exchange a few unheard words with the crew. Then he joined Sally in the fuselage. With his own static line clipped into place, he sat down opposite her.

'You never baled out in your flight career.' It wasn't a question, but a statement. He likely knew just about everything there was to know about her. 'Hopefully you never will again.'

'Fingers crossed!' Sally replied. She needed a lot more than crossed fingers, but she knew that, in his own way, Wyngate was paying her a compliment.

Being inside the plane felt so unreal. And few people knew she was here. As far as her family and friends knew, Sally had arrived in Scotland, and was about to curl up in bed.

Instead she was wearing a parachute and, sooner than she cared to think, she would be jumping out of a plane. And if that wasn't something to make any sensible person quail with fear, then there was the countryside below them, full of shadows.

And it *did* frighten her; but she had lived with that fear since Wyngate had announced that she was hired. And she hadn't run from it. Instead, she was running headlong into it.

The engines changed in pitch as the great props whirred and the bomber began to move, slowly at first as it prepared to make its take-off. From her own experience up in the cockpit, in her mind's eye Sally could picture the crew's every move. She concentrated on that rather than what lay ahead, mentally tracking each process as the Whitley gathered speed along the runway.

Opposite her Wyngate sat unmoving, his eyes closed. He might almost be asleep, but somehow she had the sense that he was as alert as ever.

Then the plane was in the air, and the undercarriage clanked as it was raised. The sound brought back the terrifying moment when the secret Spitfire's undercarriage mechanism had jammed. Sally closed her eyes, trying to squeeze the memory out of her mind. But as she did, she reminded herself that she had got through that, a frightening experience even for experienced pilots – she'd survived.

I can do this. I can.

The fuselage of the Whitley had no windows for passengers. Sally had no idea where they were, although, as the plane banked as it climbed, she pictured the route out across the Channel. The dark waves would be lapping against the beaches, along sand tangled with barbed wire.

There were mines in the sea now, and submarines lurking in the depths. She thought of the sparkling blue water she'd flown over on her jaunts to France before the war, but it wasn't like that now. And on the other side of the sea, there was a whole continent that a madman's army had rampaged through in the name of his twisted ideology.

And Sally and Wyngate were heading straight for it.

'All right?' her companion asked eventually, though his eyes were still closed.

'More or less,' Sally replied. 'I was just thinking... I used to fly this way. And it was always sunny then.'

'The next time you do an airshow in Paris, I'll come and see you.' And he gave the slightest hint of a smile. 'Try and rest while you can.'

I hope there will be a next time.

Sally closed her eyes and thought of the sapphire sea, and

how beautiful the world once was. She must've fallen asleep, because the next thing she knew she was waking up.

'Sorry, nodded off,' she said, toying with her goggles.

There was another man in the fuselage with them, a member of the crew. He greeted her with a cheery smile as Wyngate said, 'We'll be over the drop zone soon. Time to go.'

Sally's hands shook as she put on her goggles, but once they were on she was ready. Her nerves fell away. She needed to focus, not be distracted by worries. She knew what she had to do.

'I'm ready,' she told Wyngate.

Wyngate was right; she never *had* baled out of a plane before, and certainly not out of the tail, but that was how she would exit the Whitley. Together they made their way to the rear of the cramped fuselage. It was impossible to stand upright but, the way the crewman and Wyngate moved, Sally could tell they were old hands. She would be the first to jump when the moment came, and, as she waited at the closed door, she counted the seconds.

'The very best of British to you both,' said the crewman. 'Give 'em hell.' Then he opened the door onto the pitch-black sky.

The cold air rushed into Sally's face and it took her breath away. But only for a moment. She didn't stop to think, because if she did she might not do it.

She jumped, plunging into the night, the wind whipping past her face and roaring in her ears.

TWENTY-EIGHT

Sally felt like a stone dropping into a well, until her parachute billowed open above her seconds later and slowed her fall.

France lay below, sleeping uneasily, the fields and villages shadowy patches of dark grey in the scanty moonlight. Sally's eyes welled with tears. She'd been in England, safe from the occupation, and as the vast countryside spread beneath her she was racked with guilt. She'd abandoned the country of her birth.

I'll make it up to you, I promise I will.

Wyngate was somewhere above her, behind her. She knew he had a connection with the country. He wouldn't be able to speak French like he did otherwise. She wondered what was going through his mind in the minutes that passed as they drifted down.

The enemy, it seemed, were quiet tonight. There'd been no gunfire rattling at the plane, and there was none now. Just the wind rushing by as Sally drifted to earth. It was oddly peaceful.

Until she realised how close she was to the ground. She took the impact of the soft earth with her feet, folding herself up and rolling to the side. For a moment, she lay still. Nothing hurt. She'd landed safely.

Then she sat up, looking for Wyngate.

He emerged from the night sky a few feet away, landing smoothly just as Sally had. She was still sitting on the ground as he stood and began unbuckling the parachute.

'Welcome home,' he said.

'Thank you, Guy,' she replied in French; they had both now switched from English. She got up and started to unbuckle her parachute as well. 'Welcome home, too.'

She bundled up her parachute, glancing right and left. The field was bounded by trees on three sides, while a hedge ran along the fourth. Somewhere, Henri was watching for them, waiting.

And I sincerely hope he's the only person who is.

As Sally scanned the edges of the fields, she saw a figure moving by the trees. 'Guy... is that our man?' she whispered, her lips not moving.

'No moon tonight,' Wyngate called. It must be a code, intended to identify both the agent and his contact.

'And clouds over Rouen,' a man's voice called in reply.

Sally's stomach somersaulted. She looked at Wyngate.

Please let it be Henri.

'Henri!' Wyngate greeted the figure, then looked to Sally as he started to shed his flight suit. 'This is our man. You need to get down to civvies.'

'Y-yes,' Sally replied.

What the heck am I doing? But she didn't waste time on that thought. She took off the flight suit, and, once she was down to her dress, realised it was a warm night even without the suit on. She swung the bag of French clothes over her shoulder, ready to go.

She glanced at Wyngate, and was astonished when she saw how he was now dressed – as a farm labourer. Even his bearing had changed, the elegance of England replaced by something that suggested a man who had been raised on the land. It was remarkable.

Henri had crossed the field now, and was bundling up the parachutes and flight suits. 'The others will collect them from the woods. Guy, Josette, good to meet you.'

He was a wiry man, his dark hair streaked with grey, his face weathered by the outdoors.

'Henri's a good man,' Wyngate said to her as he and Henri shook hands. 'Anything you need, speak to him.' He turned back to Henri and asked, 'How's the sheep?'

'Recovering well,' Henri replied, beaming. Sally was surprised that the first person they saw in this occupied land was smiling, but then maybe she would've done as well in his shoes. He was fighting back. 'He's happy and wants to go home.'

With a gasp, Sally realised that Henri was talking about Freddy. *The sheep.*

He's not far away. I'll see him again. Oh, thank heavens!

Was he really recovering well? Sally crossed her fingers. She hoped so. She really did.

'Josette's the shepherdess,' Wyngate told Henri as they walked across the field. 'She's going to drive the tractor.'

'I can't dri—' Sally stopped herself. Of course, he didn't literally mean a tractor. *He means the plane.* 'Oh, yes, that's right. I'm driving the tractor.'

Henri nodded, looking impressed. 'I've got some food ready for you, and somewhere to sleep. It isn't much, but it's safe. It's not far.'

They reached the woods, and Henri stopped to conceal the parachutes and flight gear behind a tangle of brambles that grew beside a row of broad trees. Then they carried on, Sally wincing at every step in case she snapped a twig underfoot. The woods appeared to be empty, but she couldn't shake the sensation that she was being watched. It might be paranoia, but at least it was useful; she was on her guard.

They came out of the woods into a small field, and on the other side of it Sally saw a small stone farmhouse, shutters over its windows as if it was keeping its secrets to itself. There were barns and stables surrounding a yard and, as they approached, the chickens woke up and clucked.

Henri murmured to them, and the birds settled again. Then he opened the door and ushered Sally and Wyngate inside. 'I cannot offer you a coffee, you know,' he said with an apologetic shrug. He gestured to the wooden chairs round the kitchen table.

The space was chaotic, with pots and pans here and there, laundry hanging from a frame, and tractor parts on the table. It was if Henri never put anything away. The calendar on the wall was still showing February, and balled-up newspaper filled a crack in the window.

Sally took a seat. Her eyes roamed the room, a French farmhouse kitchen. When had she last been inside a French home?

Henri dished up some soup from a pot on the stove and handed the bowls to Sally and Wyngate, then gave them cups of water. There was no bread, despite Sally never having seen a French table without it before. But of course there wasn't. France under the Nazis was not the place she remembered.

'Now, I should tell you who you can trust in St Aubert,' Henri told them as he sat down at the table. 'Colette Auclair is your grandmother's sister, Josette. She lives in a cottage at number 22 rue de l'Eglise. That's where you'll be going tomorrow, and she's expecting you. She's in the Resistance too. There is Leah Chastain. She's friends with Colette, but she's much younger. She has a son, Armand. You know what boys are like, they run here and there, they are often our eyes and ears.'

Sally thought at once of Freddy's brother Peter. She knew

he would've been just the same if, God forbid, the UK had been invaded.

'Leah's husband is a prisoner of war.' Henri sighed. 'He was in the French army, you see. But... it could be worse for him.'

Sally knew what he was driving at. Leah's husband could've been killed. At least there was a chance he could come home once all of this was over.

Wyngate nodded as he ate. 'I'll be gone by dawn,' he told Henri. 'We need Josette on a bus from far enough out of the village that nobody will notice her getting on, to arrive mid-morning. You know the drill.'

Henri nodded, and Sally wondered how many people had landed in that field under cover of darkness. Wyngate and Henri knew each other, that was clear – they had met before. Just how many times had Wyngate made that jump?

'It's all taken care of,' Henri replied, then told Sally more names, which she committed to her memory, all people who were in the Resistance and could help. There was Veronique Maillard who worked at the grocer's, and Gérard Bertin at the mayor's office. Anna Duhamel, the parish priest's housekeeper, could be relied on, as could Dr Vautier, the local medical man. Pierre Laurent, a farmer, could help too. And that was before Henri listed the names of the older children at the village school – Eugène and Lili Gosselin, Jean Lefevre. It was an extraordinary list, people from different walks of life who were all, in their own ways, undermining the enemy that had taken control of their home.

It was humbling to hear all those names, because Sally could only imagine the dangers these people were putting themselves in. Flying a plane was one thing, but what they did... her admiration was beyond words. She imagined – God forbid – the Nazis invading England, and who in Bramble Heath would join the Resistance.

Every one of us, she decided.

'I want you to take good care of her.' Wyngate slapped Sally's shoulder as he addressed Henri. 'She's the only shot we've got. That shoulder will take too long to heal.'

'I understand.' Henri raised his glass of water to Sally with a smile. 'The sheep might've mentioned something about a girl who could drive tractors. I'm very pleased to meet you. And don't you worry, I will take good care of you, and you'll be home in no time!'

Hearing Freddy's codename again, Sally smiled. *He's told them about me. He's thinking of me.*

'I can't wait to see the sheep,' she said. 'If I can. I realise it might not be possible.' There were risks, and, if it meant Freddy's safety was compromised, then Sally wouldn't see him. But she was *near* him now, and that gave her comfort in the face of danger.

'We'll see,' Henri told her.

Wyngate pushed his empty bowl away and sat back in his chair. He stifled a yawn, then told them, 'I'll be in touch when I've got news on the trawler.'

The trawler. That must be Freddy's boat out.

'Good,' Henri replied. 'Now, I'll show you your beds. This isn't a luxury hotel, but...' He shrugged as he got up from the table.

He led them along a corridor. The rooms felt unused and chilly despite the warmth of the evening. He opened one door and gestured for Sally to enter. The metal bedstead with a crucifix hanging above it reminded her of the bedroom she'd stayed in at Mémé's house. For a moment, she forgot about the war, and instead was back in the happy days of her childhood. The blanket on the bed was old and patched, and there was only one rather thin pillow, but she didn't mind.

'And Guy, you're just over here,' Henri told Wyngate, opening the door opposite Sally's. She was glad that Wyngate wouldn't be far away, even though he wasn't staying for long.

Henri then pointed to a room further along the corridor and said, 'I'm just there if you need anything. Goodnight – and good luck.'

Once Henri had left them, Wyngate put down Sally's bag. He looked around the room then said, 'The first chance you get to fly, take it.' He held out his hand to her. 'No risks, no heroics.'

'Got you. Don't linger. Get out as soon as I can.' Sally took his hand and shook. 'I know you're heading off soon and I won't see you again before you go. But do take care, big brother Guy.'

'I always do,' he assured her. 'Goodnight, little sister. And take care.'

TWENTY-NINE

I'm not in Bramble Heath any more.

That was her first thought as she was woken the next day by a cockerel crowing so loudly he appeared to be directly under her window. And this wasn't her bedroom in the cottage at Bramble Heath; there was no photo of Freddy beside the bed, no quilt handstitched by Mémé. Sally rolled over and sighed before consciousness fully took hold.

An oppressive weight pushed down on her as she got ready to leave for St Aubert. The farmhouse was like any other, as was the countryside she could see from the window, but the knowledge that the country was occupied was inescapable.

And what she was about to do terrified her.

Henri prepared some breakfast for her, giving her a freshly laid egg. She sipped the chicory he poured for her that stood in for coffee. How Wyngate would survive on that, she didn't know. It certainly wasn't steadying Sally's nerves, and only added to the strangeness of her situation, even though she was in a country she knew. Or once had, at least.

After breakfast, she picked up her bag, and she and Henri left the farmhouse, heading for his van.

'There's a town a few kilometres away,' he explained. 'You can get the bus there, and it will take you to St Aubert. It's market day in the village on the other side of St Aubert today, so the bus stop will be crowded. There's not much for sale, but...'

Henri's van creaked and rattled as he piloted them through the lanes, past orchards, green fields and dark woods. Sally wasn't sure what to expect. There were signs here and there of what had happened to this country – a burnt-out car by the side of the road, the skeleton of a cottage with blank, empty windows – but the Nazis themselves didn't seem to be around. Sally kept alert, though; even if you couldn't see them, it didn't mean they weren't there.

They arrived at the town, with its stone and timber-framed houses, and Henri drove to a quiet road near a large square. They climbed out, and he led Sally up an alleyway that smelt of boiled cabbage and soap and opened into the square. It must've looked grand once, she was sure, but there was an air of tiredness about it now. A fountain stood in its centre. Not even a trickle of water flowed from it.

Women with baskets and string shopping bags were already waiting at the bus stop, and Henri led Sally towards them. Sally did her best to appear, and to feel, as nonchalant as she did waiting for the bus in Bramble Heath with the women off to do their shopping in East Grinstead. The women were busy chatting and, although some of them glanced Henri's way, they didn't seem particularly interested in Sally.

She was relieved. She'd passed her first test, at least. She'd blended in; she was just one more woman standing at a bus stop in France.

Henri waited with her, but he didn't speak much, only to mention that he'd be going to the market later himself to sell some eggs. Sally nodded, but at the same time she was listening to the conversations of the women around her. Would any of them say something that would prove useful to know?

But there was nothing, just conversations about how bored they were of eating root vegetables all the time, and how they wished they could have real coffee.

They couldn't say much else, Sally suspected, in case they were overheard. She didn't glance around, even though she was tempted to. It would make her look uneasy and nervous, which was tantamount to wearing a target.

The bus finally arrived. It was just like the ones Sally had seen in France before the war, a Citroën bus with the distinctive chevron on its radiator. But it had seen better days. Some of its windows were cracked and the tyres were patched. It sighed as it came to a halt for the passengers to get on.

Sally turned to Henri. 'Good luck at the market,' she told him. She wished she could say so much more. She was in awe of his bravery.

Henri merely nodded, and, once Sally had got on the bus, he leaned against the wall of a nearby building, looking at his watch.

Sally found a seat about halfway down the bus. She'd be too obvious at the front, and look too secretive at the back. When the bus started off she saw Henri give an almost imperceptible nod; then he was off, heading back to his farm and goodness knows what else.

The bus conductress moved from seat to seat, looking bored, so bored, in fact, that she didn't really look at Sally. Sally paid for her ticket, and was relieved when the conductress moved on. Each of these encounters was a hurdle to cross. She was doing well so far, she knew, but she couldn't risk getting complacent.

The bus jogged and coughed its way out of the town, and along a road that cut through a field of wheat, but Sally knew what would happen to it – the Nazis would take it as soon as it was harvested. No one around here was destined to eat it.

Sally recalled the maps that Wyngate had shown her in her

training, and was fairly sure she knew where she was: just a few kilometres away from St Aubert.

Not long now, she thought.

The bus slowly passed a pair of grand gates, and she could just about see an elegant brick-and-stone chateau at the other end of a long, tree-lined avenue. But she suspected the family who usually lived there had been forced to give it up – and not as willingly as Sally's own family had given up Heath Place.

And then, for no apparent reason, the bus wheezed to a halt. It was evidently unexpected, as the women all around Sally started to moan and complain.

'I just want to go to the market, and I can't even do that!' one of them moaned.

'Run out of petrol again, it always happens!' another chimed in.

Sally hoped that petrol was the only problem, but goose bumps rose on her arms. There was something wrong, she was sure, as the driver was making no attempt to do anything, and neither was the conductress.

Sally leaned into the aisle, like everyone else, craning their necks to see through the windscreen what was ahead. A groan of annoyance went through the women just as she saw what was holding them up.

Directly ahead of them was a beautiful, shiny Mercedes-Benz car, its roof down. But Sally had no time to admire it, because she saw two men inside it, dressed in the black uniforms of the SS. She realised now why the bus had stopped. There was plenty of room for the car to pass, but it was as if the bus had tried to shuffle aside, like a child in a playground on the arrival of the bullies.

As the car passed, the man in the back seat turned his head to gaze impassively at the faces that watched him behind its windows. His expression was unreadable, his appearance no more remarkable than that of a provincial civil servant. Yet here he was in this vast, gleaming vehicle, commanding the road in a country that didn't want his kind.

Sally made sure she followed the gaze of everyone on the bus, rather than single herself out by looking away. A shiver ran through her. The uniform the man wore was designed to intimidate and instil fear, from the thunderbolts on his collar to the Iron Cross on his chest, and the swastika on his red armband. She was close enough to see the silver design on his cap badge.

A skull and crossbones.

A uniform celebrating death and hate.

A chill ran through Sally. *And he's just been to St Aubert.*

The bus started up again. The mood on the bus had changed. The women were no longer complaining but were fretting in whispers instead, and she couldn't quite catch what they were saying. But it wasn't good news, she knew that straight away. And suddenly, Sally felt very, very alone.

She just wanted to get to St Aubert and find her next contact, but the bus stopped not much further on and the doors opened to admit another passenger.

A little boy, perhaps a couple of years younger than Peter, bounded up onto the vehicle and announced to the passengers, 'The bloody SS just rolled up! Anybody on this bus who didn't ought to be, don't hang around these parts!'

Sally didn't glance away but kept looking straight ahead at the little boy. A very brave little boy, by all appearances.

'Don't you go saying things like that, Armand,' the conductress warned him gently. 'They'll come after you!'

Armand.

Henri had mentioned him. The little boy whose mother was in the Resistance, while his father lingered in a prisoner of war camp somewhere. The little boy who was the Resistance's eyes and ears.

Armand drew his finger across his lips as though to say,

zipped. Then he asked the conductress, 'Give us a ride home, Margot?'

'All right, then, seeing as you're not going far,' Margot replied, and affectionately ruffled his hair. He hopped up onto a seat and settled there, watchful as he gazed from the window at the passing countryside.

'Armand,' whispered an elderly man on the seat behind the little boy. 'Who is here?'

Armand scrambled to turn in his seat. He told the man, 'Von Brandt. Obergruppenführer, so he's one of the big chiefs. Proper nasty so-and-so, strutting about in his dress uniform.' He shrugged and added, 'Looking for some plane or other. Chasing bloody shadows, eh?'

Sally nearly gasped in surprise and pretended to cough instead.

Obergruppenführer? The SS? Oh, no, this is serious. What on earth am I going to do...? Think calmly, that's what I'm going to do. They're looking for the plane. That means they haven't found it. I just have to hope they never will.

THIRTY

Sally's thoughts churned around her mind as she battled with herself to stay calm. She didn't take in very much of the rest of her journey; she was wondering what on earth she was going to do.

But her cover story was solid and she knew it inside out. All she had to do was be Josette. It was that simple. Josette knew nothing about the plane, and would have no reason to be scared of the SS – apart from the usual reasons that French civilians were wary of the occupying force.

Eventually the country road gave way to a line of timber-framed cottages with thatched roofs, and apple trees leaning over garden walls. Despite the war, there were still geraniums in some of the window boxes, which made Sally smile. For a moment, she could've been in Bramble Heath, and she was suddenly homesick. If only she really was in Bramble Heath, in the relative safety of her home. But she'd taken this mission on, and she had to see it through. Only then would she see her home again.

The bus continued up the road a little further, and Sally saw narrow streets leading away between the cottages.

'St Aubert!' the driver called, as the bus arrived in what appeared to be the village square.

The white stone church dominated one side of the square, while shops, a bar with the red sign of a tabac, and a café lined the others. A noticeboard stood prominently near the church, displaying a portrait of Pétain, the Vichy collaborator and head of the French state. It was a wonder no one had pelted the portrait with mud, but Sally suspected that no one dared.

On either side of Pétain were posters urging farmers to sow wheat, and young men to work in Germany. It was an ugly reminder for Sally of what the people of St Aubert, and all of France, were living through. And she fretted all over again about her cousins, wondering if they were still in France or if they'd been sent to Germany.

As soon as the bus stopped, Armand was at the door and springing down into the street.

Sally picked up her bag and got to her feet. She felt the other passengers' eyes on her, no doubt wondering why she was stopping here and not going on to the market. Even worse, perhaps they were wondering who on earth she was, as none of them would ever have seen her before.

I'm Josette. I'm going to see my great-aunt.

She got off the bus and glanced around. Henri had told her that rue de l'Eglise, where Colette lived, was near the church, as the name suggested. But Sally realised that applied to everywhere in St Aubert because the church dominated every aspect of the square and the surrounding streets.

She didn't want to wander about, lost, especially not with the SS on the alert.

Armand had settled outside the bakery, one shoulder leaning against the wall as he watched her. He wasn't the only one looking either; the passers-by also cast a second glance at this newcomer in their village.

'Wrong stop?' Armand asked.

Sally knew that if she had seen a mystery person arrive in Bramble Heath, she'd have been curious too.

'Not exactly,' she replied. 'I'm looking for rue de l'Eglise. Mademoiselle Auclair's house. Do you know it?'

Sally suspected he would, seeing as Colette Auclair and Armand's mother were friends. And besides, St Aubert wasn't a huge town. Everyone knew each other in a village like this.

'Are you her niece?' Armand stood up a little straighter. 'She'll be glad to see you, she's had a right time of it.' Then he frowned and said, 'You didn't hear me say "bloody" on that bus, did you?'

Sally smiled at him. 'No, don't worry, I didn't hear a thing. And yes, I'm Mademoiselle Auclair's niece, Josette. I've come to look after her.'

The cover story rolled easily off Sally's tongue. She had turned into Josette.

'Good day to you, Mademoiselle Josette!' Armand dropped into a showy bow. 'I'm Armand; I've been fetching Mademoiselle Auclair whatever she needs while she's been laid up. So today, I'll fetch you along to her, eh? C'mon, follow me!'

'Thanks, Armand, you're very kind!' Sally said.

The SS might be hunting around St Aubert for the plane, but at least Sally had found a friend.

They crossed the square and went down a street that ran along the side of the church. The cottages, with their timber frames, were a contrast with the church's stone walls. It made Sally feel safer, somehow. Not that she was under any illusions that the SS would spare a French church. But it was the solidness of it that she found reassuring in a world that had become fragile and full of terrors.

'I've had quite a journey coming up from La Roche, you know,' she said chattily. 'I'll be relieved to sit down!'

'Didn't see any planes on the road then?' Armand laughed

as if at a favourite joke. 'You'll get plenty of sitting down in St Aubert. Not much happens round here.'

'Planes?' Sally shook her head, as if the very idea of it was ridiculous. Even though she'd jumped out of a plane only the night before. 'No, I haven't seen any planes on the road. What a funny place for a plane!'

The little boy shrugged, then unhooked a gate and stood back so Sally could go into the little cottage garden ahead of him. 'Let 'em waste their time, eh? Keeps them out of real mischief.'

Sally went into the garden. She was impressed; it was full of vegetables, just as her own front garden was at home. She felt another pang at the thought of the cottage she shared with her parents.

At least Colette wouldn't go hungry; but Sally wouldn't have been surprised if Colette shared what she grew with the village.

Armand closed the gate behind Sally and bowed from his place on the street. 'I'll leave you here, mademoiselle,' he said, beaming. 'Welcome to St Aubert. You'll find your way round in no time.'

'Thanks, Armand,' Sally said. 'You take care.' And she meant it.

She knocked on the door, waiting to see her great-aunt – a woman she'd never seen before in her life.

After a few seconds she heard shuffling footsteps approach the door, then a quavery voice asked, 'Who is it?'

'Auntie Colette?' Sally replied gently. She was concerned about Colette; she sounded very frail. Should she be involving herself with the work of the Resistance? 'It's your Josette!'

'Josette!' A bolt slid back, then a key turned and the door opened. 'My little Josette!'

For a moment, Sally took in the elderly lady who stood before her, her face lined with time and worry. Her heart ached.

Oh heavens, she could be Mémé!

Sally stepped forward and kissed Colette on both cheeks.

'Auntie! I've missed you,' she said, with all the emotion she felt for her grandmother. 'I've been so worried. But I'm here now to look after you.'

'I've been so unwell.' Colette ushered Sally into the cottage and closed the door with a weak hand. Then, before Sally's eyes, the stooped little old lady stood up straight and seemed to grow in stature and presence. She slid the bolt back into place and said in a firm voice, 'We've had a real bastard arrive in the village today. Welcome to St Aubert, Josette, let's get you settled.'

Sally was astonished by Colette's rapid transformation. Had she been an actress before the war?

'It's lovely to meet you,' she told Colette, trying to master her surprise. 'I'm so grateful to you. I know it's dangerous for you to do this, but... thank you.'

Colette patted Sally's arm and gave her a warm smile. 'Come and see your room, then there's someone who's very keen to welcome you to St Aubert.' With a wink she added, 'I just want to be sure we're not going to get any nosey neighbours knocking before I do, wanting to know who you are.'

Colette led Sally through a room of dark wood that reminded her of Mémé's living room. She was glad to see a large sideboard with a brightly coloured tin on it, the kind that were always full of bonbons. At least... they used to be. Sally would be surprised if anyone in St Aubert had any now.

Colette took Sally up a flight of stairs, which led up to a corridor. Then she opened a door, and Sally was ushered into what would be her room for the next few nights. It was clean and bright, with a net curtain over a window that looked out across the garden at the back of the house. There was a brass bedstead, with a silk quilt laid over it. A jug and a basin stood on a table to one side, and watercolours of flowers decorated the walls.

'What a pretty room,' Sally said. It felt so friendly, and she wondered how many people just like herself had parachuted into France and found a sanctuary here, within the walls of Colette's welcoming home.

'You won't be here long, but you'll be very welcome while you are,' the older woman assured her warmly. 'This is your home, Josette, and I want you to feel at home. Settle in and come down to the kitchen when you're ready. I'll make us all some lunch.'

All. Freddy too?

Sally hoped so, with all her heart.

THIRTY-ONE

Sally unpacked her clothes, folding them neatly in the chest of drawers in her room, and laid out her toiletries on the dressing table. Josette would do exactly the same, she thought. It was strange to see her own belongings in Colette's house. It was as if they didn't really belong to her any more; now they were Josette's.

But behind her thoughts was the notion that Freddy was here, somewhere. She couldn't wait to see him, and she only hoped that Henri was right and Freddy really was recovering well.

She headed downstairs and went to the kitchen at the back of the house, with its scrubbed floorboards, stove, and a row of shiny pans hanging up on the wall.

'I've unpacked,' she told Colette. 'You've got such a cosy home.'

'You think you will be at home here with a frail, helpless, ill old lady?' Colette teased. She had seemed like all of those things standing at the open door but, here in the kitchen, when there was nobody else to see, she couldn't have been further from that vulnerable figure. Now, Sally could see the inner strength that she possessed. She'd set out a simple lunch of bread and cheese, and explained, 'We shall have something more hearty for supper.'

There on the table, Sally noticed, were three plates and three glasses, and a small flagon. Colette nodded towards it with a proud smile. 'We always welcome our visitors with St Aubert cider. We say it will keep you coming back.'

Three place settings.

Then Colette strolled across the kitchen to a spot in front of the stove that must be invisible from the window, and stamped out a short beat with her foot. It was clearly a signal, but Sally wasn't sure who or what for. Did she have a pet dog or a cat that came in when she stamped her foot?

But then a thought occurred to her, and it filled her heart with hope.

Is this a signal for a person instead, someone who's hiding?

There was nothing remarkable about the floor as far Sally could see, certainly no sign that there was anything beneath the boards but the earth. That was why it was so surprising when a portion of it suddenly lifted, opening along an unseen hinge. Then, from right beneath their very feet, Sally saw her fiancé emerging into the daylight.

Sally gasped in utter amazement and dropped to her knees, reaching for him, trying to help him up. His blue RAF uniform had gone, replaced by the simple clothes of a farm worker, and his right arm was in a sling. Sally had worried that he'd look grey and worn, but, for someone who'd fallen out of the sky and been trapped in an occupied land, Freddy wasn't looking too bad at all; his eyes were twinkling through the fading cuts and bruises on his face, and he was brimming with energy.

She shouldn't have doubted Wyngate.

'Freddy... oh, goodness me,' Sally whispered in English, the words suddenly alien on her tongue. 'You can't imagine how glad I am to see you! I've missed you so much, darling.'

He hadn't quite finished climbing out of the hole in the ground, but Sally already had her arms round him, holding him. The man she loved. The man she thought she'd lost.

'Oh, Sal...' Freddy whispered, clinging on to her with his good arm. 'You shouldn't be here. You should've stayed safe at home.'

'I had to come,' Sally told him, her voice quiet. Instinctively, she knew they couldn't talk as they normally would, in case someone overheard them who shouldn't. But it was so hard, after facing the possibility that she would never see Freddy again only to find herself with him once more. There was so much to tell him. 'I'm flying the plane back home. But I couldn't miss the chance to see you, could I? I love you, Freddy.'

She held his face with both her hands and, forgetting for a moment that Colette was in the room with them, kissed him on the lips.

The kiss went on and on, chasing away the grief and fear Sally had felt since that awful day when he was reported missing. They were a long way from safe, but they were together. For now, at least.

When they broke from the kiss, Sally couldn't help but stare at Freddy, her precious Freddy. She was still amazed to see him right there in front of her. Dear, darling Freddy.

'I hope you've been brushing up on your French,' she teased him affectionately.

'Doing my best,' he said, smiling, his eyes glittering as he gazed at her. 'They said they're going to try and get me out too.'

'Children, come now,' Colette said gently. 'Enjoy lunch. I shall eat in the sitting room today, I think. The kitchen is yours.' She added, for Sally's benefit, 'Our sheep must keep to the left of the door. That way, he cannot be seen even if someone was in my little garden with their nose pressed to the glass.'

Colette had thought of everything and was now giving up her kitchen to the newly reunited couple.

'Don't worry, I'll— *We'll* be careful,' Sally promised her. She was on a see-saw, one moment thrilled beyond words to see her fiancé again, the next reminded of the extreme danger she and Freddy were in every second that they were in France.

'Thanks, Colette,' Freddy told her in French. Luckily he had some command of the language, even if he wasn't anywhere near fluent. With a gentle smile, Colette picked up her plate of food and glass, then took her leave.

'Help me up, Sal?' Freddy said.

Sally slipped her arm round his waist, anxious to avoid his shoulder, as she helped him get up to his feet.

'You look so different, but you look exactly the same too,' she said, gazing at him. 'I'm sorry, I need to stop gawping at you. You'll feel like you're in a cage at the zoo!'

Freddy laughed, then kissed her again. It was almost overwhelming; she couldn't quite believe it was real.

She returned his kiss, so warm and tender, holding him as tightly as she could without hurting his shoulder. Their kiss ended and she told him, 'I never stopped wearing the ring. At least, until the last moment before I had to leave. I couldn't risk wearing it here. I've never stopped loving you, Freddy. Not for a second.'

'I couldn't believe it when they said you were in France,' he said. 'I didn't know until this morning. There's a pile of letters downstairs for you...' He wiped the back of his hand against his eyes. 'Oh heck, sorry!'

Was he wiping away tears? Even though Sally's eyes were blurring with tears too, at the thought of all those unsent letters, she passed him her handkerchief.

She didn't want to embarrass him if he was crying, and his mention of the *letters downstairs* made her curious about his hiding place. Sally went over to the hole in the floor and dropped down inside it.

The space was wide enough for a bed and small table, but not much else. The bed had a bright, cheerful quilt, and the walls were lined with wooden boards. Sally smiled to see that Freddy had pinned up a photo of her. There was an English–French dictionary on the table, along with some books in English – *Jane Eyre* and *Great Expectations*. Sally supposed they must have belonged to people in St Aubert who had learned English. There was a pen and a pad of paper, along with a cigar box that Freddy no doubt kept bits and bobs in. It wasn't luxurious by any standards, but it was safe and it was comfortable. And at least he wasn't trapped down there all the time.

Sally climbed back up to the kitchen.

'How do you like my place?' Freddy teased, already nibbling a thick piece of bread. 'Little bachelor den out in France!'

'It's very bijou.' Sally giggled. 'I had no idea it was there. I was so surprised when Colette stamped on the floor and you appeared! I'm so relieved you've found somewhere safe. It can't be fun, being stuck indoors for weeks and weeks on end, but better that than...'

She didn't need to elaborate. They both knew what could happen.

They sat down at the table, their chairs close together, and started to eat.

'I'll have to read those letters before we leave,' Sally told Freddy. 'And you are going to leave, too. We'll be back in England again soon, I promise.'

The presence of von Brandt and his SS troops wouldn't make the mission any easier, but Sally was determined that she and Freddy would see their home again. She didn't want to worry Freddy about it, but maybe he'd already heard about who'd arrived in St Aubert.

'That plane is really something, isn't it?' Freddy said as he poured two glasses of cider. 'Jerry couldn't get anywhere near her. She's almost as special as you, but not half so pretty.'

Sally chuckled. Freddy was his adorable self, thank goodness. 'It really is an amazing plane. We're incredibly lucky to have flown her.' She took a sip of her cider, then asked, 'So what happened? I was told it was a lightning strike.'

He nodded. 'Just sheer rotten luck.' And Sally knew all about that. 'I know you haven't flown her with her weapons readied, but she's revolutionary, Sal. I came out here on a mission and she sailed through it.' Freddy shook his head with obvious awe. He'd always been mad about planes; it was one of the things Sally adored about him. 'The storm broke as I headed home, so I pulled the canopy shut, and a moment after I did... *bam!*'

Sally knew better than to ask him what mission he'd been on. Just as she hadn't been allowed to tell anyone, even Freddy, about the secret Spitfire's test flights, he couldn't tell her why he'd been flying over Normandy.

'Lightning just comes of nowhere,' she said, and nodded. It had been no one's fault, as Wyngate had said. She glanced at Freddy's shoulder, wondering about his injury. 'And it smashed the canopy?'

Freddy nodded and jerked his head towards his sling. 'I've got a real corker of a wound under here, but luckily the local doc's on the side of the angels. And – praise be – he speaks the lingo.' He reached out and squeezed Sally's hand. 'The strike knocked me clean out. I woke up about a hundred feet from the ground feeling like my arm was hanging off.' He gave a theatrical shudder. 'I'm still not sure how, but I managed to put her down.' He took a bite of cheese and added, 'If I hadn't closed that lid, you'd have a fried fiancé!'

Sally winced at the thought. But even so, he'd been hit by the flying shards of the smashed canopy. She couldn't begin to imagine the agony he'd been in; and how he'd managed to land the plane with one hand amazed her. She hated thinking of him being in pain, and alone and terrified on top of it. But Freddy was Freddy – he always found a way to be chipper.

'Oh, Freds, you've been through so much,' Sally whispered. 'It must've been so painful.'

'I got lucky, because Henri found me,' he assured her. 'If I'd been in any old Spit, I wouldn't have put you and the folks through this, or put the people here in danger. But we can't let Fritz get hold of the technology on that plane.'

'You've taken a big risk, Freds,' Sally said, not that he needed her to tell him that. 'You could've sat out the war in a prisoner of war camp. But you're right – you're absolutely right, because if you'd surrendered, they'd have taken the plane, and... I can't bear to think about it.'

Freddy raised Sally's hand and kissed it tenderly. Then he closed his eyes and pressed it to his cheek, holding her hand as he asked, 'How's Mum and Dad and Pete? Is Wilbur looking after everybody for me?'

'They all miss you terribly,' Sally assured him, not wanting to tell him the whole truth. How would he feel, knowing that his parents' hope had abandoned them? 'Peter's excited – he wants to throw a huge party for you when you get home! We can't disappoint him, can we?'

'You must've all been having a rotten time.' Of course he would've guessed; Freddy was far from unintelligent. 'I wish I could've got word to them. I know it sounds daft, but I hoped maybe Wilbur might keep folks smiling. Stupid, aren't I?'

'Wilbur runs to the door every time someone knocks,' Sally told him. 'I know he was always keen to meet his visitors, but the way he barks when he does it now... I'm sure he's hoping it's you. It's been so difficult keeping everything a secret, knowing that I was coming to bring the plane back, and that I might see you... If only I could've told them.'

Sally rubbed the back of her hand across her eyes. Her tears were rising again and she didn't want Freddy to see. Not now they were together again.

THIRTY-TWO

Darkness began to fall over St Aubert, drawing a line under a day of contrasts. Sally had been ecstatic to be with Freddy again, and they had snuggled and whispered together, safely away from the windows. But she had also absorbed everything that Colette had told her about life in St Aubert, the position of the plane, and who she could trust.

How could their happy reunion take place in front of such a threatening background?

But that was the reality of their situation. And Sally didn't have long now until the next stage of her mission.

I'm going to see the secret Spitfire.

The news of the arrival of an SS official had swept through the village and Colette had been visited with the news by a handful of her friends, all of whom were wide-eyed at the unwelcome new visitor. They were considerably more pleased to see Sally and, with Freddy hidden away in his comfortable little hidey-hole beneath the kitchen, she was welcomed by the elderly ladies who were her *auntie's* friends.

Sally kept up a conversation with them, telling them how things were in La Roche-sur-Yon, without giving much in the way of specifics. But it was enough to convince them that she really had just arrived from there. Colette's niece was, as far as they were concerned, Josette.

She felt safe in Colette's home, and with Freddy there too she didn't want to leave. But she was never going to fly the Spitfire home if she sat in Colette's kitchen.

Sally heard footsteps approaching the house, and froze with fear. Outside, she could hear voices speaking in German. Freddy reached out and took her hand, holding it tight as they held their breath as one. The words were fast, too fast for Sally to understand with her very thin grasp of the language. One of the men sounded gruff, his sentences staccato. The other sounded more animated, and he laughed.

The laughter sent a cold finger of fear shooting up Sally's spine. Maybe the man was only telling a joke, but maybe he was amused because at any moment they would burst into Colette's home and discover the two English people sheltering there.

Sally didn't dare move. The enemies' conversation went on for a few more moments, and finally the heavy footsteps moved away.

Sally waited in the heavy silence that followed, before she took a chance and breathed again.

Thank goodness.

Next to Sally, Freddy finally let out a long breath. He squeezed her hand and whispered, 'Are you sure you want to go through with this, Sal? If anything happens to you...' He pressed a kiss to her lips. 'You're quite something, you know.'

'I have to do this, Freddy,' Sally whispered in reply. 'I've come all this way – it's got to be done, darling. Don't worry about me. I'll be fine, really, I will.'

As Sally spoke, there came a light tapping on the kitchen window, and she recognised the same melody that Colette had used to summon Freddy.

'That's Armand,' Freddy whispered.

Colette bustled into the kitchen and indicated the entrance to Freddy's little den.

'Just in case,' she told Sally in French as Freddy kissed Sally's cheek again before descending back beneath the floor, pulling the boards back after him. Only then did Colette ask in her trembling, frail act, 'Who is creeping about out there? Is that little Armand, climbing fences again?'

There was another gentle tapping and Armand whispered through the door, 'It's me, Lettie, open up.'

Sally breathed a sigh of relief. She peered through the glass panes that took up the top half of the door and could see the boy outside. She opened the door just a crack, so that Armand could come in, and quickly scanned the garden behind him.

No one stirred.

Sally closed the door behind him. 'Hello again,' she said to Armand.

'English folk are multiplying round here!' Armand told Colette, who scrubbed his hair affectionately. When he spoke again, his voice was keen with enthusiasm. 'Where's Freds?'

Colette was already stamping out the signal as she told him, 'You can say hello and no more, then you're on your way.' She stepped away from the concealed trapdoor and addressed Sally. 'Armand has some English. His mother knows it.'

Freds. The little boy was evidently fond of Freddy. And Sally knew that Freddy must like Armand, because he was so much like his much-missed brother Peter.

'So you've been keeping each other company?' Sally asked Armand, as the trapdoor lifted.

Armand nodded, keen as anything. 'Freds is great!' he exclaimed. 'He's going to teach me how to fly one day!'

'Armand!' Freddy cried cheerfully as he emerged into the kitchen. 'You look after this girl of mine, promise?'

'Promise!' Armand gave him a sharp salute as he answered

in English. Then he told Sally in French, 'Ready to see how good we are at hiding planes?'

Sally was touched by the affection between Freddy and Armand. She hoped that one day Freddy really would be able to teach Armand to fly. But before they could do that, there was the mission to get the secret Spitfire home.

She nodded in reply to Armand. Even though she was fearful of what lay out there, she had the brave little boy as her guide. 'I'm ready. Let's see how you've done it!'

'No risks,' Freddy warned her. She could see love and concern warring in his gaze. 'Armand knows the place better than anyone.'

Armand nodded proudly. 'Stick by me,' he said. Then Colette turned out the light and Armand opened the door onto the dark garden.

As soon as she stepped outside, Sally was on alert. She listened as hard as she could, trying to pick out any footsteps, or anyone speaking German. But the SS troops who had walked down rue de l'Eglise had gone.

For now, at least.

Armand moved quickly and stealthily through the shadows on the grass towards the fence. Pausing only to beckon to Sally, he scaled it and disappeared down into the alleyway behind.

Sally hadn't been expecting to climb fences, but all of the getting in and out of planes that she had done had more than prepared her. She grabbed the top of the fence and pulled herself up, swinging her legs over before dropping to the ground on the other side.

They were breaching the curfew.

We'll just have to avoid being caught.

The alleyway was narrow and dark, and at the top of it Sally could see the white stone of the church opposite. She followed Armand to the top of the alleyway, and they carefully peered out.

Coast's clear.

'If we see any Germans, don't you fret,' Armand whispered with all the bravado of a child. 'I learned a thing or two from Guy.'

'I bet you did,' Sally said under her breath. She almost chuckled.

But this was no time for laughter. Sally and Armand crept along rue de l'Eglise, step by painful step. The village was so quiet that every sound they made was amplified. Sally could barely dare to breathe. Once they reached the square, Armand gestured towards an alleyway on the opposite site. That was where they were now aiming for, but how on earth they could get there, unseen and unheard, Sally couldn't imagine.

And yet, the Nazis had told the French to keep their curtains and shutters drawn, so it was unlikely that anyone would see them. It was like walking through Bramble Heath in the blackout. As Sally had learned, footsteps could just as easily be Nazis as anyone from the village – few, if any, of the villagers would risk peering outside and drawing attention to themselves.

Keeping close to the walls of the shops that ringed the square, Sally and Armand crept carefully, Sally's heart in her throat at every step. She heard someone cough, and froze, only then realising that it was the sound of someone in an apartment above the butcher's shop. They kept going and Sally nearly jumped out of her skin at the sound of water running down a pipe – it was only someone getting ready for bed.

And so they went on, past one shuttered shop after another. Some were evidently very empty, faded TO LET signs fluttering against them. The bar was closed for the night, as customers would have had to break the curfew to drink there. But quiet as it was, the whole village was stretched taut, and it would only take the slightest thing for the silence to break.

Eventually – though it could not have taken more than a

minute – Sally and Armand reached the dark, shadowy alleyway.

She glanced back, just in time to see two German soldiers emerge from the gloom of a street on the other side of the square. They paused to light cigarettes, and one of them laughed.

They're the ones who walked past Colette's house!

Sally didn't want to wait another second, and she and Armand hurried away down the alleyway as quietly as they could, leaving the soldiers behind them.

It was just as well that Sally had Armand as a guide. She would never have found her way without him. The alleyway twisted and turned as it ran between first one house and then the next, by outhouses and small stables. Sally heard French voices behind the shutters. A man laughing, a woman singing a lullaby. Snatches of other people's lives, being lived as normally as they could, despite the war.

Finally, they emerged from between two houses, and were in an orchard. Thank goodness for the Normans' fondness for cider. The trees weren't as tightly placed as they would be in a forest, but they were close enough that Sally and Armand could travel across the length of the orchard with plenty of tree trunks to hide behind.

Sally kept thinking of the two men in the square. What if they'd decided to walk through the alley too? But they wouldn't, surely not. They'd stumble about and get lost. Sally was trying to regain her bearings and pictured the maps she'd memorised back in the attic at Heath Place. Back in her old home— No, she couldn't let homesickness take over her mind.

If she was right, they were now on the opposite side of St Aubert from the chateau.

Silently, she followed Armand from tree to tree. He was just ahead of her. Each time they made a move, they would glance around for danger first, then hastily make for the next tree.

Leaning back against it, they would scan again, and take another step forward.

'Shhh!' Armand suddenly hissed. He flung up one hand to halt Sally in her tracks and together they waited, listening to the night. Then Sally heard the purr of a powerful engine idling, before wheels moved slowly along the road. The little boy stepped back just a little into the trees, guiding Sally back with him as he took her hand in his.

From where they were hidden in the shadows, Sally could see the road, which ran past the orchard. The Mercedes-Benz that she had seen earlier, carrying Obergruppenführer von Brandt, was gleaming in the moonlight. Sally's stomach tied itself in painful knots.

Oh, heck. This is not good news.

THIRTY-THREE

The canvas roof was up on the car but, in its interior, Sally could see the pale face of the Nazi, illuminated only by the glowing tip of his cigarette. To her horror, he was looking out of the window into the orchard and, she was sure, right at them. Any minute now he would command the driver to stop and it would all be over. They would be lost.

But the moment passed and the car drove on, its headlamps disappearing into the darkness. As the vehicle was swallowed by shadows, Armand spat onto the ground at his feet and whispered, 'Bastard.' Then he blinked up at Sally. 'Don't tell Mum.'

'I won't,' Sally promised.

They started to move again. Sally's adventure started to take on the unreality of a nightmare. She started to feel as if she was floating through the orchard, rather than walking. She pinched her arm, and the sharp pain shook her out of it.

Pay attention, you fool. Be on the alert.

Armand touched her arm and pointed through the trees towards a hulking structure. So they wouldn't be heading to the chateau, but to whatever place this was.

A barn?

But surely a barn was the first place the Nazis would look. How on earth had they managed to hide the Spitfire here?

Armand led Sally through the last stretch of trees. Ahead of them were a handful of farm buildings, a couple of sheds, and an open-sided barn full of crates.

Sally blinked. Surely there wasn't any space in there for a plane. It was packed to the roof.

'Where is it?' she whispered.

'Right in front of you,' said Armand. He nodded towards the barn. 'Did you know we're famous for cider round here? We send it out all over the place to get folks toasted!'

'Oh, yes, I know about your famous St Aubert cider,' Sally whispered in reply. She wondered if Armand was *toasted* on cider too, although he was far too young. Was he being serious when he said the plane was right in front of her? 'But all I can see are crates!'

'Next thing you'll tell me is you can't see my Resistance pals,' he said, laughing. Then he broke into a trot, still heading for the barn. 'Come on, Josette!'

Sally followed, utterly bemused. But Armand wouldn't risk breaking the curfew just to bring her to a barn full of crates, surely? Somehow, the plane, and members of the Resistance, were hiding in there, but she had no idea how.

They reached the barn, and Sally was faced with a wall of crates, all branded with CIDRE DE ST AUBERT. She glanced at Armand, then gingerly ran her hand over the crate in front of her. But it really was a crate, she was certain of it.

Then she heard footsteps from somewhere; she couldn't work out where. And Henri was suddenly there.

He didn't speak but beckoned to Sally and Armand, before shifting a couple of the crates to reveal a concealed passageway. They went in, following Henri this way and that through the crates like a maze. Sally was reminded of the alleyways in

St Aubert, and, if Henri and Armand hadn't been there as her guide, she would easily have got lost.

Then Henri stopped in front of another wall of crates. Sally had lost her bearings. Surely the plane couldn't be here?

Henri pulled at one of the crates. Sally was amazed as it swung open, like a door.

Right there on the other side of it was the secret Spitfire.

'Your tractor, mademoiselle,' Henri said with a grin.

Sally went through the door, and saw that the entire plane was surrounded by a false wall made of crates. It was so ingenious. She'd had no idea at all that there was anything other than crates in the barn. Any curious Nazis who would've begun moving the first layer of real crates would have got bored before they'd penetrated through the inner layers.

There were figures near the plane, and Sally gasped in surprise when she realised that one of them was Margot, the conductress from the bus.

'Evening,' Margot whispered.

'Evening,' Sally murmured in reply, still stunned into near silence at seeing the plane again, and in such a clever hiding place, too.

'Good as new,' said Armand proudly. 'Except the canopy. But Freds says you don't need that!'

'It's incredible...' Sally ran her hand across the wing, smiling at the plane. All the test flights she had flown in the Spitfire over Bramble Heath came back to her. 'Hello, old girl. I hope you've enjoyed your holiday, but I'm afraid you're going home soon.'

She climbed up onto the wing and peered into the cockpit. Armand was right – aside from the canopy, the cockpit looked fine. There was no sign of damage from the lightning strike, and, as Freddy had been able to land her, she assumed there was no damage to the workings either.

Sally had been terrified when the landing gear switch had broken, but at least it had meant the engineers had since beefed up the insulation behind the instrument panel. That, she suspected, had definitely helped to reduce the damage the lightning had done.

But she couldn't turn the engine on to tick it over, or taxi the plane around the field. Von Brandt and his men would've known in seconds where the Spitfire was. At least she knew from Freddy that there was enough fuel to get her home – and that was fortunate, because she wasn't sure that the Resistance, resourceful though they were, could've got their hands on enough.

Sally climbed down from the plane. Henri, Margot, Armand and the others were waiting.

'Thanks so much for taking care of her,' Sally told them. She was humbled by what these people had done. 'You've put yourselves in so much danger, and I'm really just so amazed that you've managed to hide her so well. She's a very special pl— Tractor. You're brilliant, really.'

A woman stepped forward and Armand turned to look up at her with a smile. Sally knew without a second glance that this was the little boy's mother. Like him she was slight, with the same dark eyes. But whereas Armand's gaze glittered with excitement, hers was dulled with worry. Sally could hardly blame her; they were all taking an enormous risk, after all.

'This is my mum,' the boy told Sally with pride. 'She came up with the idea for this.' And he knocked lightly against the false wall.

His mother smiled bashfully. 'I'm Leah,' she said.

Sally went up to her and kissed her cheeks in greeting. 'You're a genius. And you have a very brave son. It's an honour to meet you, Leah. It's an honour to meet all of you, really.'

Henri shrugged, and Margot smiled. A young man standing beside Margot, with a couple of lengths of straw in his hair, shook his head as if it was nothing. Sally suspected he was one of the men who, on being told he'd be heading to work in

Germany, had gone underground and joined the Resistance instead. It was amazing to think how different people's lives were over here, when only a strip of water separated England and France.

'We hitched up the farm horses and dragged it here,' said Leah. 'When it came down, the young man was so injured... but he wouldn't leave the plane until we promised we'd hide it. It is special, yes?'

Oh, Freddy. You needed help, and you took such a risk for the secret Spitfire.

'It's very special, yes. And Freddy... he's even more special,' Sally replied. She knew that she was here to retrieve the plane, and not to rescue Freddy. But even so, no man from the ministry could tell *her* that the plane was more important than he was. 'He's been so well-looked after too. I'm so grateful to you all, I can barely... I can barely...'

Sally's voice was choked with tears, and she ran the back of her hand across her face.

Leah held out a handkerchief as she said, 'My husband is in Germany. He's a prisoner of war.' She patted Sally's shoulder. 'We'll see you both home. And my man too.'

Sally gratefully took Leah's handkerchief and dried her eyes. There was understanding in Leah's expression. They both knew what it was like for a loved one to end up behind enemy lines, the gnawing, haunting anxiety.

'We will,' Sally replied. 'We'll see everyone safely home.'

She could only hope that would really be the case. How could they move the plane with von Brandt and his men everywhere?

'Von Brandt's men came here this afternoon,' Henri told Sally. It didn't surprise her – of course they would have looked here. 'I could see them from my farm. They moved some crates, ended up seeing *more* crates, then gave up and left. Maybe the barn's been ticked off their list, and they won't be coming back here.'

Armand nodded. 'He's been all over the place, I'm hearing.' He looked to Henri. 'You hearing that too, Henri?'

Leah gave him an affectionate smile. 'My little man,' she said, then stooped to kiss her son's head. Her reward was a good-natured grimace.

'Mum!' Armand laughed.

Sally chuckled. 'There must be a whole underground network of boys swapping news.' And it didn't surprise her. 'Now, I've been told to get the tractor up as soon as I can. She looks ready, but...' She shrugged. They all knew what she meant.

'Von Brandt.' Henri nodded. 'You'll have to wait. Now is not a good time. When we first hid the plane, there weren't many Nazis here. It was dangerous, but not anywhere near as dangerous as it is now. They call him the Butcher of Breslau; it's better that you don't know why.'

Sally shivered. No, she didn't want to know. She didn't even want to guess. Because if she did, she would be even more terrified of what the future held for the village.

She would have to wait. And waiting meant more time kicking her heels in St Aubert, freezing with fear at the sound of every footstep. Waiting meant more time for the plane – and for her – to be discovered. But she knew Henri was right.

THIRTY-FOUR

'We need to find the best place to fly her from,' Sally said. 'We've got time to work it out, though, haven't we?' *Seeing as I'm stuck here until von Brandt goes sniffing about somewhere else.*

'Henri has a place,' said Leah, looking to the farmer for a confirming nod. 'It's not going to be easy, but...'

But that was why Wyngate had fought for Sally, wasn't it? Because she could take off from the head of a pin.

'It's my fallow field,' Henri replied. 'You saw the orchard on one side of the barn? Well, on the other side there's a field. It's full of rocks and stones, though – I don't think you can take off from there. But on the other side of *that* is my fallow field. We just have to get the tractor there. Don't worry, we'll handle that, then it's over to you.'

Sally nodded. It wasn't ideal, as it meant the plane would be exposed as it was moved from the barn and through a field, but it was better than nothing.

'You've thought of everything,' she said.

Leah nodded. 'It's our first plane, but it's not our first job for Guy.'

That didn't surprise Sally. She wondered what else Wyngate had had them do. 'He's a good man,' she said. 'He's very brave. Can I ask what you did with him before?' She wasn't sure they'd tell her, but she was curious.

'That's a secret for another time,' Henri said, tapping the side of this nose. 'There are many tales I could tell you, Josette, starting with the bullet I got in my arm at Verdun. I didn't think I'd live to see another war, but do we humans ever learn? Anyway, we should all go now, in case *they* come back for a second sweep. Armand, you take Josette home.'

Armand nodded, then turned his face up to his mother. 'Will you be all right?'

Leah nodded gently. 'Take Josette, and come straight home.' She told Sally, 'He's always visiting Freddy. Plane-mad, you know.' With a last scrub to her son's hair, she said, 'Now get along.'

Back Sally and Armand went through the maze of crates. Once they were outside the barn again, Sally glanced over her shoulder. It was just a barn full of crates from here, nothing more. No wonder von Brandt's men had given up and gone poking about somewhere else.

The night was dark, apart from the patches of moonlight that fell between the clouds, and the air was still warm from the heat of the day. As Sally and Armand made their way back across the orchard, Sally felt more positive. There might not be a canopy on the plane, but everything else looked ship-shape, as far as she could tell. There was just the issue of getting it on something resembling a runway; but they had time to arrange that while they waited for von Brandt and his men to go elsewhere.

But Sally wasn't going to get complacent. She couldn't risk getting caught, especially not so close to the plane's hiding place. Once again, she and Armand went from tree to tree across the orchard. Ahead of them, St Aubert sat dark and silent. Each step took them closer and closer to the village, and to safety.

Sally almost sighed with relief when she and Armand were in the alleyway again, taking them back towards the square. They were safely hidden from anyone who might be watching, as all the shutters were closed. Sally caught snatches of sleepy conversation from the houses they passed, but she and Armand trod so carefully, so quietly, that they wouldn't be heard at all.

When they arrived at the top of the alleyway, they paused, glancing around for any signs of danger. Sally could see the entrance to rue de l'Eglise, and she thought of Colette and Freddy, sitting in the kitchen, wondering when she would be coming home.

Soon, very soon! I'm nearly there!

Happy that the coast was clear, Sally and Armand skirted silently around the edge of the square, past the shuttered shops. Step by careful step, they drew closer and closer to Colette's home.

Still nothing stirred. The enemy had given up for the night, she supposed.

They passed a house on the square, next to the pharmacy. Sally could see a brass plaque beside the door.

'Dr Vautier,' Armand whispered. 'He's the bloke sorted Freddy's arm. You're lucky he's a good doctor, because that was a rotten old wound he had.'

Sally nodded to Armand, then smiled up at Dr Vautier's house. *Thank you*, she would've said to him, if she could.

They reached rue de l'Eglise. Sally heard something and glanced around, only to see a cat hurrying across the square.

I'm jumping at shadows. I just need to be calm and careful.

She could see Colette's house up ahead, but, even though most of the village was asleep by now, they couldn't take any chances. As Armand led the way down the alley that ran beside Colette's cottage, he glanced back at Sally.

'Safe and sound,' he whispered. Then, nimble as a cat, he scrambled over the fence and dropped down onto the grass. 'C'mon!'

'Halt!' The single word was loud as a gunshot in the silent night. 'Show yourself!'

'Armand, hide,' Sally breathed, before stepping back from the fence. She turned, raising her hands, and saw von Brandt.

THIRTY-FIVE

Sally felt as if the ground had fallen away from her feet. Light-headed with terror, she blinked at the man in his uniform that was darker than the night. He stalked along the alleyway towards her, the slivers of moonlight through the clouds illuminating that ghostly-pale face as he drew closer.

'This town is under curfew.' Von Brandt came to a halt in front of Sally. He took his cigarette from between his lips and asked her, 'What business could a young lady have creeping in alleyways after dark?'

What business have you? Sally wondered to herself, though she wasn't foolhardy enough to say those words aloud.

Instead, she told him, 'My aunt is ill, I need to fetch the doctor.'

'Oh, a poorly aunt?' Von Brandt tutted with mock sympathy. 'Are you sure it is not a sweetheart? A gentleman waiting for his lady?'

You swine. Sally shook her head. She tried to sound pleading as she replied, 'No, she's ill. Her breathing, it's... it's not good.'

He cocked his head to one side, watching her through

rheumy eyes. Sally felt as though von Brandt could see right through her, as though he already knew what she had to hide. A moment passed before he flicked the cigarette into Colette's immaculate garden as though it was a public ashtray.

'So,' he said, 'I will walk with you. We will go to the doctor together, you and I, Mademoiselle...?'

He wants my name.

'M-mademoiselle Auclair,' she answered. Hoping to keep him sweet, she said, 'Thank you, Monsieur. It is kind of you to accompany me.'

Von Brandt nodded and gave her a thin-lipped smile. A crocodile sort of smile.

'Mademoiselle Auclair,' he repeated. 'Then to the doctor we will go. Please, lead the way.'

Was he deliberately trying to catch her out?

But fortunately Sally knew exactly where to go. Her heart pounding, she walked back to the square, towards the doctor's house. Thank goodness Dr Vautier could be trusted, but Sally felt guilty to be bringing von Brandt to his door.

The echo of the obergruppenführer's footsteps was the only sound in the square.

Sally wanted to stop; she wanted to say that perhaps the doctor was asleep and didn't want to be disturbed. But that would be ridiculous. She had to go through with the story now, otherwise von Brandt would see right through her.

They reached Dr Vautier's door, and Sally rang the bell. She could sense something change in the air, and realised that von Brandt was disappointed. Her story was true. There was no sweetheart, no reason for Sally to squirm; instead, she was simply fetching the doctor.

Hurry up! Every second she had to spend beside von Brandt stretched out interminably.

'Nobody home,' said her unwanted companion. 'Or perhaps our good doctor is not keen to break the curfew.'

As if a doctor wouldn't have a perfectly reasonable excuse to leave his house after dark to see a patient.

But as he finished speaking, a male voice asked, 'Who is it? It's after curfew.'

'Obergruppenführer von Brandt!' the German barked. 'Open up!'

And as Dr Vautier scrambled to turn the key in the lock, Sally heard it fall to the floor and the doctor mutter a panicked oath. Von Brandt laughed at his obvious shock and discomfort and gave the door a firm kick.

'Come along!' he called. 'Let us see you, Herr Doktor!'

Nausea washed through Sally's stomach. She dearly wished she hadn't needed to involve the doctor. But what could she do, besides stand there next to this devil while Dr Vautier opened the door to him?

Suddenly, without any warning to the hapless man on the other side of the door, von Brandt drew his pistol and fired a bullet through the lock. And all the time he was laughing, as though he had never had such fun in his life.

Sally jolted with alarm. But she didn't dare say a thing, or glance at von Brandt. What if Dr Vautier had been hit, and was lying there wounded on the other side of the door?

And what on earth would everyone in the village be thinking? They would all have heard that gunshot. They couldn't have missed it.

What would Freddy think?

The door lurched open and there was Vautier, or so Sally supposed. He was a tiny man, stout as a tree and with a face that looked as though it was made to be jolly. He didn't look jolly just now though, milk white and wide-eyed beneath bottle-bottom spectacles.

'What on earth is it?' he asked in a stunned whisper. He looked from von Brandt, whose laughter had ceased in an instant to be replaced by that same stony countenance that Sally had seen in the car. 'What's wrong?'

'It's my aunt, Mademoiselle Auclair,' Sally told him, her voice tight with fear. 'She's — She's ill. Could you come and see her?'

Dr Vautier had never seen Sally before in his life. He'd think it was a trap. He'd— *Wait a second.* Surely he would've seen Sally's photograph in Freddy's hiding place. Maybe he would recognise her.

Besides, the rest of the Resistance knew she was coming, so surely the doctor did too? Wyngate wouldn't have left anything to chance.

'Of course!' Vautier said. 'I shall fetch my bag. A moment, mademoiselle.'

And he hurried away, leaving her alone with von Brandt again.

'She is an elderly lady?' Von Brandt asked as he holstered his pistol. 'Say the word, mademoiselle, and I shall cure the patient.' As he patted his holster, he laughed again, as though the very thought of it was hilarious.

That was typical of the Nazis, though, wasn't it? They were bullies, who thought they were better than everyone else. And anyone who they thought was weak could merely be swatted into oblivion.

'She just needs to see the doctor, that's all,' Sally replied quietly. What on earth would von Brandt do when he arrived at Colette's house?

'Thank you, sir,' Vautier was already saying as he emerged from the house with his bag. 'Thank you for seeing the young lady through the streets to me. I shall make sure she gets safely home.'

But as they started to walk, von Brandt stalked alongside them, silent now. Somehow, it was far worse than his laughter.

'Mademoiselle Auclair has a summer flu,' the doctor told

them, obviously trying to make things seem more normal than they were. 'She is recovering, but these things have a habit of coming back in the elderly. And she is frail, God bless her.'

Frail. Well, she was certainly good at pretending to be.

They walked quickly and in silence then, past the church and along the little street towards the cottage. The closer they got, the more frightened Sally became that the SS officer was intending to walk right into the house with them. From what she had already seen of him, it wouldn't surprise her at all.

'Perhaps I shall call in and greet the patient,' von Brandt mused. Dr Vautier had just unhooked the gate, and he exchanged an unseen look of alarm with Sally as the Nazi glanced back along the street. 'Yes, I think I sha—'

The not-too-distant sound of glass shattering silenced von Brandt. His head snapped round again and he listened. There was no other sound until he said, 'Good evening, mademoiselle, Herr Doktor.'

And with that he stalked away in search of the source of the noise.

THIRTY-SIX

'I'm so sorry,' Sally whispered to Vautier after a moment. She could only think that Armand had been watching and had broken the glass as a decoy. They went up the path to Colette's home, and Sally unlocked the door. 'You'd better come in.'

She led the way into Colette's cottage, Vautier following.

'Auntie, it's me,' Sally called gently, for the benefit of any neighbours who might be listening.

'Your niece says you are taken unwell again,' Vautier added, adeptly filling Colette in on the role she had to play, at least while they might yet be overheard. 'We shall have you right as rain, mademoiselle.'

And as they came into the cottage, he closed the door firmly and slid the bolt across. Colette emerged from the sitting room, bent and frail until she realised they were alone.

Sally relaxed a little now that the outside world was shut behind them. 'Von Brandt caught me just before I jumped over the fence into your garden,' she explained to Colette. 'I had to think of a reason why I was wandering about during the curfew. I'm so, so sorry, Dr Vautier. Colette, he followed me all the way there, then he shot through the lock! Everyone in St Aubert must've heard it.'

And Freddy must've thought the bullet was for me.

'Sal?' The kitchen door opened and Freddy flew out to take Sally into the embrace of his good arm. 'I thought—' And, without a thought for their audience, he kissed her.

Vautier cleared his throat tactfully and told Colette, 'I shall sit for ten minutes or so, then go home.' He gave her a nudge and said, 'I gave you a tonic to settle you for the night. Nothing but a little phlegm on the lungs of my frail, helpless old lady.'

'Frail and helpless as a lion.' Colette chuckled. Then she adopted a weak voice and croaked, 'Thank you, Doctor, you are so kind to an elderly lady in her twilight years.'

Sally clung on to Freddy. She knew exactly what had gone through his mind. He thought she'd taken a bullet.

'It's all right, I'm safe,' Sally told him. But the incident told her that von Brandt was deadly, a tyrant who she needed to avoid at all costs. He could've killed Vautier. By some miracle, his bullet had missed, but it had been close. Too close.

Vautier waited until enough time had passed for him to plausibly have made a visit to a patient. Then he bid his farewells and headed back home. This time, Sally hoped, without a Nazi escort.

After creeping about in the dark, and her ordeal with von Brandt, she was drained and exhausted. She and Freddy were snuggled on the sofa in the parlour and, although she wanted to go to bed and get to sleep, she couldn't let go of him.

'Bedtime,' Sally whispered. Curious, she asked, 'Do you sleep in your hidey-hole, Freddy?'

'I was weak as a lamb when I first arrived, so I slept in your bed,' Freddy said. 'But I can manage the trapdoor now, so I stick to my den. I didn't want to put Colette in danger.'

There was a gentle tap on the door of the secluded parlour and Colette called, 'Goodnight, children. Sleep tight, wherever you may choose to rest your heads!' And as she tiptoed away, she gave a very cheeky chuckle.

Freddy kissed Sally's hair and whispered, 'She's a game old gal, that one.'

Sally giggled. 'Well, I do have my own room, and so do you, but...' She looked up at Freddy. Could she suggest it? Well, why not? 'I wouldn't mind having your company tonight. What do you say?'

'I'd like to...' Freddy said. 'A couple of hours wouldn't hurt, would it?'

'It wouldn't at all.' Sally kissed him. Tenderness now filled her, instead of fear. 'Do you need a hand?'

He shook his head. 'You go and get settled into bed.' He kissed the tip of her nose. 'I'll be there in a few minutes.'

Sally went upstairs to get ready for bed. She washed and put on a nightdress that Colette had left out for her. She drew back the bedsheets, smiling as she climbed in.

I'm going to share the bed with Freddy. For part of the night, at least.

She lay back on the pillow, and tried to relax after von Brandt's terrifying visit, waiting for Freddy to join her.

There was a gentle tap at the bedroom door and Freddy whispered softly, 'Mademoiselle Josette?' Then he pushed the door open and crept inside. For a moment he said nothing, but stood and looked at Sally there in the bed. Then he admitted, 'I'm still not sure you're real.'

Sally smiled back at him. His eyes were gentle with tiredness, and his hair was rumpled. He looked adorable. 'I promise you I am. I'm just as real as you are, even though we have to pretend we're not really ourselves.'

'Whoever you are, you're still the girl I love.' He gave her a wink, then looked down at the sensible dark blue pyjama set he was wearing, his sling white against them. 'Do you like my old man's pyjamas?'

'Very fetching!' Sally beamed. But she was glad he had them. She was glad he'd been taken care of, when none of his family had been able to. 'It's just like the old days, isn't it? Do you remember, we'd come back late to Heath Place from an airshow and just collapse into the first bed we came to!'

But no matter how many beds they'd shared, they'd never done more than kiss each other and fall asleep. The other things that couples did in bed could wait until they were married.

As long as we both get home safely. And we will. We have *to.*

'Sneaking back to our own beds before anybody caught us out,' Freddy said, chuckling, as he pulled back the covers and slipped in beside Sally. He reached across and turned out the dim lamp. 'I kept thinking of how stupid I'd been when I got jealous... oh, Sal, I'm glad you're here, but I wish you were at home.'

'*I* wish I was at home,' Sally admitted, carefully wrapping her arm round Freddy. Perhaps tomorrow morning one of her fake letters from Scotland would arrive on her parents' doormat in Bramble Heath, and they'd think of her flying over mountains and lochs. It was almost as far from the truth as it was possible to get. 'I wish you were too. Especially after tonight. That man... that man is *unhinged*. I won't lie, Freddy. I'm really scared.'

Even though she felt ashamed that she was.

But she could tell Freddy. He understood. He wouldn't think any less of her.

'You're so brave... you and all these folks in St Aubert who have kept me and the plane hidden.' He held her tight and kissed her. 'I love you, Sal. I'm scared too, but we're together now.' He drew back and she heard a smile in his voice, even if she couldn't see it in the darkness. 'Against people like you and Henri and Colette, Jerry doesn't stand a chance. And look at little Armand! We're going to win this war, Sal. And bastards like von Brandt won't know what hit them.'

Sally smiled. Freddy's optimism always buoyed her up, and, deep down, she knew he was right. Von Brandt went around St Aubert intimidating the locals, firing his gun at will. But he hadn't found the plane, had he? He really wasn't as clever as he thought he was.

'Von Brandt's been outwitted.' Sally chuckled. 'Hasn't he? Because look at us – brave, resourceful – and he's just a bully in a horrible uniform.'

'I might have half a Spitfire canopy embedded in my shoulder, but all that matters is being here with my girl again.' Freddy shifted slightly, holding Sally tighter than ever. 'And soon we'll be safe back at home. When we get married, we're definitely inviting the heroes of St Aubert!'

'We will...' Sally sighed. Her eyelids were closing, and this time there was no sign of von Brandt. All she could see was their family in Bramble Heath, and their friends from St Aubert, smiling in the peaceful sunshine. 'We'll have a wonderful time, Freddy. I know we will...'

THIRTY-SEVEN

The following morning, Sally decided to go to the shops. Colette needed some groceries anyway, and Sally hoped she could find some.

Part of her wanted to stay in the house because Freddy couldn't leave it; and she fretted that, if she was out and about, von Brandt would collar her again.

But wouldn't staying indoors all the time look just as suspicious? If Sally had come to St Aubert to look after Colette, as she claimed, she'd have to leave the house *sometimes*.

She made sure she had ration coupons and Josette's identity papers, picked up Colette's basket and opened the front door. Instinctively, she glanced up and down rue de l'Eglise, but she was relieved that she couldn't see anyone in uniform about.

And I hope I won't.

Some of the shutters that had been down over shops in the square last night were now open. Even though the shops had little stock, people still enjoyed the ritual of going from store to store. Catching up on the latest village news still happened even if the shelves were almost empty. Sally understood that. She'd seen the same thing in Bramble Heath.

I wish I was back home.

St Aubert's priest was heading to his church. The café was open, with its tables and chairs out in the square. Two old men, with glasses of cider at their sides, were playing chess, while a woman with grey hair drank what looked like coffee but, thanks to the shortages, probably wasn't. They looked fairly relaxed, happy, even, snatching a moment in the sunny square.

And that made Sally happy too.

She wished Freddy could be out here, though, enjoying the sunshine. They could sit at a table, drink cider and hold hands. But it was impossible. And she felt guilty that she had freedom that he didn't. He was cared for, though. He'd been kept safe. With the world the way it was right now, that was the best that anyone could hope for.

As Sally walked past the tables on her way to the bakery, she waved and said, 'Good morning!'

The two men paused in their chess game. One waved, the other saluted her with his glass and said, 'A beautiful day!'

'Oh, it is!' Sally nodded. She felt as if she was in Bramble Heath again, and the thought warmed her heart.

The woman with the grey hair waved to Sally too. 'You must be Colette's niece,' she smiled. 'She said you would be coming. Nice to meet you.'

'And you too,' Sally replied.

As she continued on her way, she passed the entrance to a street called rue de l'Ecole. She could see the school that gave it its name just a couple of buildings down, topped with a bell in a tower. Children were playing in the schoolyard, laughing and running around. Some of them were climbing the metal fence, as if they were keen to escape.

Just like I was at school!

Sally thought of Armand, who had stayed up so late the night before to get her safely to the plane and back again. She hoped he wouldn't be too tired to play with his friends.

She reached the bakery, which had little in the way of produce; there were no cakes, and only a few loaves. There was quite a queue, mainly consisting of older women, who were all engaged in conversation. No doubt it was the latest gossip that was keeping them busy, Sally was sure. She quietly took her place, attracting a few curious glances.

One woman in particular, wearing a floral dress and a hat decorated with wax fruit, held the floor. 'Well, of course, we're not allowed to open our shutters, but after hearing that gun go off last night I couldn't resist a peek,' she said.

Oh, no! She must've seen me last night in the square. What am I going to do?

The other customers gasped in amazement. Sally wanted to retreat out of the shop, but wouldn't that look rather strange? She repressed her urge to disappear and stood her ground, trying to look quietly curious.

'Well, I saw a German right by Vautier's front door!' the woman said. 'He was with someone – a woman, I think. I couldn't see her very well, but he definitely wasn't alone.'

'A fancy woman?' one of the other women asked.

'I couldn't see,' the woman with the wax fruit on her hat replied. 'But it was definitely a woman. Goodness knows what she was up to so late at night.'

Thank goodness, she won't know it was me. Sally tried to stop her relief from showing on her face.

'Maybe someone was taken ill?' suggested a woman in a stripy dress.

'Perhaps, but what was that German doing here anyway, and shooting his gun outside Dr Vautier's?' the woman with the wax fruit wondered aloud. 'The Germans haven't really both-ered with us before. Now I hear about the SS hunting around the whole region for something – and who knows *what* that might be!'

The women all shrugged and tutted, then the baker looked over at Sally.

'Good morning, mademoiselle,' he said. 'You're new here, aren't you?'

Sally really wished he hadn't said that. Every customer turned to face her now, as if the baker had given them permission to stare.

She nodded. 'I'm Mademoiselle Auclair's niece, Josette. I've come to look after her.'

Those were the magic words, it seemed. Suddenly the baker and his customers were all smiles. Colette was clearly well-loved in St Aubert.

'Welcome to our village!' the woman with the wax fruit on her hat said warmly. 'I'm Marie-Claire.'

Sally was lost among the customers as they eagerly introduced themselves. As they did, she wondered how often they saw new faces in St Aubert, aside from those belonging to Nazis, of course.

Unexpectedly, some of the women took items from their baskets – a small bread roll, a little tin of peas, a tiny pat of butter – and gave them to Sally. She tried to say no, but the ladies insisted.

'This is for Colette, and for you, for coming to visit St Aubert!' Marie-Claire told her.

When Sally left the shop, she felt as if she was floating on a cloud of kindness. The people in Bramble Heath didn't have much, and in St Aubert they had even less. But they all still shared what little they had, and gladly.

Outside in the square, the two old men were still playing chess, and another lady had come to join the woman at the table. A bell rang in rue de l'Ecole. The children would be going back to their lessons. It was just another day in St Aubert.

The peace was shattered by the roar of engines that heralded the arrival of a ragged procession of dark green transport trucks, with von Brandt's Mercedes at its head. As he climbed from the staff car, uniformed SS troops poured out of the canvas backs of the trucks until they seemed to fill the square.

Sally shrank back, trying to make herself inconspicuous. Some of the troops marched towards the streets and alleyways; others made for the shops and the café. Two bullies went over to the chess game, and grabbed the men by their collars and yanked them to their feet. Two others pointed their guns at the women at the table, while more headed for the bakery.

The women inside had fallen silent. One of the troops stood, his gun pointed at Sally, while the women were marched out of the bakery along with the baker, their hands raised.

It was so sudden, so unreal. Sally stared at the dark mouth of the gun, and all she knew was fear.

THIRTY-EIGHT

.

'People of St Aubert!' Von Brandt bellowed, raising his arm in a brief salute. Nobody in the square reciprocated and Sally sensed the unease and loathing that greeted the casual appearance of that Sieg Heil. 'I have searched for a valuable treasure and, by a process of elimination and intelligence, I now believe beyond a doubt that that treasure is somewhere around this region – and I intend to find it!'

He took in the silent faces, his eyes cold and dark. One by one, he studied the villagers in the square until his gaze passed over Sally. It felt as though the temperature had suddenly plummeted.

'I seek a British plane. If you know where it is and are conspiring to conceal it, the consequences will be severe!' He gave a vague gesture of his hand and the soldiers scattered this way and that, disappearing down streets and alleyways and knocking on doors. 'Today, we will conduct searches of your homes and businesses for any clue as to its whereabouts. If we find anything there will be no mercy!' Then von Brandt dropped his voice to a razor-edged growl: 'And if we find the airman who was piloting it, St Aubert will watch him hang.'

Sally shivered involuntarily with terror at von Brandt's ruthless cruelty. It was horrible, too horrible. But he and his men couldn't find Freddy, could they? He was safe under Colette's kitchen floor. They'd never find him. Never.

But what about the village? What about all these people who were innocently trying to live their lives? They never asked to have a secret plane get trapped near their village. Through a veil of guilt, Sally hoped beyond hope that the Nazis wouldn't find anything.

The soldier who had pointed his gun at Sally now glared at her and pointed across the square. 'You – home,' he said in French. He evidently didn't know the language very well.

Sally swallowed as she made her way across the square towards Colette's street, the soldier walking behind her. The unblinking muzzle of the gun was vivid in her mind and the threat of it nearly made her stumble. She was bringing the soldier into Colette's home.

She racked her thoughts trying to think of anything, anything at all, that would raise the Nazis' suspicions once the search of Colette's house began. But Colette was wily, and so were her other Resistance friends. They would know how to hide things so that no one could ever find them.

That was the one hope Sally had.

Sally, with her unwanted escort, reached Colette's house. She saw other SS troops already in the street, bashing the butts of their rifles against the doors. Surely Colette had heard the marching footsteps enter her road and had sent Freddy into his hiding place in seconds.

Sally unlocked the door, fumbling the key with her shaking fingers.

'Schnell!' the soldier barked, and something small and hard dug into Sally's back.

Oh, heck, that's his rifle!

Finally, she managed to unlock the door, and stepped inside

the house. She called, her voice trembling with fear, 'Aunt Colette?' Then she looked around at the soldier, who was following her into the house. 'My aunt's ill.' She dug about in her memory and found the word in German for *ill*, and said that too, hoping it might touch the man somehow.

But it didn't. His eyes narrowed, and he gestured with his rifle for her to keep moving.

'Aunt Colette?' Sally called. 'They're searching every house in the village.'

Freddy, for goodness' sake, I hope you're in your hiding place.

'Is that you, child?' Colette's voice was weak and frail, drifting in a pained croak from the secluded little parlour where Sally and Freddy had cuddled last night. 'You have a caller with you?'

'It's the— The Germans,' Sally replied. 'They've said something about... a plane? I don't quite understand. They're going to search, from house to house.'

The soldier had started his work. He moved around the front room, eyes darting, poking cushions and curtains with his rifle. Sally wondered if he knew what to look for, or if they'd just been told to look threatening to shake tongues loose in the village. He even peered inside the bonbon tin on the sideboard.

'A plane?' From the parlour came the sound of a walking stick and soft, shuffling feet. Colette emerged from the doorway as a bowed, helpless little old lady. She was wrapped in a shawl, her back stooped and her voice thick with the imaginary summer flu when she said, 'Good day to you, young man. Where would we put a plane in a cottage like this? I barely have room for my little niece.'

And she coughed, the sound harsh and rasping.

You should be on the stage.

The man frowned at her. Sally wondered if he had only

pretended to speak little French earlier. He seemed to understand what Colette had said.

'I'm searching for clues,' he said gruffly, and carried on, this time kneeling down in front of the sideboard and rummaging through it.

It was full of crockery, and Sally winced, hoping he wasn't going to smash it. But perhaps Colette's presence stopped him. Instead, he lifted out piles of plates, a soup tureen – he lifted the lid to check inside – and a sauce boat, and placed them on the floor, then stuck his head inside. Satisfied there wasn't anything in the cupboard, he started going through the drawers, pulling out tablecloths and napkins, shaking them out as if something incriminating might fall from the folds.

Behind his back, Colette narrowed her eyes at the soldier as he searched. She turned to look at Sally and, in her expression, Sally saw the sort of steel that sent a surge of strength through her own blood. There was no fear in the old lady's face, only determination.

'A plane...' she murmured, shaking her head gently. 'Josette, child, have you passed a good morning in the village?'

'I-I went to the baker's,' Sally told her, as if a Nazi wasn't really right in front of them, peering under the furniture. 'I met Marie-Claire and lots of your friends.'

The Nazi stood up, his cold gaze on Sally and Colette as if he didn't appreciate them chatting. 'Your kitchen,' he barked.

'This way, this way,' cooed Colette, making her slow, painstaking progress on the walking stick through to the kitchen. There was no sign of anything untoward in the little room, but Sally knew Freddy would be listening below, as filled with trepidation as she was. She came to rest on the very place where Freddy's trapdoor blended into the floorboards and turned to tell the soldier, 'But do not ask for a sandwich, young man, because the answer will be no!'

A muscle pulsed in the man's cheek as he stared at Colette.

He displayed an unfathomable amount of hate for an apparently frail, elderly woman. Then he resumed his search, looking through saucepans, cooking pots, the dresser, even in jars of currants and rice. Food inevitably ended up spilled across the table, and Sally knew that was out of spite, because the Nazis knew full well how little food ordinary French people had.

He even looked into the stove; and all the time his heavy boots clomped on the floor. Poor Freddy, he must've been terrified.

And all Sally could do was watch in terror, her heart hammering loudly in her chest, as the man poked around the kitchen. She let her gaze follow the soldier so that it wouldn't drop to Freddy's hiding place and give him away.

I wish I was back home in Bramble Heath. I wish Freddy was too.

He would find the trapdoor, she was sure of it. It seemed impossible that he wouldn't as he went this way and that, searching every nook and cranny. As he roughly shouldered Colette aside to take her place on the trapdoor, she held Sally's gaze, silently telling her all would be well.

And that was when there was a sharp rap at the door.

'I better answer that,' Sally said. It would be another soldier, she expected, to poke around with his rifle. Her limbs were frozen stiff with fear. It took all her effort to walk out of the kitchen, away from Freddy. She was terrified for herself, for Freddy, for everyone in the village.

She reached the front door and opened it.

'Mademoiselle Auclair!' Von Brandt's smile was like a razor blade. He stepped over the threshold and into the house, leaving Sally no choice but to retreat in the face of his approach. 'It occurs to me that you are a new face here in the village, just as I am. Therefore, I would be remiss if I did not—' With a frown, he peered over her shoulder towards the man searching the kitchen.

With that, he barked something in German to the soldier, who reacted by jumping to attention as though someone had run electricity through him. Sally's stomach flipped, her heart thudding so loudly she thought that everyone would be able to hear it.

He knows. He's telling the soldier to lift the floorboards.

A moment passed, then, with a sharp nod, the young soldier hurried from the kitchen to continue his search elsewhere. Sally could hardly believe her luck, let alone Freddy's. In his haste to demonstrate how his men snapped to his command, von Brandt had chased him from the very place where he might have found what he sought.

'Pardon me,' the SS officer said, once again wearing that pantomime of a smile. 'Mademoiselle, I'm afraid I must ask to examine your papers. You have arrived at a most unfortunate time.'

'Of-of course,' Sally replied. Trying to still her trembling hand, she reached into her pocket to retrieve the papers that had been so carefully made for her to pass muster in occupied France. She held them out to von Brandt. He took them in a leather-gloved hand and, as Sally tried not to look as frightened as she felt, scrutinised them.

Colette hobbled past, humming a gentle tune as she went, her stick tapping its way along the hall. As she passed Sally and von Brandt she told him in a gentle tone, 'Do not frighten my little niece, sir, she is here to help this sorry old lady.'

Von Brandt flicked his gaze up and Sally remembered how he had joked about shooting Colette the previous evening, as though it would be an act of mercy.

'Madame.' He clicked his heels together and greeted her with a chivalrous, sharp nod. 'I believe you will be robust again soon enough. A mere summer affliction!'

'Yes you *are*,' Colette said, her eyes twinkling with mischief. 'Forgive an old lady her joke, sir.' Then she hobbled off after the soldier, leaving von Brandt to hold out the papers to Sally.

'She is a spirited lady indeed,' he observed, watching Colette until she ascended the stairs out of sight. Then he nodded towards Sally. 'La Roche-sur-Yon? I was briefly stationed there myself last summer. My sweetheart's home!'

Fear lanced through Sally. He could ask her something about the town, anything, and she'd have to know the answer to it. But, what if she didn't?

But maybe he was calling her bluff? Maybe he was just claiming that he knew her hometown because he wanted to frighten her.

His sweetheart... Sally tried to imagine the cold-hearted monster in front of her being sweet with anyone, and the thought made her skin crawl. And how could a French girl go with a man like *him*...?

'It's a lovely town,' Sally replied, smiling nervously. 'Don't you think so?'

'Very picturesque,' said von Brandt. He rolled his eyes. 'But Adele has eyes only for Paris. Alas, it is an expensive city, but La Roche-sur-Yon holds few charms for Adele against your beautiful capital. Mademoiselle, you and I must speak of our memories of La Roche-sur-Yon again, but today I have business to conduct.'

There was one of those sharp bows again before he said, 'Good day, mademoiselle.'

Sally sincerely hoped she'd get the plane airborne and back to England before being forced to have a tête-à-tête with von Brandt about Josette's hometown. But the thought that she might not be able to escape the conversation alarmed her more than she could say.

'G-good day,' she said, with a small, stiff curtsey. She was rigid with fear. She hated herself for curtseying, as if she was showing this demon respect, but she couldn't antagonise him.

He opened the door and stepped out onto the path just as Sally saw Leah on her way through the gate. At the sight of von Brandt she froze, then called, 'I wanted to see that Colette wasn't upset, Josette.'

She ignored von Brandt's nod of greeting and stood back until he was on the street and she could hurry up the path.

The soldier who had been searching the house pushed his way past them, shaking his head at von Brandt. The two men began to walk away.

He didn't find anything. Thank goodness.

But Sally's fear hadn't left her.

'Thanks for coming, Leah. It's very kind of you,' she said. 'Threw tablecloths all over the place, and left flour all over the kitchen table, but... Colette was quite shaken.'

That wasn't *exactly* the word, seeing as Colette had been determined to make the Nazis searching her house feel as uncomfortable as she could.

As Sally and Leah went back into the safety of the house and closed the door, Leah told her, 'Our shepherd thinks the sheep should stay in his pen until night falls.'

Poor Freddy, stuck in that tiny little living space until sundown.

'It's for the best.' Sally sighed. Horrible though it was for him down there. And it wouldn't be for much longer, surely. 'I hope they won't be back. They didn't find a thing. And you're... you're all right, aren't you, Leah?'

She laid her hand gently on the other woman's arm. The risk Resistance members like Leah took, day after day, astonished her. How on earth did they keep their nerve?

Leah nodded. 'I was worried for you when Armand told me what had happened last night.' She gave Sally a gentle smile. 'You have friends here, Josette. We will win this war.'

THIRTY-NINE

The next day, Sally and Freddy woke up together in her bed. She had been so frightened by the search – for herself, and for him – but she'd eventually fallen asleep, her head against his chest.

'Good morning,' she whispered. She was surprised he hadn't gone down to his hiding place in the night. 'You decided to stay up here last night, then.'

'I didn't decide,' he murmured sleepily, snuggling closer. 'I got very comfy with my girl and nodded off. A day stuck in that little cell of mine feels like a year now I know you're around.'

Sally ruffled his hair, smiling. 'It won't be long now.' But her smile faded from her face as she recalled what had happened yesterday. She shook her head, still in disbelief. 'He stood right on top of the trapdoor...'

'Oh, believe me, I heard him!' And because Freddy was Freddy, he laughed. 'Lucky for us they're bloody idiots. Searching every thimble as though they're going to find a Spitfire in there!' He lifted Sally's hand and kissed it. 'We've got to get out of here soon, Sal, for everybody's sakes.'

Sally nodded. 'I know. Then, if they *do* spot the trapdoor, all they'll find down there will be potatoes.' She stroked Freddy's cheek with her fingertip. 'They're so brave. If the Germans had invaded England, I don't know if I would've been anywhere near as brave as them.'

'You're here,' he reminded her. 'You're one of the bravest people I've ever met.' With a sigh, he admitted, 'I'm angry at myself for bringing her down. I'd dodged Luftwaffe all the way from Germany but that bloody lightning did for me. They must've known I'd come down... the patrols would've been watching for me after the merry dance I'd led them.'

Sally gently squeezed Freddy's hand. His words warmed her, even if she didn't feel very brave at all. 'It wasn't your fault. Not even *you're* fast enough to escape lightning. The only person to blame for all of this is marching about in a uniform in Berlin – not you.'

'At least I wasn't over the Channel when I got zapped.' Freddy gave a shrug, then kissed Sally's cheek and settled his head against her shoulder. 'Everyone's taking all these risks and I'm stuck in a spud cellar. I feel like I should do something, but they won't let me out of the house.'

Sally could understand Freddy's frustrations; he was used to being impetuous and brave, to racing out to save the day whenever the siren sounded, but all he could do now was sit it out. It made sense though; there was no point putting all of them at risk after they'd come so far.

'You're taking a risk every second you're here,' she reminded him. 'And whatever reason you had for flying here – well, that was a risk too. We're nearly there. We're going home, Freddy. We're going back to Bramble Heath.'

She smiled at him. She really wanted to believe that they would make it, but von Brandt had cast an impregnable shadow. She suppressed a shudder at the thought of that man. Home seemed a very long way away now. But at least she had this – some snatched time, just for herself and Freddy.

Suddenly, the air was split by a metallic shriek, and a voice outside announced, 'Residents of St Aubert – assemble in the square immediately!' Then the order was repeated, and repeated, the loudhailer making the voice sound like a machine.

'What on earth?' Sally gasped, her fear erasing her contentment. An order like that could only mean something serious had happened – or was about to. 'What can they want? Oh, Freds, I'm so sorry, you better hide again. This *can't* be good. I hope to heaven they haven't found the plane.'

Freddy was out of the bed a moment before Colette knocked urgently on the door and said, 'Children, come along! Sheep should be safely away!'

Sally hurried out of bed and grabbed Freddy's arm. Her heart hammering against her ribs, she kissed him on the lips, then said, 'Freddy, run!'

The metallic voice was still giving its order, and Sally heard someone banging on the front door. *No, no, we can't get caught now!*

Freddy dashed a kiss to Colette's cheek as he ran for it, and whispered, 'Sorry, Lettie!'

And the banging at the front door was repeated.

'A minute, monsieur, a minute!' called Colette in her shaky voice. 'My niece is helping me dress. What kind of person are you to harass a poor, helpless old woman?'

Sally gave Colette a wink as she threw on her own clothes, the ones she'd worn yesterday. Colette's nerves of steel were a marvel, playing her part to buy Freddy much-needed seconds.

'I'm ready now,' Sally said, once she was dressed. 'Have you got everything you need, Colette?' She was genuinely concerned. Colette played up to the idea that she was a frail old lady, but still, Sally did worry about her host. And she couldn't help the feeling of dread snaking through her stomach.

Colette took Sally's hands in hers. 'Courage, little one,' she told her. Then, with a kiss on her cheek, she said, 'Let's get on.'

Together, they descended the staircase. Whoever had been hammering on their door had moved on now and Sally could hear that furious bark being repeated up and down the street as the metallic voice went on issuing commands. Colette wrapped herself in her shawl, took up her stick and let Sally take her arm as they walked out into the morning sunshine.

The mist was beginning to dissolve in the summer air, but there was nothing beautiful about this morning. From every house, there was a stream of people heading to the square; old, young, nobody had been spared. Some glanced anxiously at their neighbours, as if they could tell them what was going on. Others stared blankly ahead, their emotions kept under stony wraps.

And up and down the street, the soldiers pounded on doors with their fists and their rifle butts.

'I don't like this one bit,' Sally whispered urgently to Colette.

A mother rocked her crying baby in her arms and a soldier shoved her, yelling, 'Silence!', which only made the baby cry harder.

An elderly couple, arm-in-arm, stumbled on the cobbles, which earned them a bellowed, 'Faster!' from one of the SS bullies in uniform.

Colette seemed to know everybody and, despite the fear in the air, her neighbours still found the time to ask how she was feeling and to greet her visiting niece. Sally wondered at Colette's subterfuge, and her neighbours' worry at their robust woman having become a frail patient, struck down by the summer flu.

'I shall soon be right as rain,' she assured those who asked. 'Not too long now.'

'Thank goodness,' Colette's friends replied.

Sally recognised one of them from the bakery yesterday, one of the women who had welcomed Sally so warmly to their village. They didn't deserve to be treated like this by the Nazis. Nobody did.

But what of Freddy? This was the first time he'd been alone in the house and, with the village swarming with Nazis, what if one of them decided to go in? What if this was all a cover?

It wasn't something Sally could let herself imagine.

They reached the square, where the Butcher of Breslau was waiting, standing ramrod straight in his shiny Mercedes-Benz. Parked not far off was a green transport truck. Von Brandt's soldiers shoved the villagers into position in a crowd in front of him, under his unrelenting stare. Sally was amazed at the number of people forced into the square. She recognised some faces among the crowd – the two chess players, and Leah. Even the priest had been taken from the presbytery, and he stood in the crowd among his parishioners, just as frightened as everyone else.

No one spoke. That was the worst thing about it. The silence, apart from the hurried, anxious footsteps, the occasional cry of a baby, and the barked orders from the soldiers.

'Faster! Silence! Faster!'

Heads turned one by one, and Sally followed the direction of the villagers' gazes. They were all looking towards rue de l'Ecole, and, with a sense of horror she had never felt before, she saw a line of ashen-faced children and their teachers being marched by shouting, shoving soldiers from the school into the square. Sally was appalled, and glanced away, her attention turned to the crowd. It was obvious who the children's parents were; fear of a kind Sally had never seen before had taken possession of them. They stiffened, their eyes widened in terror in their blanched faces. They held their hands over their mouths, as if they were desperate to cry out their children's names but didn't dare.

'Not the children, please,' the priest pleaded, but a soldier knocked him in the chest with his rifle butt and he winced in pain.

And as Sally watched, shocked, she saw Armand among the children as they were shoved into a group in front of von Brandt. The little boy who had turned the village into his hiding place – not even *he* could escape.

Then everything was still, the voice on the loudhailer silent. Even the baby had stopped crying. It was odd, disorientating, like being trapped in an unmoving photograph.

A soldier marched up to von Brandt and saluted. He announced something in German, which Sally almost understood. It sounded as if he was saying that everyone had been brought to the square.

Everyone, except Freddy.

Von Brandt gave a stern nod, then turned his dark gaze on the villagers.

'Several weeks ago, a British plane came down somewhere in this region,' he told the assembled crowd. 'I have been searching for that plane and its pilot. I have been searching for those who would shelter them.' Nobody moved. There wasn't so much as a flicker. 'Yesterday, I searched your homes and village and found evidence that one of you has aided the escape of that pilot and the removal of that plane!'

A jolt ran through the crowd. They were horrified, but didn't risk making a sound. They glanced from one to another, and Sally gripped Colette's hand, terrified.

But then Sally's reason began to take hold over her fear. What had von Brandt just said? *The removal of that plane?* Did he think it was no longer here? Or had something been missed in translation? What on earth had he discovered?

Sally glanced at Colette, wishing she knew what the brave lady was thinking.

Colette looked as bewildered as everyone else, but, where her arm was wrapped round Sally's, Sally felt the older woman grow tense. Von Brandt looked to the soldier who had saluted him and gave a sharp nod.

'Behold the traitor!' the obergruppenführer announced.

The soldier marched to the transport van and, with two others, pulled down the panel at the back and drew back the canvas. Sally's stomach turned over and over as two of the men went into the transport van and dragged someone out.

He was wearing the ordinary clothes of someone who worked on the land, his torn shirt spattered with blood. His hands were secured behind him, and he struggled to stand on the cobbles. His blackened eyes were swollen shut, his lip split, and his face smeared with dried blood.

It took a moment for Sally to recognise him, but then she realised who it was.

Henri.

She wasn't the only person to recognise him. The crowd stirred, gasped, whispered his name.

'It's Henri....'

The man who had so many tales to tell. The man who'd taken a bullet at Verdun. The man who had fought one war in uniform, and another underground. The man who had helped to hide the plane, and to get Sally and Wyngate into France.

And he'd been caught.

With what looked like a great deal of pain, Henri lifted his head. He was dignified, despite his injuries.

'*Vive la France!*' he croaked. Then louder, finding strength from somewhere, he shouted it. '*Vive la France!*'

And it echoed around the square.

Von Brandt settled his gaze on Henri, his face twisted with revulsion and hatred. He said in a cold, low voice, 'Ein Volk, ein Reich, ein Führer!' Then, in what seemed to be slow motion even though it happened in a split second, he drew his pistol and shot Henri between the eyes.

For a moment Henri was still on his feet, then he crumpled

to the ground. A ribbon of red blood ran from the bullet wound, and his eyes were still open. Glassy, unseeing.

The man was dead.

Sally had to look away. There were gasps and moans of terror in the crowd. The children cried. Sally couldn't believe what she'd just seen. What if this happened in Bramble Heath? If one of the farmers was dragged from his farm and executed in front of everyone in the village? It was too dreadful to contemplate.

The priest rushed forward, trying to reach Henri's body. 'I must give him the last rites,' he insisted, but the soldiers held him back.

Sally clung to Colette. She couldn't imagine what her friend was going through right now, seeing her friend murdered in the street, right in front of her. The old lady gave a low gasp and clapped her hand to her mouth, but it was Armand who broke from the crowd, dodging around the soldiers as he flew towards von Brandt's car.

'You bastard!' the child howled. As he did, von Brandt turned to face him, his face placid as he lifted his revolver again and pointed it not at Armand, but at Leah.

'Henri—' cried Armand.

'Shall I, little boy?' asked von Brandt, his finger tightening on the trigger. Leah appeared frozen to the spot in terror as he shifted the gun to point at Armand. 'The mother, or the child?'

Sally forced herself not to react. She couldn't risk intervening, even though these were her friends. She could do nothing.

'Then it must be me, the mother.' Leah lifted her chin defiantly. 'Not my boy. Please, sir, he's upset—'

'I have sons of my own,' von Brandt told her. 'If they behaved like this, I would whip them. Rats like you are not fit to be mothers.'

This butcher had children of his own, and he'd think nothing of whipping them? Some father he was. And not much of a husband, with his sweetheart. Not much of a human being either.

But Armand shook his head and spat on the gleaming Mercedes. And when he did, the man who had just shot a hero of the Resistance in cold blood finally betrayed his anger.

'You filthy peasant!' Von Brandt snarled at Armand. As he did, a farm labourer rushed across the square and scooped up the boy as though he were weightless. He bowed his head to the Nazi, muttering apologies as he did.

'He doesn't know his sense, sir,' said the labourer desperately, rubbing the car clean with his tattered sleeve. 'He's just a daft lad. His mother won't let him get out of hand again.'

Leah nodded, her eyes cast down. 'I won't, sir, I promise.'

Sally was rigid with fear. She could hardly breathe. Von Brandt was a monster. What would he do? Would he really spare the boy and his mother? She knew very well how happily he fired that gun.

But he can't shoot them. He can't.

Two of the soldiers headed towards the labourer with slow menace, cruel smiles contorting their lips.

Von Brandt cast his gaze across the square again, then barked a command in German. At his word, the soldiers ceased their advance and headed back towards the transport. He spat another command at his driver and resumed his seat in the car.

'Clean this filth off the street! Heil Hitler!' was von Brandt's parting shot for the village as his staff car purred into life and drove slowly out of the square, followed by the truck. Armand was sobbing desperately in the labourer's arms, and as Leah took him in her embrace he clung to her. He was helpless with grief, and all around the square the people of St Aubert wept.

Doctor Vautier went forward with the priest, the first people to break from the shocked crowd. Only then did the labourer who had scooped Armand out of von Brandt's sights turn from the little boy and glance towards Sally and Colette.

Sally had started to cry. She wiped away her tears, and looked back at the labourer.

She blinked. She couldn't believe it.

The labourer who had rescued Armand was none other than Wyngate.

'What about his farm?' Armand was asking. 'What about all his stuff? And the chickens? Why did he have to do that to Henri?'

'Don't worry about the chicks. We'll take them,' Leah whispered to her son, who was shuddering with sobs. It seemed like such a small thing, but at least it was a crumb of kindness they could offer him. 'I bet they'd love to live in our garden.'

Wyngate patted the boy's shoulder. 'We'll go over in a bit and gather them,' he promised Armand. 'Henri wouldn't trust anybody else to care for his chickens, Armand.'

Around them, the people of St Aubert were beginning to head back to their homes. The teachers let the parents lead their children away. There would be no more school for them today. What a dreadful thing to force everyone in the village to see – a murder. A public execution. And in front of the children.

Sally looked up at Wyngate. How hard it must've been for him, pretending to be respectful *and* scared of von Brandt, when Sally knew he was nothing of the sort. 'Thank goodness you're here. That man... that monster, von Brandt...'

'It's a bad business, miss,' Wyngate told her, playing his part perfectly. 'But we'll see the little lad right. We'll see to the chickens and whatever else we've got to sort. Sheep... tractors... farmers have all sorts of things going on.'

Was that a clue? Was the time near?

'I understand,' Sally replied. But she knew it wasn't safe to say anything else, especially in such a public place. She would need to be patient, but surely it couldn't be long now?

She leaned down to speak to Armand. 'You're a very brave boy. I'm sure Henri would've been proud of you today. One day

– soon, I hope – von Brandt will be stopped. But you *must* be careful. I know you want to stop him, but it's better to let a grownup do it.' She smiled gently at Leah. 'I'm so sorry,' she whispered.

'He was a good man,' Leah whispered. And he had laid down his life to send von Brandt on a wild goose chase. 'Oh, Josette, what sort of people have come to our village?'

'Evil, nasty brutes,' Sally replied. She put her arm round Leah. 'Henri didn't deserve to die like that. He made the ulti-mate sacrifice, and... I can't let him down, Leah. I can't let any of you down.'

FORTY

Henri's death had cast a shadow. Even hours later, Sally still couldn't believe it'd happened – still less that she had *seen* it take place. She shivered as the images came back to her. That brave man, murdered by a monster.

And the people who'd known Henri far longer than Sally had were mourning him. Sally hadn't been surprised to hear Armand's tap at Colette's kitchen door. The little boy wanted to see Freddy, another hero he could look up to.

'How's your mum?' she gently asked Armand once he was safely inside Colette's home.

He gave a little shrug and said, 'Margot's come round to sit with her. She says she's fine, but...' Armand shook his head. 'She's in charge now, you know.' He bit his lip and admitted, 'I wish she wasn't.'

'Adolf doesn't stand a chance if Leah's the boss.' Freddy scrubbed Armand's hair. 'You all right, chum?'

Sally held Armand's hand. She was sure under normal circumstances he would've thought himself too grown up for that, but she knew he needed comfort. He'd experienced something that no child ever should.

'Your mum's a very clever lady,' Sally reminded Armand, thinking of Leah's plan for hiding the plane within its maze of crates. 'She'll be fine. You just need to look out for her. But you already do, don't you?'

Armand nodded. 'Until Dad comes home,' he replied. Then he turned to Freddy. 'I don't want to never see you again. But you'll be going soon, won't you?'

And Freddy would miss the people here too, Sally was sure. They were brave and selfless and they'd become his guardian angels, no matter what the cost to themselves. But in Armand he'd found another little brother, just like Peter back home, who refused to mourn for him.

'Come and sit down,' Freddy told him, nodding to the kitchen table. Armand towed Sally with him by her hand as he settled, watching Freddy intently, just like Peter had watched Sally when she'd visited the Carr house every morning after Freddy was lost. 'You're not going to never see me again, pal. When this is all done and your dad gets home, all three of you are coming over to England and me and Sally will take you up in a few of our stunt planes. You've got to start your flying lessons one day, after all.'

For the first time since the awful gathering in the square that morning, Sally smiled as she listened to Freddy's careful French pronunciation. She caught Freddy's gaze, and her heart filled with love. He was such a kind, thoughtful man.

'Won't that be fun?' she said to Armand. 'And you'll meet Freddy's brother Peter, too. I know for a fact that you'll be wonderful friends.'

'And Wilbur.' Freddy smiled. He reached into his pocket and took out a dog-eared photograph that showed Wilbur sitting in his Harrods basket in the Tiger Moth, a stray puppy on his way to live like a king. Sally remembered snapping that picture, in what seemed like another lifetime. 'Wilbur's the sort of dog who brings good luck. So this photo is going to bring you and your family good luck too.'

Armand took the photograph and blinked down at it through tear-filled eyes. Then he threw his arms round Freddy's neck and hugged him.

Sally bit her lip, trying not to cry too. Armand needed luck.

'Before you know it, you'll be coming to visit us,' Sally promised Armand, hoping against hope that she would see Bramble Heath again. 'As soon as the world's gone back to normal, you'll see us again.'

'Now get off home before curfew,' Freddy said kindly, glancing towards the clock on the wall. 'And say goodnight to those chickens you've adopted!'

Armand looked a little happier as he shot Freddy and Sally a salute and told them, 'I will.' He looked down at the photograph again, then slid it into his pocket. 'Night-night, Freds. Night, Josette.'

With Armand gone, Sally and Freddy sat together, talking about the future. A future that was by no means certain; but they couldn't allow themselves at that moment to let any dark thoughts in. The things they would do together, the places they'd show Armand when he came to England. Soon, if luck was on their side, Freddy would be back in England, and would once again feel the sunlight and the wind against his face. They'd be free. One day, Sally hoped against hope, the whole world would be free. Only who knew how long they'd have to wait?

In the silence of the village streets, the sound of a purring engine outside was loud as a siren. It would've gone unnoticed but for the eerie emptiness that seemed to have deepened after Henri's death, and Freddy jerked his head up, suddenly alert.

And a few moments later, there was a sharp rap on the front door. Sally's stomach flipped because she already had an idea who this would be.

'You've got to hide,' she whispered urgently to Freddy. 'Quickly. It's *him*. It's that *monster*. You've got to hide.'

'One moment,' called Colette as usual, from where she was settled in the sitting room with her book. 'When you are old as I am, sir, you will take your time greeting callers too!'

Sally lifted the trapdoor for Freddy, her arms straining with the weight of it. The scent of earth reached her, the dark little cell opening towards them like a mouth. Freddy dashed a kiss to her lips and climbed down, drawing the trapdoor closed behind him.

Sally could still feel the warmth of his kiss against his lips, like a promise waiting to be fulfilled. But what could be fulfilled if von Brandt found Freddy? She saw again Henri's staring, glassy eyes as he lay on the ground in the square. Von Brandt didn't take prisoners – he only killed them.

Sally got to work, sitting at the table industriously shelling a bowl of peas from Colette's garden, as if there was nothing out of the ordinary here for von Brandt to discover. But her heart was pounding so loudly in her ears that she could barely hear anything else.

She could hear Colette's frail voice at the door and von Brandt's smooth responses, although she couldn't quite make them out. After a minute or so though the voice grew louder, accompanied by footsteps as the old woman and her unwanted visitor made their way towards the kitchen.

'A caller for you,' Colette told Sally. 'I have told him, we are after curfew. It isn't right.'

Sally got up from her chair. At the sight of von Brandt, she felt hot and sick all at once, as if she was coming down with a fever. Why was he here? 'It's not right at all. *We're* following the curfew rules. What do you want with us, von Brandt?'

'A social call.' He tucked his cap beneath his arm and told them, 'You will please sit, ladies.'

'We can't offer you a coffee,' Sally said. 'No one has any.'

Barging into Colette's house and telling us what to do. The nerve of this man. And what tosh about a social call.

But she sat back down again anyway. Maybe it was best to let von Brandt think he was getting his way. Perhaps he wanted that conversation, reminiscing about La Roche-sur-Yon? Sally tried to bring to mind her memories of the town in readiness. She hoped that was all it was, anyway. But she didn't trust von Brandt one bit.

Colette sat too, her walking stick held across her knees. Von Brandt stood in front of the concealed trapdoor and regarded them, a quirk of mirth in his expression when he asked, 'Did you enjoy our show today?'

'Oh!' Colette clutched her hand to her breast, fingers finding the cross she wore. 'You must not say such terrible things! I have never seen such a sight in all my years...'

'And you, miss?' he asked Sally.

Sally's skin crawled. She wanted to scratch and scratch, as if it would rid her of von Brandt's presence. 'It's not the sort of show I enjoy,' she replied, choosing her words carefully.

'What sort of show *do* you enjoy?' Von Brandt enquired placidly, his eyes unblinking. And there on his hip, the pistol that had shot Henri.

'The circus, and magic shows,' Sally replied without pausing. Because the buff folder that held everything about Josette's life had mentioned them. 'Of course, I haven't seen either in a long time...'

Although a magic show had taken place moments before. A grown man had vanished into thin air. And Sally made sure her gaze didn't wander towards the trapdoor and spoil the trick.

'Do you know what kind of show I enjoyed before the war?' Von Brandt asked brightly. 'Airshows. Oh, I was never one to fly, but I might perhaps embarrass myself by admitting that I would go from show to show with my notebook, marking down the registrations of each plane I saw.'

A cold finger of fear ran the length of Sally's spine, but she kept her expression neutral. She wouldn't let it show. She was Josette. Not Sally, she was Josette. And Josette had never been to an airshow in her life.

Sally shrugged. 'You must forgive me, I don't know anything about airshows. I suppose you must miss them?'

'Oh, on the contrary. With our glorious Luftwaffe, I am honoured to see the finest planes in the sky. One day, I hope, my own son will fly for the Führer. It is a sorry thing to leave one's wife and family in Germany, but a French sweetheart will always occupy the mind, eh?' The glorious Luftwaffe that the allies had sent running, fleeing back to Germany as the Battle of Britain had turned against them. And von Brandt would offer up his own child like a lamb to the slaughter. Meanwhile, he was romancing a woman behind his wife's back. What there nothing he wouldn't stoop to? 'But some of the pilots, one could not see. Because they would not come to Germany. Because they thought themselves too good to perform for the volk.'

More like we didn't want to look like we were in league with the fascists. Sally quickly buried the thought. She was Josette. She had to be Josette.

'That's a shame,' she replied as casually as she could. 'Perhaps it was a long way for them to fly?'

'An awfully long way,' Colette twittered, stifling a cough. 'Why, I—'

'In the end, to complete my collection, I had no choice but to travel to Paris with my boy, just to catch the last few planes at the airshow there.' Von Brandt reached into his tunic and took out a tiny notebook. He flicked through it with his gloved hand, through the pages filled with row after row of immaculate, minuscule dates and aircraft descriptors.

'Here, you see.' Very deliberately, von Brandt put the book on the table and tapped one finger on a page. 'I had wanted to see these two pilots in particular.'

Sally blinked, pretending to be confused, feigning polite interest in something that Josette would have had no clue about.

But Sally knew. Her heart raced. She felt too hot, too sick. She swallowed as she read what he'd written down.

Toussaint, Sally and *Carr, Freddy.*

And the numbers of their planes.

'What is it?' Colette asked, squinting at the book. 'Josette, child, fetch my spectac—'

'Fetch nothing, Miss Toussaint.' Von Brandt snatched the book back and closed it. 'I knew I had seen your face somewhere... I thought perhaps when I was stationed in your hometown. Then this evening, as I came out to my car, I watched one of our squadrons soar through the clouds, carrying the Führer's message to the people of your country. And as I watched, I remembered. You almost had me, Miss Toussaint, but the game is at an end.'

No, no, this can't be happening. It can't.

As frantic as Sally felt inside, she concealed it with a shrug. 'Bof. I don't know what you mean. I don't know any Miss Toussaint. Perhaps I happen to look a little like her? I have never met her.'

'You will accompany me to the chateau for questioning.' He jerked his head towards the door, the ill-fitting mask of affability cast aside. 'If you are innocent, you have nothing to fear.' Von Brandt smiled his razor-blade smile. 'But you are *not* innocent. When word reaches Berlin, you will have doomed this village.'

So you haven't told Berlin yet... there's still a chance.

Sally shook her head. If he took her to the chateau, how would she ever escape it? 'You've seen my papers, you know I'm not Miss Toussaint. I don't need to go to the chateau. I won't!'

'You will have seen her in your sweetheart's town,' Colette

assured him, rising to her feet. 'She is a good girl, sir, please do not—'

Von Brandt's hand lashed out and connected hard with Colette's jaw, sending her sprawling back towards the table. His attack shocked and disgusted Sally as much as if she'd seen her own grandmother struck.

Yet the supposedly frail old lady moved just as fast as her persecutor and, as Sally caught the suggestion of movement from behind von Brandt, Colette lifted her walking stick above her head and swung it like a poleaxe against the Nazi's temple. He staggered backwards towards the trapdoor that Freddy was lifting, letting out a cry of alarm when Freddy seized his ankle. The German's flailing fingers tried in vain to reach his gun, then Freddy pulled him down into the dark cell that had been his sanctuary.

Von Brandt gave one more cry as he fell, a shriek of terror that ended abruptly when the back of his skull slammed into the floorboards.

The loud *crack* seemed to reverberate around the room.

Everything had happened so fast, and suddenly there was silence. Sally dared herself to peer over the edge, into Freddy's hiding place. There at the bottom, sprawled at an unnatural angle like a puppet with severed strings, lay von Brandt.

And his unblinking, glassy eyes told Sally everything she needed to know.

'Good lord, he's dead...' she whispered in shock. But the man had been a monster.

And now, he couldn't hurt anyone else ever again.

FORTY-ONE

'Go to Leah's house,' Colette instructed urgently. She put her arm round Sally's shoulders and embraced her as Freddy climbed up into the kitchen, his attention still fixed on the body of the man that was sprawled on the floor of his hiding place. 'Tell her we need Guy. He will know what to do.'

Freddy nodded, as though the instructions were for him. His French had improved enough to understand that Sally was being sent off.

'I'm coming too!' he told them, but Colette shook her head, cool and calm as ever despite the bruise that was already colouring her jaw.

'Go,' she told Sally. 'And go carefully.' Then she slammed the trapdoor down, sealing von Brandt in his temporary tomb.

Von Brandt's chauffeur was outside. How long did they have before he became curious and knocked on Colette's door?

Not long, Sally was certain.

She kissed Freddy's cheek, and nodded to Colette. 'I'll be careful,' she promised.

She was sure she knew the way through the alleyways as, on Armand's visits, he had told Sally how he knew his way around, the features he looked for. All she had to do to find Leah's home was to turn right and carry on until she saw the empty house with the broken red shutter, and look for the house with three chimneys.

She opened the back door and stepped outside, then climbed over the fence, as quietly as a cat. As she crept away down the alley, she pulled her cardigan around her. It had started to rain.

Sally tried to keep in the shadows. Von Brandt might be dead, but there were still the other Nazis in the village. And she couldn't risk being spotted. Von Brandt's death might cause horrendous consequences for the people of St Aubert. As she passed the end of an alleyway that led up to the street, she heard voices chatting in German. The soldiers looked bored.

You really have no idea what's just happened, do you?

Sally silently passed out of their sight and kept going, the rain falling more heavily all the time. It rattled in the gutters, and splashed off the leaves, but still she forged on.

Finally, she spotted a broken shutter. And, in the weak moonlight, she was sure it was red. It hung drunkenly from its hinge, on a house that didn't look lived in. A fence ran along from it, where a garden was blooming, and the scent of rosemary filled the air. At the other end of the garden was a house. And Sally looked up at the roof.

Three chimneys, Armand had said, and that was exactly what she saw.

She slipped over the fence and crept up the garden path, past vegetable plots, and chickens, who clucked in their coops as she went by – the new residents brought to Leah's garden from poor Henri's farm.

Sally reached the back door of the house and, hoping she really had found the right place, emulated Armand's knock and waited.

She heard footsteps approach, then Leah asked, 'Who's there?'

'Josette,' Sally whispered, standing close to the door to try to get out of the rain. 'I need to speak to you, urgently.'

A key turned and Leah opened the door. 'Come in out of the rain,' she said. Her brow furrowed as she took in Sally's ashen appearance. 'What has happened?'

Sally went inside. She was shaking; maybe it was just from getting caught in the rain, but— No, she knew why.

There in the kitchen were Wyngate and Armand. They would all hear this together. Wyngate looked like a coiled spring, as if he had known trouble would come.

'Von Brandt's dead,' Sally said. The words didn't feel real on her tongue, so she said it again. 'He's *dead*.'

Armand's mouth fell open, but Wyngate rose from his chair, immediately alert.

'What happened?' he asked.

'He recognised me,' Sally admitted. She felt as if she was to blame. She shook her head, and raindrops spattered against the floorboards.

'He's – he *was* – a plane enthusiast. Freddy and I wouldn't fly in Germany once Hitler took over, and there were others who wouldn't either. So, he went to an airshow in Paris to watch us. He was going to take me to the chateau... Colette tried to intervene. He hit her, she hit him back with her stick, and Freddy – well, he just burst out of his hiding place and yanked von Brandt off his feet. Von Brandt cracked his head as he went down, and it killed him. Right there. He— He's dead. He's under Colette's kitchen floor right now. But... oh, heavens, what on earth are we going to do?'

Armand's eyes were wide as he murmured, 'Well done, Freds.'

Leah handed Sally a towel and patted her arm gently. 'You must have been terrified,' she said. 'Guy, what do we do?'

'He was alone?' asked Wyngate. His gaze was fixed on Sally and she got the impression that he was likely already running through every possible avenue in his mind.

Sally tried to dry herself off and patted her curls. It was such a normal thing to do, and she could feel herself becoming more grounded by the second, her fear receding. Wyngate would know what to do, surely?

'No, he wasn't alone,' she replied. 'His chauffeur was with him. He's parked right outside. I came as fast as I could. He's going to be wondering where his boss has got to soon. If he hasn't already...'

Wyngate nodded slowly, thoughtful again. He looked to Armand, then flicked his gaze back to Sally. 'He didn't bring anyone with him to make the arrest?'

'No. He pretended, to start with, it was a social call,' Sally replied with a shiver of distaste. Then she remembered something that von Brandt had, in his arrogance, let slip. 'He hasn't told Berlin yet. No one knows. I doubt he's even told his chauffeur, you know, because he only realised – he only remembered me – when he was getting into his car just now. No one knows!'

Wyngate nodded again and for a moment the kitchen was silent. Even Armand, usually so full of life, watched Wyngate as they waited for his decision.

'Leah, get on the radio and get the message out to the network. The tractor moves tonight.' Then Wyngate turned to Armand and told him, 'Gather everyone you can, Armand. We need to get her ready.'

The next instruction was for Sally, who was still reeling from the realisation that she would be leaving France before the night was over. 'You and I have work to do.'

Sally went back out into the rain. She didn't notice it now, though. All she could think of was her flight back to England that very night. But there was no other option – with von Brandt dead, everything had changed.

She felt like Armand now, as she led Wyngate through the alleyways back to Colette's, although she was sure he had taken this route before. Unseen, they arrived back at Colette's, climbing over the fence and heading to the kitchen door.

Sally knocked using Armand's rhythm. Colette was at the door in a moment, ushering them inside to where Freddy was waiting, pacing the floor.

'We go tonight,' Wyngate said in English, not waiting for pleasantries. 'Flight Lieutenant, First Officer, gather what you need, then head to the barn. We'll need everybody we've got to shift the tractor, sling or not.' His next words were in French, addressed to Colette and Sally. 'I'll deal with the rubbish in the cellar.' He glanced towards the front door. 'And I'll clean up the street.'

And without another word, he yanked up the trapdoor and descended into von Brandt's tomb.

Colette turned to Sally and Freddy, her eyes glistening with tears. 'God bless you both,' she said tenderly, before repeating the sentiment in halting, careful English. 'We shall drink to tonight in peacetime.'

Freddy stepped forward and took Colette's hand. He lifted it to his lips and kissed it, courtly and respectful.

'I'm hoping Sal will translate for me if I make mistakes,' he said in his careful, halting French as he glanced towards his fiancée. 'Colette, you've kept me alive. You're one of the bravest, kindest people I've ever been lucky enough to know. I'm never, ever going to forget you.' He put his arm round her shoulders and hugged her. 'And I'm going to miss you.'

'Of course I'll translate, Freds,' Sally told him. Then she repeated his words for Colette, in French, the first language Sally had ever learned. 'And I'll miss you, too,' she added. 'You're an amazing bunch in St Aubert and you, Colette, you astonish me. Take care, and don't ever give up. We'll see you one day. *Soon*, I hope.'

FORTY-TWO

Could they make it home safely? Especially in this weather. Would she ever come back?

Sally's mind raced as she and Freddy retraced the route to the barn that Armand had shown her. She couldn't believe that this was the last she would see of St Aubert. The little town looked quieter than ever, all the shutters closed as the rain kept falling, glistening in puddles in the square and pooling in the alleyways.

The rain had kept the Nazi soldiers off the streets, Sally realised. No doubt they had decided that the village was too subdued by what had happened earlier to carry out acts of outrage against them in the rain.

Oh, if only you knew...

Hand-in-hand, they picked their way through the orchard, the soil now turned to mud, sucking at their feet as they went. Sally kept an eye on the road that ran past the orchard, but there was still no sign of the soldiers. Perhaps they'd all gone back to the chateau and, with von Brandt away, were taking the chance to enjoy themselves.

Sally tried to keep her mind on what was happening

moment to moment, rather than let the thought of her sudden flight dominate her thoughts and overwhelm her. With Freddy's hand in hers, she felt stronger. Even though she'd have to let go soon, so that he could make his own escape.

We're Toussaint and Carr, stunt pilots extraordinaire!

At last, they brushed past the trees that ran around the barn, and Freddy could finally see how well the secret Spitfire was hidden. The crates were already being removed from one side of the barn by figures in macs shiny from the rain. Armand had rounded up more people than Sally had thought – Henri's death had galvanised the people of St Aubert into action.

'Aren't you impressed?' Sally whispered, wondering if Freddy would be just as thrown as she had been. His jaw dropped as he watched the activity, everybody working in unison to get the Spitfire ready for its flight.

The flight home. For Sally, at least.

'Sal,' Freddy whispered, drawing her closer. 'What you've done since you got here... you're bloody remarkable, you know.'

Sally slipped her arm round Freddy's waist, resting her head on his shoulder. She felt bashful about his praise. 'Oh, I wouldn't say that. I've just done what anyone else would do. Whereas you – you took down a monster, Freddy. You're so brave! But then I always knew that you were.' She turned her head and kissed him, her lips lingering on his as the rain continued to fall.

'I love you,' he murmured. 'Now let's go and ready your carriage, ma'am.'

FORTY-THREE

Each second that ticked by took Sally closer to the moment when she would have to say goodbye to Freddy again. She would take to the air, and he would escape by sea. Wyngate would handle that. Sally trusted him to get Freddy to the coast. But what if she didn't make it? What if Freddy didn't? They would both face danger.

But no, she couldn't think like that. Moment by moment, they were closer to making their separate escapes. They would meet again in England. Sally couldn't allow herself to question that for a moment, or else she would risk shredding her nerves.

They went over to the barn, where the crates had now been cleared and the false wall was coming down. Sally and Freddy did what they could to help. Sally could guess what Freddy would be thinking once he saw the plane again – the secret Spitfire was an incredible sight. But it also meant that, very soon, she would be in the air – over an occupied country.

Margot came up to them, lowering the hood of her raincoat. 'We have a problem,' she whispered. 'Look at the field. All this rain has turned it to mud. The wheels will be stuck fast, won't they? What will you do for a runway?'

Sally's heart plummeted. She remembered Henri's words, that the field was very stony and couldn't be used for take-off. With patience, perhaps, the stones could be trodden down, but what on earth could they do about the mud? Sally had flown from grass runways before, but one made only from soil, claggy with mud from the heavy rain, wasn't good news at all.

'I won't need a very long runway...' she said, trying to think of a solution. But a short runway consisting of stones and mud was hopeless.

Armand trotted over to stand beside Freddy and, together, they watched the plane gradually appear. Freddy looked thoughtful, his brow furrowed, until he said with dawning realisation, 'Use the flats.'

This time it was Armand who frowned, unable to understand what the Englishman had said. He blinked up at Sally through the rain. 'Whatever Freds said – was it a good idea?'

Sally bounced on her toes with excitement. *Of course!*

'The fake wall,' she told Armand. 'That's what Freds has thought of. We'll lay the fake wall down over the mud!'

Sally repeated it in French, explaining that it was Freddy's idea, and Margot beamed from ear to ear, then hurried off to tell the volunteers what they would need to do. Sally and Freddy pitched in with Armand and the others, lifting sections of the lightweight fake wall and laying it from the barn out across the mud.

The rain was relentless, and the stones and mud in the field made the job even harder, but with everyone helping the runway soon extended several metres from the barn. Sally tested the wind direction. She knew just how she could get into the air with the wind this way. She had to – there were no other options left now.

Leah slapped Sally's back. 'Is it good enough?' she asked, searching her friend's face. 'Can you do it, Josette?'

Sally nodded. 'Oh, yes! Don't you worry, I can do it! Thank

you, Leah. Thank you for everything. And good luck. *All* the luck – St Aubert is in a very safe pair of hands with you.'

For the first time since they'd met, Leah smiled. She nodded and took Sally's hand, then glanced back through the orchard and whispered, 'Oh no.'

Sally froze. There was something in Leah's tone that she didn't like one bit. Rather stiffly, she followed Leah's gaze. Driving towards them over the grass that led from the road was von Brandt's staff car, the powerful roar of the Mercedes-Benz engine filling the night.

FORTY-FOUR

The volunteers heard the sound of the engine and they all stopped, their attention focused in the direction of the car.

We're so close. This isn't fair. Fifteen minutes more, and I'd be gone with the plane. This isn't fair.

As one, Armand and Freddy stepped forward, putting themselves between Leah and Sally and the approaching car. But what could they do? They'd been discovered, and this time they wouldn't be lucky enough to be facing one man and his chauffeur.

'There's our tractor!' called the driver as he opened the door and climbed out. But it didn't make sense. He wore the familiar black uniform of the SS, but he spoke in French, with no trace of a German accent. 'Good job, comrades!' he went on.

'It's Guy!' Armand cried, his voice betraying his relief.

Wyngate!

Sally laughed with relief and said to Wyngate in French, 'Guy, you scared us witless! Why on earth are you dressed like that?'

But it was part of his plan, wasn't it? He had to dispose of von Brandt's body. And, she now realised, that of von Brandt's chauffeur, too. Because how else could Wyngate have taken the car?

Sally didn't want to think about that. There'd been more than enough deaths for one day.

Wyngate reached into the car and took out a battered leather valise. He carried it towards them across the mud as Freddy reached for Sally's hand again, holding it so tight that she wondered if he would ever be willing to let go.

'Your uniform, Obergruppenführer.' Wyngate held out the case, but Freddy still clung to Sally with his good hand. 'The boat won't wait for us, so we need to move. Nobody will stop the SS on the road, even after curfew.'

'You want me to wear...' Freddy's words petered out and he dropped his gaze to the case. He gave a decisive nod. 'It makes sense. Can I say my goodbyes?'

Wyngate glanced at his watch and gave a long sigh. 'Make them quick.'

'Remember what I said?' Freddy released Sally's hand and stooped to embrace Armand. As he spoke, Sally translated his words. Emotion had robbed Freddy's French of its new-found competence. 'Wilbur's photo will bring you all the luck you need. And we'll see each other soon.'

He and the little boy embraced. 'We will,' Armand whispered, sniffing back a tear. 'Take care, Freds.'

'Leah.' Freddy and Leah exchanged the next hug. 'Sally will have to tell you what I'm saying. And maybe you'll tell all the folks who are helping too... you've risked everything for me and this plane. And I'm always going to be in your debt. Thank you.'

Sally quickly translated, then asked, 'Is there anything you'd like to say to Freds?'

Leah nodded. 'Please tell him that we will never give up fighting for our freedom. And that Armand has struggled since his father was captured... he made my little boy happy again, with their talk of planes.' She reached down to put her arm round her son. 'Even if it was a bit of a muddle sometimes. We will work on Armand's English, and you must work on Freddy's French.'

Armand nodded. 'For when we see each other again.'

'Don't worry, Freddy will *definitely* be getting lessons once we're back in England,' Sally promised. *As long as we do get back to England.* 'And we'll definitely see you again.'

Then Sally translated for Freddy, her heart swelling with pride. Freddy had done a great deal, while stranded in St Aubert, for a little boy who needed a hero to look up to. As Leah and Armand took their very diplomatic leave to pass Freddy and Sally's thanks to the rest of the workers, even Wyngate turned and took a few steps away. The man from the ministry had a heart after all.

'And now I need to say goodbye to you,' Sally said to Freddy. She wrapped her arms round him. They were both taking huge risks, but it was the only way for each of them to get home. 'Just be careful, darling, please. I love you so much, and I thought I'd lost you... then when I was told you were still alive, I was so, so grateful that you'd been given a second chance. Please, Freddy, please be careful. I can't lose you again. I love you.'

Freddy kissed Sally, letting it linger as though that alone could stop the clock. Then he drew back just a little, studying her face.

'I'll be fine,' he promised. 'But you don't take any risks in that plane, all right? You're the best pilot there is, but you're still my girl. I love you so bloody much, Sal...' He kissed her again. 'Get home safe.'

'And you too,' Sally replied. She kissed the tip of his nose. 'Peter said there's going to be a huge party in Bramble Heath when you get home.' Her breath caught as she said the name of their village aloud. 'We can't disappoint him.'

'And Wilbur'll be missing his dad...' Freddy smiled. 'Time to go home.'

'The boat won't wait.' Wyngate had returned, the case held out in a way that suggested he wasn't about to take it back again. 'Josette, you'll have the cover of an allied raid. Flight Lieutenant, it's time. You'll have to manage without the sling, but the doctor tells me that won't be a problem.'

Freddy kissed Sally one more time, then took the case. With a glance back at his fiancée, he headed off towards the barn, ready to change. Sally knew the uniform wouldn't be a perfect fit, but it would be the perfect disguise.

'I best get into my flight suit,' she said to Wyngate, after a last wave to Freddy. 'Colette told me they've kept Freddy's safely with the plane. But answer me one thing before you go, Guy – what did you do with the bodies?'

'Very roomy boots, these Mercedes.' Wyngate glanced back towards the car. 'It was lucky in its way though, because I *did* need a car and von Brandt arrived in one.' He gave Sally the briefest ghost of a smile. 'This storm... it wouldn't surprise me if this staff car isn't found in a ditch tomorrow morning, the chauffeur and the Obergruppenführer unfortunate victims of the treacherous roads.'

Sally stared at Wyngate in amazement. 'I knew you'd sort it out somehow, but that really is... my goodness. And the people of St Aubert... There won't be any repercussions at all! Thank heavens for that.' Relieved at that thought, Sally went on, 'Take care, big brother. I want you to get home in one piece. And please, *please*, look after Freddy for me, won't you? I don't know what I'd do if...'

She couldn't put her fears into words.

'If I start a job, I finish it,' Wyngate said, recalling their meeting in the church all those weeks ago. 'I'll get him home, though if he suffers from seasickness he may be in for quite a crossing.' He held out his hand to Sally. 'Bring her home safe, little sister. And yourself too; we need all the miracle workers we can get.'

Sally took his hand and shook. She'd enjoyed working with Wyngate, even though the pressure had been on every moment. 'Never fear, I'll do my best.'

Never fear. Sally couldn't afford to. She would have to keep her wits about her and fly like the wind.

'I'm ready.' Freddy's voice was quiet now, as the moment for goodbye finally arrived. 'I don't like wearing this get-up, but if it gets me home...'

Sally hadn't even heard Freddy's quiet return and when she turned to look at him, she blinked in astonishment at the transformation. Freddy, in a dead man's SS uniform. He was almost unrecognisable as the gentle, funny, brave man she loved. 'I prefer your RAF uniform, I must say. But this really is a super disguise.'

She took Freddy's hands and kissed him once more.

'I've got your letters safe here. You can read them over breakfast tomorrow.' Then Freddy stepped back and rested his forehead against Sally's. He swallowed hard. 'I love you, Sal. You know the way home... second star on the right and all that?'

'And straight on 'til morning.' Sally nodded, her eyes blurring with tears. Those letters, the ones he'd written from that cell when he had no idea if they'd ever see each other again. But they had. And they would do again. 'I won't get lost, I promise. We'll both find our way home.'

FORTY-FIVE

Sally had waved off Freddy and Wyngate, and now it was her turn to leave St Aubert and the friends she'd made there. She was nearly home – she just needed to get up in the air and fly – but it wasn't as simple as that. It was dangerous. An almost impossible gulf separated her from Bramble Heath.

The weather was getting worse, the rain heavy and the wind bending the branches of the trees in the orchard. Sally changed into Freddy's flight suit, which was too big for her but was much better than nothing at all.

The impromptu runway was a pale patch across the dark, muddy field. Sally's heart was in her throat as she looked across at it. But it was the only way she could get airborne.

Before she could get started, though, she walked round the plane, checking that all was well. The vents on the plane's nose were clear, the propeller's surface was smooth, the wings and the tail had no problems at all. She crouched to peer underneath. The wheels had some dried earth on them from Freddy's landing, but she couldn't see—

What's that?

Sally crawled under the plane and peered up at the undercarriage. On one side, up at the top of the landing gear where it connected to the plane, she could see some stones. They must've got in there from Freddy's emergency landing in the field; but they couldn't stay there or they might damage the landing gear. She'd already had problems with that – she really didn't need any more. She wished she'd seen the stones when she'd come to see the plane before. But she'd been so astonished to see it again, and in its ingenious hiding place, that she just hadn't noticed.

She reached up, trying to dislodge them, but the space the stones had jammed themselves into was too small.

'Has anyone got a toolbox? I need a screwdriver or some tiny pliers, something like that,' she asked urgently. Someone could go back to the village to fetch one if there wasn't one there, but every extra second she was on the ground was an extra moment in which they could be found out.

Margot looked to Leah, then to the other volunteers. They were all shaking their heads.

'I need to get these stones out from under the plane,' Sally explained, trying not to let the panic she felt show in her voice.

'It won't fly?' asked Leah as she stooped to peer at the Spitfire's belly.

'I won't be able to get the wheels up safely,' Sally told her. 'They'll be sticking out from under the plane for the whole flight, which'll slow her down – or if I *do* manage to get them up they might not lower properly when I land.'

Leah nodded. She slicked her wet hair back from her face, then gave a firm nod. It looked as though Wyngate had made a good choice, putting her in Henri's role as the person in charge.

'Armand,' she said. 'Run home and bring your dad's toolbox. Be as fast as you can.'

FORTY-SIX

But Armand wasn't listening, it seemed. He dodged round his mother and darted up beneath the Spitfire, gripping a shielded torch. The little boy shone the low beam on the landing gear, then held up the torch to Sally and said, 'Grab this, Josette.'

Sally took the torch, shining it towards the stones. She wondered what he was going to do, but she trusted him. The war had made him wise beyond his years. 'What's the plan, ground crew?'

'Sometimes, you just have to get your hands mucky.' And Armand reached into the recess above the landing gear and began swiftly plucking out the caked mud and embedded stones.

Sally watched as Armand's hand, smaller than her own, worked at the recess. 'Be careful, Armand, don't hurt yourself,' she whispered with concern. She glanced back and saw the volunteers from the village staring in amazement at the boy before smiling proudly at Leah.

Eventually Armand stood back and dusted off his hands briskly. He nodded towards the plane and said, 'Clean as a whistle.' In the distance, the drone of incoming aircraft could be heard. Wyngate's promised diversion was on its way. 'Now get yourself home, Josette. I'll look after my mum and St Aubert.'

Sally climbed up onto the wing, then into the plane. She dreaded what would come next. Spitfires weren't very manoeuvrable on the ground and, even though the secret plane had been modified to improve that side of things, it still wasn't perfect. Added to that was the rough floor of the barn, and the fact that she was the only person present who knew how to get the plane ready and into the air.

And the plane had to warm up, too. Although the wind was howling, there was still the risk that someone not far away would hear the engine. And if that *someone* happened to be a Nazi, everyone was in trouble. But then, with Wyngate's air operation, they'd have more to worry about than just one Spitfire taking off from a field.

Sally started the plane, and its deep growl as the engine fired and the propeller spun took her back to another barn, another field, where she had first crossed paths with the secret Spitfire.

We flew well back then, girl. We can do it again.

Sally bit her lip, waiting, listening to the engine and watching the dials. The plane had been mothballed for several weeks, and yet everything was in fine working order. She gave a thumbs-up to the volunteers who were waiting around the plane, and they cheered – quietly, but the look of joy and excitement on their faces sent a thrill through her.

'Good luck, Josette!' Armand called from his place on the ground. 'I'll see you for my flying lessons before you know it!'

'You're a natural, I'm certain!' Sally beamed at him. Despite the danger of being here with the clandestine Spitfire, she knew he'd remember this moment for ever, watching the Spitfire that had waited so patiently in the barn spring into life. 'Goodbye, St Aubert! And good luck!'

The volunteers stood back, giving Sally and the plane

space. She looked down at the dials, waiting and waiting for the moment when the pressure and temperature were just right and she could get going.

Finally, the moment came. Sally's heart squeezed with terror and excitement as she moved the plane towards its temporary runway, the wheels crunching over the floor of the barn. As soon as she left the cover of the barn's roof, the rain rushed in as there was no canopy to stop it. She sighed. Getting wet was the least of her worries.

She wondered how the flattened wooden crates would cope with the heavy rain and the weight of the plane, but she didn't have time to spare it much thought. There was so little runway that she had to get the aircraft into the air quickly, and she knew the secret Spitfire could do it. As the engine roared over the noise of the wind and the approaching planes from the air operation that was providing cover for her, Sally pushed the Spitfire to accelerate and it rushed forward.

She pulled back on the stick and the secret Spitfire was in the air and climbing – just in time, as the plane cleared a copse of trees at the end of the field by only a few feet. The wind buffeted the plane, and Sally did her best to respect the wind's direction while checking the compass and pointing the plane where it needed to go.

The plane climbed higher and higher, St Aubert and her new friends disappearing into the rainy night below.

She would never forget them.

But first of all, Sally had to get home. The dark night yawned open ahead of her, scraps of moonlight and stars occasionally visible through the heavy clouds. The wind kept trying to throw her off course, and without a canopy the relentless rain was pelting her. However much she kept wiping her goggles and the dials clear of the raindrops, they were soon covered again. All she could hear over the radio was static, and she felt very alone.

But the miles were rolling by beneath her, and a change in the air told her she was nearly at the coast.

Once I get to the sea, and the radio isn't just static, I can tell myself I'm almost home.

Despite how soaked she was and how uncomfortable and difficult the flight was, that thought perked Sally up. And, against all the odds, she was airborne. Von Brandt was dead and, now that the plane was no longer in St Aubert, the brave people who lived there were safe. She just had to bear with the rain and the storm, and its onslaught against her. One more hurdle before she reached home.

But just as she was settling in, Sally heard the throbbing of aircraft. Only there was something about the timbre that set her nerves jangling. With her heart in her throat, she heard gunfire. And when she looked in the mirror, she couldn't believe it.

There was a Messerschmitt right behind her.

FORTY-SEVEN

They're following me.

Because now, in Sally's mirror, she could see more of them. But she didn't want to stop and count the number of enemy planes pursuing her. All she knew was that she had to get away from them. There was still nothing over the radio. She remembered her last encounter with a Messerschmitt – Wyngate's voice through the airwaves then had given her courage. But now she heard nothing at all.

She pulled back on the stick, forcing the plane to climb against the gusting wind. There were too many for her to loop overhead and get behind them, but just getting higher meant she was out of the way of their guns – for a moment, at least.

Freddy had been so enthusiastic about the armaments on the Spitfire, but Sally had never been trained in even the standard equipment, so she would hardly know where to start if it came to a dogfight. All she could do was keep outmanoeuvring them and hope that she could lose them. Far beneath Sally's plane lay the yawning darkness of the sea, and somewhere on that sea was a boat carrying Freddy and Wyngate, just as

Commander Seaton had promised there would be. She had to make it back to Bramble Heath.

Sally checked her mirror as she was still climbing and saw the Messerschmitts following, although not as fast as she could go. Then, turning her stick sharply down and to the left, she forced the plane straight into the storm's westerly wind while heading towards the sea in a corkscrew. She knew that the secret Spitfire could take it – and she hoped it'd make it far harder for the Messerschmitts to take aim.

In the night behind her a cannon roared, but Sally flew on in the darkness, listening to the static that was all the radio could give her. She had never felt more alone than she did now.

Is there anybody there? Please, there must be someone!

She kept going, heading down in a corkscrew towards the waves that roared beneath her. She quickly wiped her goggles and her altimeter free of raindrops again. Just in time she pulled up on her stick again, hurtling skywards. She spared a glance in her mirror, and saw a Messerschmitt hit the sea with one wing tip and cartwheel away, smashing to pieces.

That was one less plane pursuing her, but she still had to evade the others. This time she turned sharply with the direction of the wind as she climbed, her speed accelerating.

'Is anyone there?' Sally pleaded over the radio. There couldn't be, she knew; there could only be silence. But if she spoke as if there was, maybe it would help her feel less alone, even if she was only pretending. 'I'm over the Channel, and I'm pursued by the Luftwaffe. Is anyone there? Please!'

FORTY-EIGHT

And out of the static, as another cannon roared into life, a faint voice cut in: '—hear me? This is Flight Lieutenant Carr. Respond if you can—' Static buzzed through again, before Freddy repeated his plea.

'Freddy?' Sally gasped in astonishment as she sent the plane into an aileron roll. 'It's me, Sally! I mean, First Officer Toussaint!'

What was he doing on the radio?

'Sally!' Freddy's voice was distant, but it was there. 'We're out to sea. Stay on this channel, the cavalry's on its wa—'

'Don't go, Freddy, please!' Sally begged. His sudden appearance over the airwaves gave her hope. She wasn't alone. And Freddy had met the boat and was making his escape too. 'I'll stay on this channel. Please don't go.'

The cavalry, though – what did he mean? Was someone coming out into the storm to save her?

'I love you, Sal!' Freddy assured her. 'Stay on this channel so we can find you!'

The static buzzed again and, for an awful moment, Sally

thought she was alone again. Then, out of the night, another voice spoke.

'This is Group Captain Chambers, First Officer. You should be seeing your escort party any time...' He paused before saying, 'Now.'

And as Sally lurched the plane into a roll to evade another burst of cannon fire, she saw soaring shapes emerge from the storm clouds up ahead, their weapons already blazing. The boys from RAF Bramble Heath had arrived.

'Group Captain Chambers, it's you!' Sally said excitedly. He was in Bramble Heath, he was in her old home, and he was talking to her over the radio. 'And I can see them! They're here! The cavalry's arrived! Oh, what a magnificent sight!'

She certainly wasn't alone now. Her courage renewed, she wiped the raindrops off her goggles and pushed the plane to climb through a gap the boys from Bramble Heath had left for her, a safe path through their fire. The Luftwaffe were still following her through the slanting rain, but their job had just got a whole lot more difficult.

'Leave Jerry to the lads,' Chambers said. 'And head for home.'

The air fizzed before Freddy's distant voice cut into the frequency to tell Sally, 'Show them how a Spitfire girl flies, Sal!'

Sally laughed as the rain lashed against her. 'Oh, don't you worry, I will!'

She kept the plane on course as best she could despite the terrible weather and the evasive moves she needed to keep up, just in case any of the Luftwaffe managed by some fluke to get past the boys who'd come to save her. Bramble Heath was ahead, through the clouds and the rain.

She looped, she rolled, she kept wiping away the rain and fighting the wind. And each minute that passed brought her closer and closer.

The airwaves weren't silent any longer, with Group

Captain Chambers there to talk her in over the coast of her homeland. And the fighters at her back now weren't those bearing swastikas, but the Polish and British pilots she knew so well, escorting her safely in to land.

There'd been so many times in the past few days when she thought she'd never see the village again, but now... now she was nearly back again at Bramble Heath.

Home. I made it home.

FORTY-NINE

Sally had landed so many times at Bramble Heath that she barely blinked an eyelid – normally. But not tonight.

As she descended, spotting the landmarks she knew so well through the rain streaming across the windscreen, her heart was so full of love for her home that she had to sniff back her tears. She saw the spire of the church, and the ribbon of the high street winding through the centre of the village. In the houses and cottages below, almost everyone would be sleeping soundly, and the last few stragglers from the George and Dragon would be dropping into bed.

'Group Captain Chambers, I'm on the descent to RAF Bramble Heath,' Sally told Chambers over the radio, hoping he wouldn't hear the wobble in her voice as she said *Bramble Heath*. 'Am I cleared to land?'

'Bring her in, First Officer Toussaint,' Chambers told her brightly. 'It's good to see you home.'

'It's good to *be* home!' Sally chuckled. 'On my way. Over.'

She bit her lip as she flicked the switch to lower the flight gear, wondering if it would work. But, there it was – the reassuring sound of the mechanism. She was going to have a safe landing, even in the rain, thanks to the engineers after her test flight – and to a little boy in France.

She wiped her goggles and saw the landing lights through the clouds. She descended through the rain, her body flooded with relief. It was all over. Nearly all over. It wouldn't be over until she saw Freddy safely back in Bramble Heath again.

The wheels met the runway and, finally, Sally was back home.

She taxied the plane towards the hangar, directed by two ground crew. And through the rain, she suddenly recognised them. It was her father and Freddy's. She waved to them and the two of them waved back.

Once Sally had brought the plane to a standstill in the dry of a hangar, she peeled off her goggles and started to climb out. The wing was slippery with rain and she nearly lost her footing, but François and Arthur rushed to help her down.

'Papa! Arthur! Oh, it's wonderful to be home!' Sally told them, and gave them both a hug.

'But you've only been in Scotland a few days!' Her father chuckled. He was glancing at the plane, looking surprised. He'd noticed it wasn't the usual kind of Spitfire. 'And you're soaked! What happened to the canopy?'

'It's a very long story,' Sally replied. And one that she wasn't able to tell, no matter how much she wished she could. They would be so proud, if only they knew.

Arthur stepped back and looked up at the Spitfire. 'This is a new one...' He gave Sally a rueful smile. 'Still no news about our Freds, love, but Peter'll be happy to see you home. We've all missed you.'

Sally patted Arthur's arm, trying to find words. She was bursting to tell him that Freddy was almost home, but she had to keep the news to herself. 'I've missed you too. I'm so sorry I wasn't around. And you never know, we could hear something about Freddy any day.'

'First Officer Toussaint?' Group Captain Chambers was striding across the airstrip towards the hangar, a large umbrella protecting him from the rain. At his side beneath the sheltering umbrella was Lane-Bannister, the man who had started her on this unexpected and perilous path. 'Too late for the brolly, I'm afraid. But perhaps we could see you safely home at least? Dashed poor business, letting an Attagirl fly by night with Jerry buzzing around.'

Of course, Chambers knew that it was no such thing, but the message to the ground crew was clear. There was nothing unusual to see here at all.

François glanced at the Spitfire again and smiled proudly. Sally knew what he was thinking – that his daughter was involved in the delivery of a new kind of Spitfire. And he couldn't know anything more than that.

'I wouldn't mind a lift home if there's one going,' Sally said with a grin to Chambers and Lane-Bannister. 'I'm thoroughly soaked, and the cockpit's full of water, like a leaky boat. But at least I got it— At least I'm home, that's the main thing.'

'If your father has no objections, my driver is at your disposal,' Lane-Bannister told her as he looked to François for an answer.

'No objections at all,' François said with a French shrug, and Sally felt a pang for the people of St Aubert. But they were safer now, without the secret plane or the downed pilot in their midst.

Sally kissed her father goodbye, and gave Arthur a companionable hug. She could feel Arthur's desolation, but she knew it would very soon come to an end.

'Don't give up hope, Arthur,' she told him.

Arthur gave a sad nod. 'Elsie and Peter are staying with your mum tonight, to take their mind off Freds,' he said. 'So if Wilbur starts barking when you go in, don't be scared.'

'I won't be,' Sally assured him, touched that he would think of her being alarmed at hearing Wilbur. After what she had faced, hearing the little dog's bark again would be a tonic. 'Goodnight, Papa, goodnight Arthur.'

Then she glanced at Chambers and Lane-Bannister. Their expressions were giving nothing away, even though they knew that Freddy was on his way back to Bramble Heath.

'Let's get you home,' said Chambers, holding the umbrella over Sally as they set off towards Heath Place and Lane-Bannister's car. He was right, it was far too late for the brolly, but she appreciated the small gesture anyway after the night she'd just endured. Once they were safely out of earshot of the hangar, he said, 'That was quite the flight, First Officer. Absolutely remarkable.'

'There'll likely be a decoration in it for you,' Lane-Bannister assured Sally. 'You'll soon be seeing a lot more of these planes overhead.'

'Thank you. But of course, she's a remarkable plane,' Sally replied. 'The thing is, she would never have been hidden for so long, or even got back up into the air again if it wasn't for the peop— My *friends* in St Aubert. I wouldn't mind having a decoration, of course I wouldn't – but I want, more than anything, for *them* to be recognised for what they've done. They're so brave.'

Lane-Bannister nodded. 'I'll speak to some people in the know,' was all he said. They had reached Lane-Bannister's car, which glistened in the rain that kept relentlessly falling. He opened the door for her and said, 'Hop in.'

'Good, I'm glad to hear it,' Sally replied with a smile. She got into the car, feeling rather guilty about the puddles she would inevitably leave behind. It was a luxurious vehicle, especially after the flight in a plane with no canopy. She wondered where Freddy was now; whether still at sea or back on solid ground, she had the idea that he would be safe with the man she'd come to regard as a big brother.

'Flight Lieutenant Carr is going straight to the medics when he lands,' Lane-Bannister said, as though reading her mind. But he had been widowed in the Blitz, so of course he knew that Sally's every thought was for the man she loved. 'I'll make sure his family are the first to see him when he arrives in Bramble Heath.'

'Oh, Mr Lane-Bannister, thank you so much.' Sally smiled even as she wiped away a tear, not that it made much difference on her already wet face. 'He might need a little bit of patching up, but he never once gave up hope that he was coming back. And once he does... I don't know what it took to bring him back, but I want you to know that me, Freds, our families – we'll be eternally grateful that you did.'

'Flight Lieutenant Carr did a considerable service to the country, as did you,' he replied. 'We all owe you both a debt.'

They travelled through Bramble Heath's dark, rainy lanes, and, once they reached the cottage Sally had learned to call home, she climbed out of Lane-Bannister's car. She let herself in at the gate, and hunted for the spare key to the kitchen door under a flowerpot. As soon as she turned it in the keyhole, Wilbur started to bark, and Sally laughed. She was so glad to be home.

'Wilbur, it's me,' she whispered, opening the kitchen door.

'Shush, Wilbur!' Peter ran into the kitchen and scooped up the little dog into his arms. 'Sally! You came home!'

'I'm back!' Sally hurried over to Peter and hugged him and Wilbur together. She might be soaking wet but she didn't care. Some things were more important. With a grin, she asked him, 'I hope you've been good while I've been away?'

Peter laughed and assured her, 'I'm always good! I knew somebody was on the way, because Wilbur wouldn't settle. I knew you or Freds was coming home.' In his arms the little dog squirmed, and Peter put him down on the kitchen floor. 'Look at him, he's still carried away.' Peter blinked up at Sally. 'Maybe somebody else is coming home too?'

'Maybe he is,' Sally told him. It was remarkable how Wilbur knew. Sally wondered if the dog could detect Freddy's scent on her, somehow, despite the rain that had pelted her. Or did he simply know, deep in his heart, that Freddy was nearly home? 'Wouldn't that be wonderful?'

Peter beamed. 'It would be. But you're here, and that's wonderful too.'

Sally needed to get to bed. The initial excitement of being home was passing, leaving exhaustion in its wake. She kissed Peter and Wilbur goodnight, then, as she was about to make her way up to bed, Emily and Elsie appeared at the door.

'We heard Wilbur barking, and we wondered... Look at you, soaked through! You best get to bed before you catch a chill!' Emily told Sally, but she still gave her a hug, welcoming her home.

Sally hugged Elsie too. She could feel Elsie's grief, like a cold, hard stone inside her. But she knew it would be gone in almost no time at all.

Once Sally's bedroom door was closed behind her, she went straight over to the loose floorboard and lifted it up, removing the tin she'd hidden there. She opened it and, even in the weak light of her lamp, the diamond on her engagement ring glittered.

'I love you, Freddy Carr,' Sally whispered, as she slipped the ring back on her finger.

Then she remembered something else – the letter she'd written to her parents in case she didn't make it home. She opened her dressing table's drawer and took out the envelope that concealed it, then she stood over the grate and tore it up.

I made it home again. And soon Freddy will too.

FIFTY

The next morning at breakfast, the Toussaints' kitchen table was almost full, as François and Arthur had got back from their night shift, and Peter, Elsie and Emily had all sat down with Sally to tuck into their porridge. One chair was empty though, and Sally noticed Elsie and Arthur stealing sad glances at it.

While they ate, Wilbur ran barking to the front door and scratched at it.

He knows Freddy's on his way. I don't know how, but he knows.

'Come on, you,' said Peter. He padded after Wilbur to the door. 'Jamie's not due for half an hour, Wilbur. You're early to say hello.'

Sally heard the front door open as the little boy let Freddy's dog out. A second later he shouted with obvious excitement, 'Mum! Dad! Everybody!' And Sally knew then that Lane-Bannister had kept his word: Freddy was home.

Sally leapt up from her chair, beaming at everyone. 'Come on, come on!' She beckoned to them to follow her as she hurried out to the front door. And there, walking up the path, was Freddy. Just as if he'd never left.

Elsie gasped as she saw him, and grabbed Arthur's arm, who was beaming with joy and relief. 'It's our boy! It's our boy, Freddy!'

He was back in uniform, his arm held in a fresh white sling, and on his face, as he stooped to hug Peter and scoop up Wilbur, was the brightest smile Sally had ever seen. Her heart swelled with love when he stood straight and asked with his familiar brightness, 'Is breakfast on?'

'Oh, yes,' Sally told him. 'You've arrived just in time!'

'Come here...' Elsie chuckled affectionately, and Freddy was soon lost in the embrace of his parents and his brother. Elsie stroked Freddy's cheek, staring at him in amazement. The son they thought they'd lost had returned. A little worse for wear, but still smiling.

And Sally was smiling too. She wasn't sure she'd ever stop.

FIFTY-ONE

TWO DAYS LATER

The sun shone brightly on Bramble Heath, and on Freddy and Sally too.

Now, as Sally and Freddy sat together in the George and Dragon's garden, the sun sparkled against the diamond on her ring.

We're home.

And that meant that the party Peter had longed to have, to welcome his brother home, was in full swing.

The pub's garden was full to bursting. RAF and ATA uniforms mingled with the civvies of Bramble Heath's locals, and laughter filled the air. The village was welcoming him home.

Even Father Piotrowski, who had arrived in the village with the Polish refugees, and Reverend Ellis had come to the party, and were laughing with Laura and Ewa. Rose from the tea rooms was handing around plates of sandwiches, while Peter and Jamie were chatting with the RAF pilots.

'It is a miracle that he's home, a miracle!' François kept saying, and it made Sally giggle. *Oh, Papa, if only you knew!*

Arthur and Elsie kept smiling at their son. And Wilbur had

planted himself in Freddy's lap and was refusing to move for anyone.

'I still can't believe it,' Elsie said, her voice almost a whisper as she leant across the table towards him. 'I thought we'd lost you, Freds. But you came back. You came back, and here you are, as if you'd never left.'

Freddy was all smiles. He turned his face towards the sun, making up for all those weeks he'd been forced to hide indoors. 'I never thought for a moment I wasn't coming home. There wasn't a chance I wouldn't see you lot again!'

Of course, he couldn't tell his parents everything that had happened, only that he'd been downed over France and was eventually helped to escape. The rest would always have to remain unsaid.

Annie came over with Group Captain Chambers, her fiancé. They were full of smiles.

'It's so good to see you back in Bramble Heath, Freddy,' Annie told him. 'You had the whole village crossing their fingers, hoping you'd come home.'

'Just a bit of a stopover in France,' Freddy breezed, as though it had been nothing but a holiday. 'Sampled the wine, ate a bit of cheese, then home! You know how us lads are.'

Group Captain Chambers gave him a comically stern look and teased, 'I can assure you that Nurse Russell knows nothing about *lads*. Gentlemen officers, on the other hand...'

They all laughed at that.

Jakub, one of the Polish ground crew, and Betty, his girl-friend, were arm-in-arm, and drifted over too.

'What's this about wine and cheese? What have I missed?' Jakub chuckled. He nudged Freddy, then affectionately patted him on his good arm.

'State secret,' Freddy told him, tapping the side of his own nose. 'Between me and Winston!'

Jakub laughed it off, of course, but Sally knew there was more truth in that than anyone would ever suspect.

Peter took a break from touring the beer garden with Jamie, gathering good wishes, to tell Freddy, 'I never gave up – I knew you'd come home. Wilbur did too. He's a smart little dog!'

Freddy smiled warmly at his brother. He slipped his good arm from Sally's shoulder and reached towards Peter, rubbing his hair affectionately.

'And Wilbur says you gave him all the treats he wanted!' Freddy said, with a quick glance at Sally. He was thinking of Armand, Sally was sure. 'I met a little lad just like you in France. You'll be mates one day, I hope.'

I hope so too, Sally thought. As nerve-wracking as it had been in St Aubert, she missed it. At least, the friends she had made. And the older brother she'd gained – but Sally had no idea when she'd see Wyngate again, the mysterious man from the ministry. If she ever would – she was sure he had other adventures awaiting him, maybe more dangerous than the last. But when she was alone with Freddy, they could talk about them.

'That's a swish motor...' Peter murmured appreciatively, shielding his eyes against the sun as he watched a low-slung blue sports car purr along the village street. Other people in the beer garden were watching too and Sally couldn't help but smile to herself. So Mr Wyngate was still safe in Blighty.

The car slowed almost to a halt and the window opened to reveal the driver. From within, Wyngate lifted his hand to the brim of his hat and shot Sally a very sharp salute indeed.

Do take care, Wyngate. My big brother.

While everyone's attention was on Wyngate's car, Sally gave him a small wave. With that, the window was raised and the car sped on, its engine roaring into the distance. Freddy looked to Sally with a smile, not saying anything. He didn't need to.

Sally returned Freddy's smile, then rested her head against his good shoulder. She had read his letters, which he'd written in his hiding place under Colette's kitchen floor. Freddy had been cheerful and upbeat in every one, wondering what Sally was doing and where she was off to next. And every word had been filled with love.

Because love had kept everyone going, hadn't it? Love for each other, love for a country, love for climbing into a plane and flying into the blue sky. And love for home. Wherever that might be.

EPILOGUE

1945

The bells of Bramble Heath church rang out as Sally, in a parachute-silk dress, headed up the aisle on her father's arm. Standing up by the altar rails was Freddy in his RAF uniform, with Wilbur at his side. It wouldn't be long, though, before he went back to civilian life and Toussaint and Carr would take to the air again. His face was illuminated with joy and love, and Sally felt as if she was floating over the floor towards him.

They were going to be married. They'd waited out the years of the war, as patiently as they could, because they didn't want to do this without having all their friends with them on their special day.

The pews were full of people from Bramble Heath, as well as Sally's friends from the ATA, and Freddy's from the RAF. Mrs Farthing sat with Betty, and Zofia and Szymon smiled as their daughter walked down the aisle in front of Sally, scattering wildflower petals. Annie and Group Captain Chambers shared a pew with the Attagirls, and, as ever, Mr and Mrs Gosling were with their Land Girls.

There was even a little space at the back of the packed church for the fans of Toussaint and Carr who had so loved to see them fly before the war. They would now witness a very special moment for the couple, something everyone had hoped would come, even in the darkest days of the war – Sally and Freddy especially.

And among them were their other friends, from St Aubert, along with Sally's family from France. Mémé and Colette had become firm friends within moments of meeting, and Sally had been so proud to discover that her cousins had fought in the Resistance. They, like Colette, Leah and Armand, had witnessed dreadful things, but they had survived to see liberation. And nobody was beaming more broadly than Armand, who stood proudly between his mother and father. When the ceremony was done, she knew, he'd be back in a friendly huddle with Peter and Jamie; the three lads were already as thick as thieves.

The war was over and France had been liberated; Sally and Freddy getting married wasn't just a celebration of Sally and Freddy's love and their promise of a future lived together, it was a celebration of the end of tyranny and the return to peace.

Sally reached the altar rail. Her heart full of love, she took Freddy's hand and whispered, 'I love you, Freddy.'

'I love you, Sal,' he whispered. 'My very own Spitfire girl.'

A LETTER FROM ELLIE CURZON

Dear Reader,

We want to say a huge thank you for choosing to read *The Spitfire Girl*. If you enjoyed it, and want to keep up to date with all our latest releases, just sign up at the following link. Your email address will never be shared and you can unsubscribe at any time.

www.bookouture.com/ellie-curzon

There may only be one Ellie Curzon, but she consists of two authors, and we both hope that you enjoyed *The Spitfire Girl*. It was a privilege for us to spotlight the brave work of SOE and the members of the ATA, who did so much to contribute towards the Allied victory. We'd love you to sign up to our newsletter to find out all the latest news about our series, A Village at War, the residents of Bramble Heath, and even the man from the Ministry!

We would be very grateful if you could write a review. We'd love to hear what you think, and it makes such a difference helping new readers to discover one of our books for the first time.

We love hearing from our readers – you can get in touch on our Facebook page, through Twitter, Goodreads or our website.

Thanks,

Ellie

www.elliecurzon.co.uk

facebook.com/elliecurzonauthor
twitter.com/MadameGilflurt
goodreads.com/ellie_curzon

ACKNOWLEDGEMENTS

Huge thanks to the team at Bookouture, especially our editor Natalie Edwards, whose unflagging enthusiasm and perceptive feedback has helped *The Spitfire Girl* take flight. Thanks also to Rick and Gordon for the tea, and Pippa and Vincent for the cuteness.

Reader, thank you for reading our book, you're awesome!

Printed in Great Britain
by Amazon

30173069R00179